DEVIL BOATS

MICHAEL AYE

C.S. DUNCKLEE

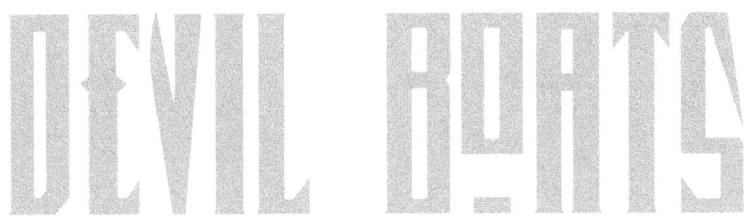

MICHAEL AYE

BITINGDUCK PRESS
ALTADENA, CA

Published by Boson Books
An imprint of Bitingduck Press
ISBN 978-1-68553-025-9
eISBN 978-1-68553-026-6
© 2024 Michael Fowler
All rights reserved
For information contact
Bitingduck Press, LLC
Altadena, California
notifications@bitingduckpress.com
http://www.bitingduckpress.com
Cover art by C. S. Duncklee
Photos courtesy Frank J. Andruss, Sr.

Author's Acknowledgement

A special thanks to Frank J. Andruss, Sr., owner and curator of the Mosquito Fleet Exhibit. Without Frank's untiring devotion to the Mosquito Fleet, this book would not have been nearly as historically accurate as it is. The Mosquito Fleet Exhibit is full of first hand testimony, artifacts, and pictures that are a treasure in themselves. I have used Frank as a character in this book as a small token of my appreciation of his endless efforts. All the pictures, unless otherwise stated, are the property of the exhibit. Again I'm very appreciative for his permission to use the pictures in this book.

This book is a work of fiction with a historical backdrop. I have taken liberties with historical figures, ships and time frames to blend in with my story. Therefore, this book is not a reflection of actual historical events.

DEDICATION

To: Bubba and Kathy Blue, and Katie Blue Griffin
In Loving Memory of Matthew Cox Blue

To: Dianne Hinson Capps
In Loving Memory of Sidney Ellison Hinson

To: Roy West Singleton
Memories of the Neighborhood and Harold

"I wish to have no connection with any ship that does not sail fast. For I intend to go in Harm's Way."

—John Paul Jones

FOREWORD

WHEN PEOPLE THINK OF PT boats during World War II, they only have a few examples to use to form their opinion. A couple of movies come to mind demonstrating Hollywood's impression of PT boat life. A color feature called "PT109" was about our future president, John F. Kennedy. The movie They Were Expendable took us back to the days of Squadron 3, and her exploits in the Philippines. They did a pretty good job portraying the life of the PT Boat Veterans. The 1960's comedy McHale's Navy was about a wacky PT boat crew in the South Pacific. None of these portrayed real life on board the Devil Boats of the Mosquito Fleet.

PT duty in the South Pacific was nothing close to being fun. It was hard, nerve wracking duty that produced many hours of patrol in places that produced death from enemy ships, planes, barges, submarines, and shore batteries. You worked in the black of night which produced nerves that stood on end because at any moment you could be fired on. You fought the weather that in the Pacific could produce wind and waves, humidity, tropical downpours, and heat that could reach 100 degrees or more during the day. You sweat through your clothes so much that many PT sailors wore nothing more than shorts during the day. You fought many different diseases that ran amok in the hot climate of the Pacific including malaria, dengue fever, beriberi, and dysentery.

Food was always at a shortage, and unless your boat had a good cook you didn't eat very well, as things like meat and veggies were not often available. It was more like spam and powdered eggs. Most PT sailors lost anywhere from 10 to 20 pounds after being there for a while. Bathing was always limited and fresh water on the boat was always guarded for use like drinking and cooking. You took salt baths and jumped into the water to rinse off, which always left your skin dry and tacky feeling.

PT duty was nothing like what you saw when watching McHale's Navy, although PT sailors were very good scroungers. One must take into consideration that PT boats were made from many types of wood and offered no protection against incoming enemy shells. There was no place to hide, and you depended on those 3 Packard engines to provide your boat with enough speed to get you out of harm's way. Sometimes even I forget that these boats, as pretty as they are, were made for one thing, to destroy the enemy.

—Frank J Andruss Sr.

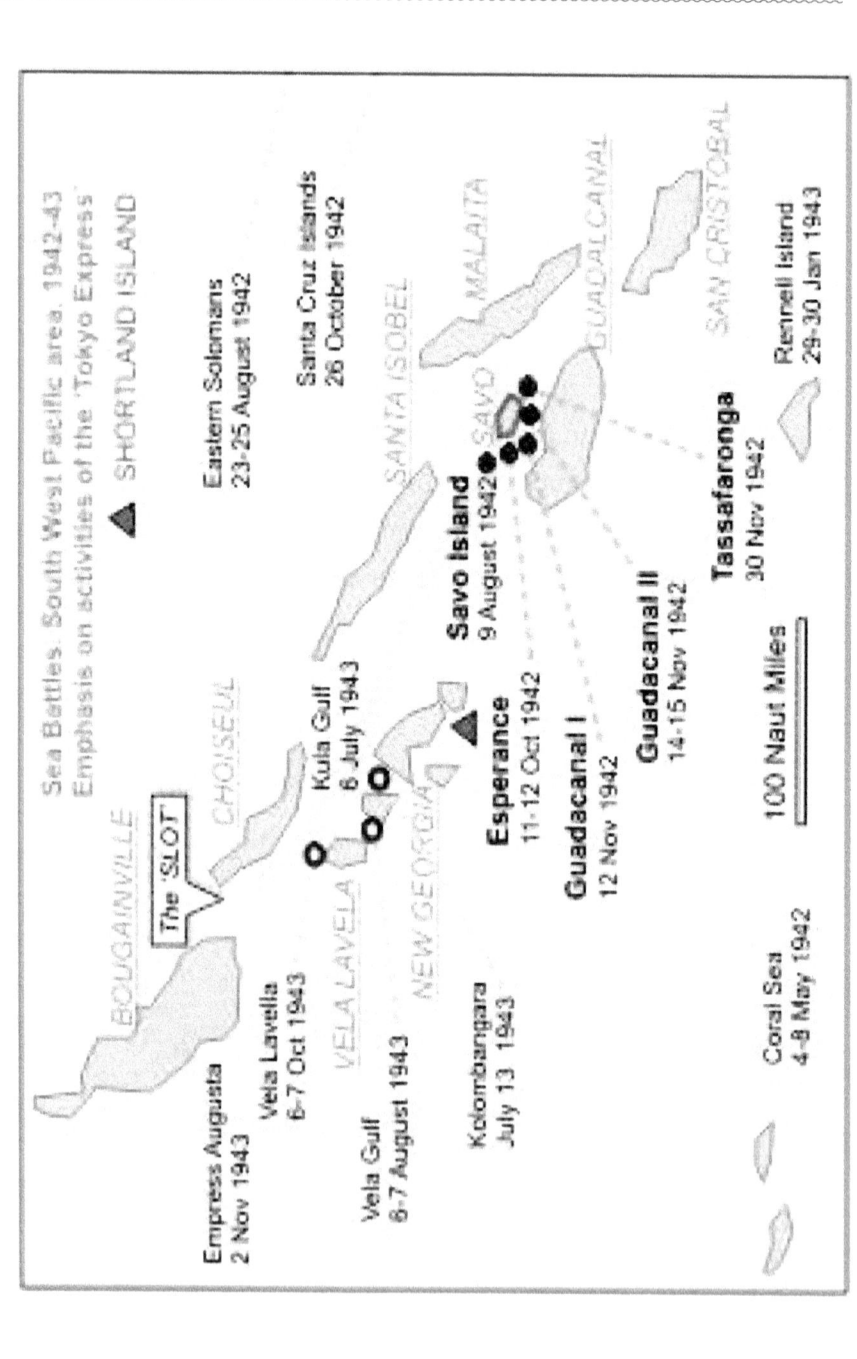

Sea Battles. South West Pacific area. 1942-43
Emphasis on activities of the 'Tokyo Express'

▲ SHORTLAND ISLAND

Eastern Solomons
23-25 August 1942

Santa Cruz Islands
26 October 1942

SANTA ISOBEL

MALAITA

GUADALCANAL

SAN CRISTOBAL

Rennell Island
29-30 Jan 1943

SAVO

Savo Island
9 August 1942

Tassafaronga
30 Nov 1942

Guadacanal II
14-15 Nov 1942

CHOISEUL

Kula Gulf
6 July 1943

BOUGAINVILLE

The 'SLOT'

Esperance
11-12 Oct 1942

Guadacanal I
12 Nov 1942

100 Naut Miles

VELA LAVELA

NEW GEORGIA

Empress Augusta
2 Nov 1943

Vela Lavella
6-7 Oct 1943

Vela Gulf
6-7 August 1943

Kolombangara
July 13 1943

Coral Sea
4-8 May 1942

PREFACE

THE HEADLINES OF THE MONTGOMERY Advertiser, like other newspapers in every major city, read "General Douglas MacArthur, family, and staff escaped death in tiny PT boats."

Suddenly the entire nation is enamored with the Navy's little warriors, PT boats. Foot for foot it was the deadliest of the Navy's fighting ships. They were the fastest thing on the water. Like David and Goliath, they proved their fighting capabilities every time they were tested. To add to this growing reputation, it was the PT boats MacArthur chose to transport himself, his family, and his senior staff out of the jaws of death to safety.

December 7, 1941, the Imperial Japanese Navy Air Service took off from a carrier task force and launched a surprise attack on the United States Naval Base at Pearl Harbor, Honolulu, Hawaii, just before eight a.m. on a beautiful Sunday morning. The attack destroyed, or put out of action, twenty warships. The Japanese planes also concentrated on nearby airfields, destroying three hundred airplanes. By the time the Japanese broke off the deadly attack, over 2,400 people were killed and another one thousand were wounded, of which some would later die. The United States was suddenly at war.

December 8, 1941...Nine hours after the attack on Pearl Harbor, the Japanese attacked Clark Airfield in the Philippines. General MacArthur's air force was nearly a total loss. Due to the lack of air support, Admiral Hart ordered his fleet to set sail and depart from the Philippines. The only ships to remain in port were Lieutenant Robert J. Bulkley's small squadron of PT boats. Two days later on December 10, 1941, a group of Japanese bombers attacked the Cavite Naval Base, where Bulkley's Squadron 3 PT boats were head-quartered. Cavite was soon in complete ruin. Fires raged all over the base, with black smoke billowing up into the sky. As soon as the air raid sirens went off, Bulkley got his squadron of PT boats under-way as quickly as possible and out into the open waters of Manila Bay. As a result, none of Bulkley's boats were damaged in the raid. Japanese pilots saw the boats, however, and thinking them easy targets, they attacked. The Japanese soon found out differently. The commanding officers of the boats would hold a course until a bomb was dropped. They would then push the throttles forward to full power and turn the boat so that the bombs would miss the zigzagging boats. This kept the boats away from danger as they kicked up rooster tails and roared across the bay. During this time the PT boat gunners filled the air with thirty and fifty caliber lead projectiles. Before the Japanese broke off the attack, three of their planes had been shot down while none of the boats had been dam-aged. The little boats no longer looked so tempting.

As Japanese forces continued to advance, taking over the Philippines, President Roosevelt felt that he couldn't risk MacArthur's capture and sure death, so he ordered him to leave the Philippines. MacArthur was considered an American hero and one of its most famous generals. His capture would be devastating to American morale.

When MacArthur received his orders to leave Corregidor, his choice of escape was Lieutenant Bulkley's PT boats, now called the "devil boats" by the Japanese.

Bulkley's squadron had been forced to fight with little or no support, since the Japanese had bombed the support facilities, destroying them. This left his boats were in dire need. He chose four boats to attempt the escape. PT Boat 41, with Bulkley in command, would transport the general, Mrs. MacArthur, their son and his nurse, as well as General Richard Sutherland, Chief of Staff, Major Charles Morehouse, MacArthur's personal physician, and two other officers on the general's staff. The 34 boat, under Lieutenant Robert Kelly, would carry Admiral Francis Rockwell, General Richard Marshall and two other officers. PT boats, 32 and 35, also sailed with several officers. It was decided that if the boats were attacked, the PT boat 32, the PT boat 34, and the PT boat 35 would put up a defense while the PT boat 41 would flee and try to escape. The boats were overcrowded, making for poor conditions for both the passengers and crew. This was especially true when foul weather was encountered, which was a frequent occurrence in the area. Nevertheless, on the evening of March 11, 1942, the boats rendezvoused at eight p.m. and, with their passengers on board, they started the trip.

For fear of airplanes and Japanese ships, the trip would be made in several legs with travel only at night. On the morning of March 13, 1942, PT boat 41 made the big island of Mindanao, their final destination. This was where they'd meet a plane that would take MacArthur to Australia.

Bulkley's boats traveled the five hundred sixty miles in a hair raising thirty-five hours. They had encountered stormy seas, mishaps to PT boats, avoided mine fields, Japanese warships, and big guns on some of the Japanese held islands.

MacArthur told Bulkley at the end of the trip, "You've taken me out of the jaws of death."

PROLOGUE

T HE JAPANESE BOMBED PEARL HARBOR on December 7, 1941, where most of the United States Pacific Fleet was destroyed. The President said that it was a day that would live in infamy.

Matt didn't dispute Roosevelt's words. He was sure that Roosevelt, being the President, knew more than an ensign in the Naval Reserve. One thing that he was sure of, however, was the outcome of the Pearl Harbor attack had stretched as far as Bullock County, Alabama. There were two thousand plus killed that day, which included one of their own. In front of the Singletary house, both sides of the road were lined with cars and trucks. They had parked alongside the ditch, leaving just enough room for a car to pass. In the pecan trees across the road from the house, three wagons were standing, which had been pulled by either horses or mules. The trees provided some shade for the animals. As they got close, Matt could see the handles of a plow in the back of one wagon. Ready to go to work after the owner paid their respects.

Matt's dad saw a place to park and expertly pulled into the space. His dad was Bubba Blue, the only highway patrol for Bullock County. "Kathy, watch your step getting out," Matt's dad said. "That ditch looks deep."

Matt noticed a black ribbon on the mailbox as he slid out of the car. It caused a shiver to run down his back. The yard and front porch were full of people. Many of them spoke to Bubba and Kathy. Bubba was considered the law and people parted out of respect, giving them a clear path to the porch and front door. Matt felt the people looking at him and holding their gaze. He didn't care if they stared. It was not often that they saw a naval officer in dress whites. Matt wore the white dress uniform out of respect, and because he didn't have a set of dress blues, which he thought would have been more appropriate. But out of respect for the deceased, he should be in uniform. It was, after all, Ensign Lamar Singletary. The friend who had talked Matt into joining the Naval Reserve a few years ago.

When they were in the house, they got in line to pass by the casket, which sat in the corner. Lamar had been critically wounded while firing one of the ship's machine guns at the Japanese planes. He'd been in the hospital since the attack until he died a week or so ago. The family had gotten his body back quickly, Matt thought. He wasn't sure who would be sitting up with the dead, but Matt was glad that he hadn't been called to do so. Matt couldn't see himself doing that, even as much as he liked Lamar.

Martha, Lamar's mother, saw Matt and, with a cry, she ran to him. Matt stood out in his uniform, and now he questioned his decision to wear it. "Oh Matt! Matt, they've killed my boy, damn their heathen souls." He hugged Mrs. Martha until Mr. Homer pulled her away.

"You'll mess up his uniform crying on him, Martha," Homer said. As they stepped away, Homer asked Matt to see him before he left.

Matt touched Lamar's hand as they passed by the casket, and then moved on. Lamar was gone before his time, like many of the young men that the Japanese took that day.

Seeing a flash of white on the back porch, as he was walking back towards the kitchen, Matt headed that way. Picking up a glass of sweet tea that still had ice floating in it, he hurried to the back porch. He immediately saw the man in his dress whites. It was Lieutenant Sidney Hinson, USN. Sidney was smoking a Lucky Strike cigarette. He tossed it in the yard, and then he stood up and shook Matt's hand, introducing himself as he did so.

Two teenage girls had just gotten up from the porch swing, so they went over and sat down. Sidney lit up another Lucky Strike and asked Matt when he was to report for active duty.

"March 1st," Matt told him. "I report to the 3rd Naval District Headquarters at 90 Church Street." He was proud that he'd memorized the name and address.

"They'll probably want to send you to torpedo school as soon as you get there," Sidney said, thinking aloud. He looked at Matt then and said, "You don't want that. You'll be just one more ensign. How would you like to go where you'll really do something for the war effort and enjoy yourself at the same time?"

"Sure," Matt said.

Sidney then told him about the PT boats. "I'm going to the MTB School in April. It's in Melville, Rhode Island. Would you like to come with me?"

Matt was soon mesmerized, listening to Sidney as he painted a picture of the dashing motor torpedo boats, shortened to PT boat. He was soon won over, and when Sidney asked if Matt would like to join, he said, "You bet." If it was good enough for Sidney, who was already a full lieutenant, it was good enough for Matt Blue. It was like one Bullock County boy looking out for another one.

"If you are not doing anything tomorrow, we'll go over to Montgomery, to the Reserve Center, and you can put in your application. We can maybe get orders to the same PT boat," Sidney said.

Damn, two of Union Springs finest, serving on a PT boat together, Matt thought.

Sidney left soon after with a promise to pick Matt up at 08:00 the following day. Mr. Blue walked out and asked Matt if he was ready to leave. Matt looked up and could see that the sun was going down. Matt hadn't realized that he and Sidney had talked for so long. He found Mr. Homer in the kitchen eating some pecan pie.

Looking up, Mr. Homer asked, "Are you ready, Matt?"

"Yes sir," Matt replied.

He took one more swallow of tea, wiped his mouth on his shirt sleeve and told Matt to follow him. They went to Lamar's room...a room Matt had been in many times. He'd slept there often. These thoughts got to him and it was hard to hold back the tears. It suddenly hit home that one of his friends was gone forever.

Mr. Homer picked up a box and handed it to Matt. "These are Lamar's uniforms. You were close to the same size so we want you to have them. They'd just be a waste staying here. Likely they would rot." Matt took the box and turned to go. "Wait a minute," Mr. Homer said. "You may as well have his long knife too."

"That's his sword," Matt replied. "You should keep it."

"No, we don't want to keep anything from the Navy," Mr. Homer said.

Matt took the beautiful sword with a promise to give it back if they ever wanted it. Mr. Homer shook his head and stated that they never would, so Matt's dad took the sword, while Matt carried the box. No one spoke as they headed out the door to go home.

PART ONE

CHAPTER ONE

I
T HAD BEEN SOMEWHAT OF a sad departing. Matt's parents were not just sending their son off to join the Navy, they were sending him off to war. Matt's dad had been very manly, trying to hold back the tears, while his mom and sister, Katie, were crying. A wounded marine, getting off the train with bandages on his head and face, didn't help matters. Further proof that the war was touching home.

Matt quickly got on board the train car and easily found a seat, just before he started crying. The car was only half full, so basically everyone had their pick of seats. Matt mentioned it to the conductor, who smiled and said, "Just wait, by the time we get to New York, you'll wish that you had this much room."

The seats were not that comfortable, so Matt put his sea bag on the seat and leaned against it. His mind soon began to wonder, thoughts on when he'd first gone to the recruiting office. There wasn't a recruiting office in Union Springs, at that time, which was the county seat for Bullock County. Lamar Singletary was driving, so they went to Eufaula, Alabama, which was right on the Georgia line. Matt filled out the application, which the recruiter just glanced over.

"You've had three years at Alabama?" The recruiter had asked.

"Yes sir, but I already have enough credits to graduate," Matt replied.

"Uh huh," was all he said. "Your father is a highway patrol." This seemed to arouse his attention. Looking back at the application, the recruiter continued, "You like to play football, hunt, and fish." Matt nodded his head. "You like to fish," the recruiter said again, more a statement than a question. "I bet that you have a nice boat."

"My dad does," Matt responded. For some reason, he knew that the recruiter's mind was on the speed boats that zipped across Lake Eufaula on the weekends. Matt didn't tell him that his dad's boat was a ten foot jon boat made for fishing in ponds. Matt was not sure if the recruiter thought he might need Matt's dad's help some time, or his thoughts of Lake Eufaula were what moved him. The next thing he knew, though, Matt was assigned a billet. Ninety days later, after completing midshipman's school, he was commissioned an ensign in the Naval Reserve. Returning home, Matt finished his fourth year at Alabama. He now had more than enough credits to graduate, but his orders had him reporting to active duty before the actual graduation. Alabama would send his diploma to the house, Matt was told. He had no doubt that his mom would frame and hang it on the living room wall.

***

MATT HAD DOZED OFF SOMEWHERE in his reverie. When he woke up, the train had stopped and people were entering the cars. A couple looked at his seat and then moved on. He wondered if his officer uniform scared them off. Matt asked the conductor where they were and he said, "Columbia, South Carolina."

The conductor then asked, "Did you get your nap out?"

Smiling, Matt admitted that he had and then some, "I tried to cram a lot in my last two weeks at home."

"Don't all you guys," the conductor said before moving on.

The next stop was Wilmington, North Carolina, where Matt met a guy who would turn out to be one of his closest friends throughout the war...Frank Andruss. Striking up a conversation with Frank proved to be no problem at all. In less than a minute, Frank asked where Matt was from.

Matt told him, "Alabama."

"I knew it was Alabama or Georgia. That southern drawl was a dead give away," Frank said.

It was plain to Matt that Frank was a Yankee but he didn't ask from where. Matt figured Frank would tell him at some point. Matt's dad had always told him, 'don't ask the obvious'. After a bit of silence, Matt said to Frank, "What have you been doing south?"

"I got a call from a boat dealer in Boston. It appeared that a guy from Wilmington bought a new sailboat. It was bigger than what he was comfortable with sailing by himself. I had the time and the money he offered was good. On top of that," he said with a big smile, " he had a good-looking wife and she could really cook." Matt was smiling now, as Frank continued his story, "She looked good in a bathing suit, also."

Frank raised up his head, closed his eyes and went, "Mmm uh...I can still see her. I thought about going A.W.O.L. before ever signing in." Matt laughed as Frank gave a big sigh and then said, "But, I didn't want to screw up a chance at P.T. boats."

"Are you going to MTB School?" Matt asked after hearing Frank's comments.

"Yeah," Frank said.

Matt then told Frank about Lieutenant Sidney Hinson. "I'm expecting orders to Melville's MTB School as well. I was told that orders would be waiting once we checked in to New York."

"Looks like we'll be classmates, maybe," Frank said.

For the rest of the trip they talked about sports, played cards, talked about girlfriends, dozed, and then talked some more.

When they got to New York, Frank said, "Let me do the talking, Country, ain't nobody likely to understand you."

A petty officer heard their discourse, and seeing their officer's uniforms, asked if they were headed to the Third Naval District Headquarters.

"We are," Matt answered.

"Buses are to the right and around the corner," the petty officer said.

Matt thanked the guy and then looked at Frank, "He understood me well enough."

"Lucky," Frank responded and gave a Matt a push towards the bus.

At the Third District Naval Headquarters, a first class petty officer with a badge and armband directed the enlisted men one way and the officers another way.

"He must have been a traffic cop in another life," Frank mumbled.

Matt and Frank entered into a large room that was filled with, at least, a hundred other officers. Most of them were smoking and a dense haze hung over the room.

"Dang," Matt complained, the smoke burning his eyes. "Anybody think of opening a door or window?"

"I don't see any windows," Frank answered.

At four o'clock, or as the Navy says, sixteen hundred, a navy lieutenant came in the room saying, "Okay, you men, we are shutting down for the weekend. If you need a bunk, see Chief Meeks." The lieutenant pointed to a man standing at the entrance to the room.

"He obviously doesn't like the smoke either," Matt said.

"Shh..."

The lieutenant had just finished saying, "Otherwise, you are on your own until 0800 Monday."

"I guess that even with a war going on, the navy doesn't work overtime," Matt volunteered. Frank just grunted, and Matt could tell that he had other thoughts running through his mind. "Do we get in line to get a bunk?" Matt asked.

Frank's response was different than what Matt expected. Frank cut his eyes at Matt and said, "Have you ever been to New York City?"

"No," Matt responded.

"Well, its country comes to town," Frank replied with a big smile. "Your tour guide awaits you, young sir. Let's go see the sights of the big city."

The weekend was a blur. They took a cab downtown and for the next hour they just walked up and down the main streets. Matt had never seen the like and in his mind he tried to form a letter to his parents. Times Square had to be the most fascinating and busiest place in the world.

"I've never seen so many people, not even in Montgomery at Christmas time," Matt volunteered to a pleased appearing Frank.

They walked up and down Broadway, stopped in a lounge that Frank had visited before, and with them being in uniform the bar-keeper gave them their first round of draft beer on the house.

"Much obliged," Matt said, thanking the man.

"He's from Alabama," Frank said, to explain Matt's comment.

"People don't say thank you in New York?" Matt asked.

"Yeah, they say 'thanks,'" Frank replied.

Matt was not yet twenty-one, but since Frank gave the order, Matt wasn't asked for any identification. *I guess they don't question you if you're in uniform*, Matt thought.

While they drank their beer, a group of people were arguing over which movie had been the best, *Tobacco Road* or *Doctor Jekyll and Mr. Hyde*. The guys liked Spencer Tracy and Ingrid Bergman in *Doctor Jekyll and Mr. Hyde*. The girls liked *Tobacco Road*, since it was more of a love story.

"What's your favorite?" Matt asked.

"I'd go with Ingrid Bergman," Frank answered. "She's a beautiful dame."

As they finished their beers, Frank looked at his watch and said, "Let's go to the movies, Country."

Matt was game, but was not expecting to see such a theater. It was nothing like the theater in Union Springs or those in Montgomery. It was nearly nine p.m., and time for the second feature. They crossed the street, dodging cars and cops, and went to see the Errol Flynn movie, *"They Died with Their Boots On."*

Frank said the theater was called a 'movie palace.' There were so many lights outside that it looked almost like daytime. The inside of the theater was, for lack of a better description, elaborately decorated. It was indeed a luxury palace and made so that people could watch a movie in comfort. No wonder so many people were nicely, almost formally, dressed, with the men in suits. Matt felt out of place in his Navy uniform. A woman at the ticket window spoke to her husband who turned to look at them. He either felt patriotic or felt that dressed in uniform as they were they couldn't afford the price of a ticket, so he bought their tickets to the show. It was ten cents for each ticket, as it was a late show.

Matt haphazardly watched the movie but spent most of the time people watching. He wished, at one point, that he had a camera with him to record the things he'd seen that evening to show the folks back home. They'd never believe it if he just told them. Waiting for the show to start, Matt said, "The prices are pretty much the same as at home."

"Yeah," Frank replied. "It's hard to jip you on popcorn and a coke."

***

MONDAY MORNING CAME AND THE officers were being sent to torpedo school in droves, just as Sidney had said. Frank got out of line and walked over to an ensign. "Perhaps you can help us," he said. "We've been told that special orders would be awaiting us here, so I hate to waste time in line with the officers headed to torpedo school."

The ensign responded, "Most special orders come after torpedo school."

"Not these orders," Frank said, speaking very firmly, in spite of the fact that neither he nor Matt knew for certain that the orders had come through.

Finally, after a long moment, the ensign sent them over to a chief petty officer's desk. The ensign sarcastically told the chief their story and then he walked off.

"Twit," the chief said as the idiot walked off. "He's the kin of some admiral."

Frank and Matt could understand the chief's dislike. Frank then told the chief that they'd both received verbal orders to MTB School at Melville for the first class. Matt felt that Frank may have been stretching the truth a bit, in his case anyway.

"Do you have a point of contact?" the chief asked.

"Lieutenant Commander Specht, William C. Specht," Frank rattled off just like he knew what he was talking about.

The chief smiled, "Specht tech. I'm not sure that I envy you guys."

There were no orders awaiting them, but the chief made a phone call. He came back and said, "Snafu, but they are expecting you, so I'll have your orders cut. Go find a coke or take a smoke and come back in an hour."

Good as the chief's word, they were soon on a bus to Melville or Rhode Island's little Annapolis. Within a few weeks, Matt had come to know personally what the acronym, SNAFU meant.

CHAPTER TWO

WHEN FRANK AND MATT ARRIVED at Melville, almost the first person they saw was Lieutenant Sidney Hinson. Sidney came over and shook Matt's hand. Sidney had already checked in but he walked with Matt up to the petty officer who was checking the officers in. Matt introduced Sidney to Frank and they chatted for a while. When they got up to the petty officer, Matt handed his orders to the man.

"Petty Officer Barnes," Sidney said, calling the petty officer by his name. "I'd consider it a favor if you could put Ensign Blue next to me in the First Housing Building. I know that there's an empty bunk and if we could be in the same training group that would be good also."

Barnes looked up and asked, "This officer as well?" He was referring to Frank, and Sidney nodded his head, 'yes.' The petty officer said, "Sure thing, Lieutenant."

After checking in, Sidney took Matt and Frank down to the water where they instantly fell in love. There sat a seventy-eight foot Higgins PT boat. For the next half hour, Sidney filled them in on her engines, her speed, and the torpedoes, which he said were the least reliable aspect of the boat. He pointed out each of the machine guns and the big gun aft.

"Can we go on board?" Matt asked.

"No, it's look but don't touch at this point. You'll get on board soon enough," Sidney replied.

They returned back up the hill where Sidney stopped at the little exchange and bought a coke and a pack of Pall Mall cigarettes.

"Changing brands?" Matt asked.

"No, I noticed that they were what Petty Officer Barnes smoked," Sidney said, and then he walked back into the administrative building. "Excuse me," he said to an ensign as he shouldered the man aside. Sidney then sat the bag down on Barnes' desk, without saying a word.

Matt learned quickly that Lieutenant Hinson firmly believed in taking care of his men, regulations or not.

A voice called out as they were walking back out, "Lieutenant Hinson."

They turned and Sidney smiled, "Damned, if you didn't make it." He then introduced Matt as a hometown boy and Frank as a friend. The man that Sidney was speaking to was a first class quartermaster named Al Ross. He and Sidney had been on the same minesweeper. After they talked for a while, Ross ran back to take his spot in the line.

Sidney said, thinking aloud, "I'll have to speak to Commander Specht about Al."

Matt found out then that Sidney and Specht had been shipmates in the past and it was Specht who had talked Sidney into applying for the PT boats. It was never said, but Matt believed that Sidney had also been promised to be a skipper...but why not, he was a full lieutenant.

✱✱✱

MTB School proved to be tough at times, but not overly so. This was partly because Sidney took Matt under his wing and also partly because Matt loved it. It was soon obvious that Lieutenant Sidney Hinson was the best in the class with Frank in second place. It was not surprising to Matt that First Class Quartermaster Ross seemed to go out each time that they went for training.

"I don't know if I'm going to make it," Matt volunteered to Sidney after a class. "This navigation is kicking my butt."

"Not to worry," Sidney responded. "I'll see that you pass." He looked around, spotted Al Ross and called the quartermaster over. "Al, I'd take it as a favor if you'd get Matt caught up on navigation."

"No, problem, Skipper, consider it done."

Matt found that Ross was able to teach him navigation much better than the school instructor. After a month, Matt actually felt like he might pass and make a passable PT boat officer.

"Thank you, Al," Matt said to Ross, after passing the navigation test. "I appreciate you."

"My pleasure," Ross said, making light of his efforts. Still, Matt knew.

The next weekend, Sidney borrowed a car from a friend and they took a ride to Newport, Rhode Island.

"Goodness," Matt exclaimed, totally astounded to see the summer homes of all the millionaires. He thought to himself, that even their local congressman's house in Union Springs was not much more than a gate house or servant's quarters for these homes. Matt had come better prepared this time and brought his camera. He took a dozen or so pictures of the homes to show his parents. They went by the Yacht Club then. He took more pictures, since the yachts were bigger than most people's homes back in Union Springs.

When they were alone later, Sidney said, "I wanted to get you out of your shell and show you there's a different world outside of Bullock County."

"I'll say," Matt replied. "I've never seen such...such opulence."

"Aye," Sidney replied. "A lot of your MTB classmates come from houses such as these. They've handled yachts the size of our P.T. boats all of their lives. Still, I think you're better at handling a PT boat than most of them are."

Graduation day came at last. Matt was not surprised to see Sidney was number one and given command of the 48 boat. Matt was to be Sidney's XO (executive officer). Frank was given the 46 boat, and Ensign Ted Walters was his XO. Another friend that Matt had made was Lieutenant (j.g) Chris Duncklee. He was given the 60 boat, and Ensign Robbie Turner was to be his XO. Little did Matt know of the living hell that this group would go through in the following years.

Matt walked up to Sidney after graduation. "What do you have there?" he asked.

Sidney was looking at a sheet of paper that had the names of their crew members written on it. He handed it to Matt, who read over the names. Some of them he knew. It wasn't surprising to see that the name Al Ross, Quartermaster First Class, was the first name on it. Matt pointed it out to Sidney, who nodded.

"He'll be chief of the boat," Sidney said.

Matt nodded his head, but he didn't really have a clue as to what it meant. *I'll find out soon*, he bet himself. It was the school's philosophy that every man should be able to perform the next man's duty. A great theory, and in school it seemed to work. Matt took the list and went down it; *to get everyone cross-trained would be a job.*

Reading Matt's thoughts, Sidney said, "It's your job, XO, but we've got the crew to do it."

Matt nodded, feeling the responsibility coming down on his shoulders. He looked at the list again.

Al Ross, (QM1) – Quartermaster First Class

Joseph Morales, (GM2) – Gunner's Mate Second Class

Tom Clark, (MOMM2) – Motor Machinist Mate Second Class

David Hall, (QM2) – Quartermaster Second Class

Charles C Steffey, (BM2) – Boatswain Mate Second Class

Tony Brown, (RM2) – Radio Man Second Class

Allen Miller, (GM2) – Gunner's Mate Second Class

Rob Ruby, (MOMM3) – Motor Machinist Mate Third Class

Anthony Anderson, (SN) – Seaman

Greg Dermody, (TM2) – Torpedoman Second Class

Houston Dale, (TM2) – Torpedoman Second Class

David Gill, (SN) – Seaman, striking for RM (Radio Man)

Mike Phagans, (MM3) – Machinist Mate Third Class

Dale Byhre, (GM2) – Gunner's Mate Second Class

It looked like they had a good group of mature petty officers, on paper, with only two seamen. It was surprising that the PT-48 was blessed with one extra crew member. Somehow, they had a seaman that somebody didn't know what to do with. The seaman was striking for Radioman, so Sidney gladly accepted him.

"There may come a time that we'll be glad we have an extra hand," Sidney said. Matt didn't disagree with that, after all Sidney was the skipper.

Matt and everyone else were authorized two weeks leave and then it was off to war. Matt thought to himself, *am I ready...is anyone ever ready?* He wanted to try to put the war out of his mind and just enjoy the next two weeks, if for no other reason than to keep from worrying his parents and sister.

***

MATT FOUND SIDNEY ON HIS bunk, reading letters from home. "I feel hemmed in," Matt said. "Let's get off the base for a while."

"Alright," Sidney replied. "Let's see if the others want to go."

It was Saturday and while they didn't feel like going off any distance, they decided to go in to Melville to this little tavern and get one of their delicious steaks. Melville would be shut down on Sunday and with them expecting orders on Monday, Sidney, Frank, Ted, and Matt loaded up in a taxi and went to eat.

They had each ordered and were drinking Cokes, as the beer truck had been delayed due to the foul weather, and the tavern was out. Matt had noted a naval line officer when they sat down, but the man across from him had his back to them, so they didn't recognize him. It didn't take long for his voice to grow louder, as he seemed to grow angry at something the line officer said. Matt suddenly knew who was talking. The officer with his back to them was their commanding officer, Lieutenant Commander Specht.

"What do you mean a school for rich frat boys so that they can continue to play and have fun during this damn war," Specht asked angrily. "PT duty is anything but fun. If you don't believe it, ask Lieutenant Bulkley. Read his reports on what his squadron has gone through, or read MacArthur's reports and comments. Fun...I don't think so. The Navy is going to need more than the big battleships and carriers. Even destroyers can't do the things that Bulkley has done with his small boats. They have patrolled areas where death is a constant reality. They've faced all types of enemy ships, planes, submarines, and shore emplacements and the list goes on. They patrol in the black of night expecting to run up on the Japanese at any moment. Talk about nerve-wracking, and let's not forget about the sudden and frequent squalls that drench the men and the wind that chills them as they patrol in an open boat. When they're not being soaked, they are constantly faced with temperatures of one-hundred degrees or more. Your clothes are constantly wet so they chafe the body. Many of them wear nothing more than shorts and soggy boots that rot on your feet. They are assaulted with every kind of disease that you can imagine, malaria, dysentery, dengue...I could go on. But let's talk about nourishment? How often do you eat powdered eggs or spam, Henry?" *Henry must be the line officer*, Matt thought.

"I can't recall the last time," Henry replied.

"That's a mainstay for them. Bologna is called round steak and is a treat," Specht said.

Captain Henry Hull, USN smiled, "You remember when it used to be called 'horse cock'?" Both men laughed then.

Matt and his group couldn't help but snicker, even though they didn't want to alert Lieutenant Commander Specht that they were eavesdropping.

Specht continued, "While there's been some improvement, minimal I'll add, getting parts and finding suitable repair facilities is abysmal. Bulkley had to scavenge just to put enough boats together to transport MacArthur and his family and staff. Don't come at me with this rich boy crap. Send young Andrew to us when he graduates, and see what he tells you."

Captain Hull looked across to his friend, "I believe you've enlightened me, John. I will do more to see that you get funding."

Lieutenant John Specht gave a sigh. Hopefully, his hometown friend and neighbor would come through. If so, the steak had been a small price to pay. When Specht and Hull left, they never noticed Matt and his friends.

CHAPTER THREE

MATT'S TWO WEEKS AT HOME flew by, and he was glad that he had the time with his family and friends. He couldn't explain it, but he was anxious to get back to Melville, though, to see where their orders had them going.

Matt got a copy of their orders first and took them over to Sidney. "You hear about this yet?" he asked.

"Unfortunately," Sidney replied.

Their orders were not straight to the South Pacific as hoped for, but to deliver the 48 boat to the Brooklyn Navy yard where she was loaded on board the *Kitty Hawk,* APV1, for transit to Balboa, Panama. There the crew put theory to test. They found out what it was really like to be engaged in combat patrol and training exercises in all types of weather.

They had gun drills, but because ammunition was in short supply they didn't fire the guns. They also had torpedo drills that were probably the closest thing to actual firing.

"How can we really train without actually firing?" Matt griped. To his surprise, during their time in Panama, Matt came to realize that he could actually handle a PT boat. It also came with a deep satisfaction. *How I wish that father could see me now*, he thought.

It had started during an exercise when Sidney called to Matt and said, "I've just been killed and Ross is wounded. It's your job to finish the mission and get us back home."

Matt stumbled through the drill without crashing into any of the other boats, simulated firing the torpedoes and hauled ass back to port. Matt was smart enough to follow the 46, since he knew Frank would know the way home.

The next day, Matt took her out and played skipper all day while Sidney smoked and ate peanut butter and jelly sandwiches. The hard part came at the end – docking the boat by backing her in. He learned that it takes a bit of feel for the current as well as the throttles. The wheel was basically useless at low speeds. However, Panama served its purpose, and by the time they got orders to join Ron 3, Matt could handle the 48 with the best of them. While their exercises in Panama were not under live fire, they were, at times, tedious enough to cause tempers to flare.

They also found out the strengths and weaknesses of the crew. But with all the experienced petty officers, they were soon molded into a good crew. Houston Dale, who thought only of his torpedoes, had gray hair and so was nicknamed "Pappy." Allen Miller was six foot seven inches and became "Big Al." Greg Dermody was nearly thirty years old. He had a deep abiding faith in God. He was their Holy man and was called "Preacher" by the crew. Tony Brown, the radioman, naturally became "Sparks."

"You've done a good job, Matt," Sidney said the night before they left for the South Pacific.

"Thanks," Matt said. "There were times, though, that I wasn't so sure."

"You didn't show it, and that's what is important," Sidney replied. "The crew has confidence in you."

Matt smiled and answered Sidney, as they headed to the canteen, "Thanks, but you're still buying, Skipper."

The trip to Nouméa, New Caledonia was done by loading the boats onto the USS *Lackawanna*, AO400; and the USS *Tappahannock*, AO43. Cradles were made and the boats were lifted on board by a crane. There were two PT boats per ship.

They departed Balboa, Panama on September 19, 1942, and arrived at their final destination on October 12, 1942. It had been a most unbelievable trip. Even after they were unloaded, the boats were towed from place to place before actually arriving at their new home under their own power.

The newly constructed PT basin was on the island of Tulagi at the village of Sesapi. Matt didn't want to speak unkindly about his first base, but was only impressed in what it lacked as a base in his humble opinion. When the Japanese had left the island, they had left it in almost complete ruin, especially destroying anything that might be used by American Forces.

Sidney must have been thinking along the same lines. After a moment, he tossed a half-smoked Lucky Strike cigarette into the water and said, "Be it ever so humble, there's no place like home."

Matt, glancing about, was suddenly glad that he'd gone home on leave. He looked at Sidney and would've bet that he felt the same way. The trip home had been good. His family had dinner with Sidney's family at Holmes Café. Sidney's wife was a pretty lady and also very pregnant. She would stay in Union Springs with Sidney's parents and his sister, Dianne, who was also a pretty girl in her own right.

Matt had run up on an old football buddy from college. He was a second lieutenant in the marines, and like most of the marines, he was headed to the South Pacific. "Maybe we'll run into each other over there," Matt said. Herman didn't seem real happy, and Matt mentioned it to his dad.

"He may have a premonition," Bubba had said.

"I hope that I never get one," Matt replied.

"You just keep your mind on our Lord and Savior and on your duty, Matt," his dad replied.

"I will," Matt promised his dad. Looking at Tulagi, now, Matt was glad that he'd talked to his dad.

It had been another sad farewell with both families seeing them off. There had been no time to write in Panama, so Matt penned several letters while on the transport boat, not knowing when or if he'd have time to write again.

When they joined their squadron – Ron 3, they were told to make their own camp. Two days later their life of ease and luxury came to a complete halt, and not in a planned way. It was 2:00 a. m. or near that, when, going topside, Matt saw that it was misting rain. Was that thunder that awakened him? And then he heard it again. Pulling on his boots, Matt went out on the deck to hear better and maybe see the sky. He felt a chill as he realized that it wasn't thunder, but the sound of gunfire. The gunfire was coming from large naval guns.

**

THE THUNDER OF GUNFIRE SOON had everyone awake. As the crews of the PT boats came up on deck, the shelling became almost constant.

Lieutenant Commander Montgomery came down to the dock yelling, "They're attacking Henderson Field! Prepare for action. All boats should be underway, immediately!"

Someone asked, "Where to?"

Montgomery replied, "To the sound of gunfire," as he jumped on board the closest boat, which was PT 60. Matt thought to himself, *lucky you, Chris.*

The basin came alive as the PT boats' engines revved up. Matt's boat was the second boat and Sidney waited until the 60 boat was underway before shoving the throttle forward, lifting the bow up and shooting rooster tails sky high. The 46 boat was behind them, with Frank's boat following the 48's example. Sidney bumped Matt, getting his attention to move so that he could speak to Sparks and see if there was any radio traffic, so Matt didn't see the 38 boat get underway.

There was still a misty rain and the sky was black. "Black as the ace of spades," Sidney said. Were it not for the wake from the 60 boat, Matt wasn't sure that they could have followed it.

The flames leaping out of the Japanese big guns were now plainly visible. They were not unlike flashes of heat lightning, only they were orange and carried with it steel death.

Ross stepped in between Sidney and Matt and, speaking loudly to be heard over the gunfire and the boat's engines, said, "We're about halfway to Guadalcanal, Skipper." Sidney just nodded.

Montgomery gave the signal right after that for them to deploy in pairs. Looking back, Matt could see Frank's 46, but the 38 boat was still nowhere to be seen, but it was still black dark. A searchlight from a Japanese destroyer was sweeping the area but it didn't pick up any of the PT boats.

One of the crew commented, "Thank God for blind-assed Japanese."

Matt didn't know how they'd gone undetected but suddenly they were bearing down on a Japanese cruiser. She was lit up by her own gunfire. Easing the 48 to ten knots to reduce their wake, they closed with the cruiser. As they were getting close to the cruiser, they saw the 38 boat on their starboard side and just forward of them. The 38 boat slowed for a torpedo run. He fired his first two torpedoes at five hundred yards, and then let go with the other two fish at two hundred yards. Following the protocol that they had taught us at school, he kept the throttles to about twenty knots, or half speed, and then turned right and passed no more than one hundred yards off the cruiser's stern. The 38's deck guns were then firing into the Japanese cruiser. The 38 boat had interrupted the 48's run, but if the 38's fish ran true, so be it.

Sidney stayed at ten knots and counted the seconds. There was a violent explosion and then a second one came between the bridge and the bow of the cruiser. They were several hundred yards away from the cruiser, but when the torpedoes exploded, an intense heat wave swept over them. It lasted only moments but the preacher quipped, "That, me mates, is what a taste of hell feels like." Nobody laughed.

"Did you count the fish?" Sidney asked Matt.

"Yeah, two of the four fish exploded," Matt replied.

"That's not good," Sidney responded.

Montgomery, in Chris Duncklee's 60 boat, was trying to close with the enemy ship that was still firing at the airfield. However, luck was not on his side this time. Another Japanese destroyer had its searchlight on and it landed on the 60's port side. The Japanese immediately opened fire on the 60 boat.

Sidney opened the throttles a bit on the 48 and told the gunners to target the searchlight. The gunner opened up, peppering the destroyer with .30 and .50 caliber bullets. They continued to fire as the 60 boat continued its torpedo run. Two things happened almost at once.

Ross yelled out, "She's fired her fish." The other thing was the gunners shot out the searchlight on the Japanese ship. A welcome darkness fell over the 60 boat.

The destroyer was no longer concentrating its fire on the 60 boat. The 60 boat was now retreating at full speed. Suddenly there were two explosions where the torpedoes had run true and found their mark.

"Did they fire two or four torpedoes?" Sidney asked.

"I'm not sure," Matt answered.

Sidney changed direction and was going to attempt a run at the Japanese boat that they'd shot out the searchlight on. The crew turned on the smoke machine and laid a good layer of smoke and began a zigzag pattern. Sidney then slowed the PT boat down to limit their wake and turned to make their run. The boat had just planed out when out of the black night another Japanese destroyer crossed right in front of them. Matt thought to himself, *I don't think they even saw us but it turned on its searchlight looking for a boat.* Frank, in the 46 boat, zigzagged, laying a layer of smoke while the 48 boat fired their deck guns into the stern of the Japanese ship. Sidney was getting ready to make a torpedo run at the Japanese when it suddenly turned to port and left at flank speed.

"They've stopped firing on the airfield," Ross shouted.

Brown stuck his head out from the radio room, "We've been ordered to return to base."

Luckily, all the PT boats made it back to base without losing anyone and with no critical injuries to any of their boats' crews.

It was dawn when they tied up at the base. The gunners' mates had cleaned most of the guns on the way in. Once the boat was docked, Sidney said, "Take care of the rest of the guns and then we will get some shut eye. We can clean the rest of the boat in the morning."

All of the crew pitched in and they soon had the guns cleaned and were headed to their bunks. There were a few catching a last cigarette before turning in, and the glow looked strange in the dawn's light.

Sidney called Matt into his space where he'd already poured two fingers in a glass. Matt drank the fiery liquid straight down and then shivered. He thanked Sidney and went to his rack with a prayer on his mind and brandy on his breath. Matt was still excited...excited to be alive and completely exhausted. The exhaustion and brandy took over as soon as his head hit the pillow.

CHAPTER FOUR

THE NEXT MORNING EARLY, *WAY too early,* Matt thought, he heard Sidney tell Seaman Anderson to wake up the XO. Matt was always hard to wake up but by the time Anderson got to him, he was putting on his boots. Thanks to QM1 Ross, who had given the Commanding Officer and Matt a list of what would be needed for daily wear on the boat, Matt had been able to get his boots. The list was made for the enlisted but in these forward bases, their hats, if worn, were at times all that showed who was an officer.

"The crew knows so to hell with the rest," Sidney said.

The list consisted of twelve sets of underwear, twelve pair each of black socks and white socks, four sets of dungarees, six shirts (t-shirts), two pair of shoes, one pair of boots, a good sewing kit, one pair of swimming trunks, extra shoe strings, six towels, twelve handkerchiefs, extra shaving gear and toilet articles such as tooth brushes and scrub brushes.

There was also a list of items which were nice to have – a soap box for soap (it was also good for keeping smokes dry), cards, a cribbage board, and other games. There were also two pair of sunglasses, a pocket compass, and a waterproof watch (this could be purchased at the Exchange.) They also might need extra watch straps, a knife (possibly two), a flashlight, sneakers, a lighter with extra fluid, flint and wicks, two boxes of band aids, cheap canvas luggage, ink pens, ear plugs, fishing tackle, books, and an address book. The list had been pared down from the list given to the enlisted men. Did Ross do it, or was it given to him that way? It made no difference. Their time in Panama showed the value of it.

Matt quickly used his mouthwash, promising himself that he'd brush when he got back.

❊❊❊

Lieutenant Commander Montgomery looked worse than Matt felt. Matt would later find out that Montgomery suffered from malaria. The men quickly found seats and, seeing a few guys with coffee, Matt wished that he'd gotten there sooner to get a cup.

Someone shouted, "Attention on deck." Everyone stood up and there were a few scattered groans when their coffee spilled.

"Light them up if you got them, gentlemen," was Montgomery's first words. He then continued, "As soon as you leave here, you will go to the tender and fill your gas tanks. You will go in order of your slip. We will later reverse it. Now, let's talk about last night. You've all been well trained or you're just plain damn lucky. We sunk at least one ship and may have sunk another. Nevertheless, we stopped their firing on Henderson Field. The Mosquito Fleet did its duty once more, accomplishing its goal. We turned back the Tokyo Express."

Tokyo Express was the name given to the Japanese ships that were coming down the slot to attack Guadalcanal. The slot was the deep passage in the middle of the Solomon Islands.

Montgomery continued, "Hopefully, the top brass will soon admit to the value of the PT boats. Once you've filled up your boats and they're cleaned up and in shipshape order, you may wander around the base so that you will know it, especially the showers. A few of you reek." He made a show of smelling his armpits. "Oh hell, that's me." It got the laugh that he expected. His last comment was, "We have little here in the way of beverages. Any time you are with a large ship, beg, borrow or steal what beer you can. Usually every boat has one smooth talker, and you can bet that you have at least one man who is good at obtaining supplies in his own way. Since our supplies are slim to none, use this man's talents. I, of course, have no knowledge of it." Everyone laughed.

***

AFTER REFUELING, THEY SET THE crew to repairing the bullet holes. There were, all told, forty-seven holes in the 48 boat. They were all forward and above the water line. Thank God they didn't hit the gas tank or knock off an engine. Later, Sidney and Matt left Ross in charge of the boat and took their walk. It didn't take long to see that the native women had never heard of modest dress. A few women with babies walked about nursing as they went about their chores.

When they got back to the showers, the line was short so they hopped in. The water was fresh water and a bit warmer than Matt liked, but he realized that he was in the tropics and you can't adjust the sun.

Another thing that they learned was that rain or tropical showers sprung up at any time and frequently when you wished that they wouldn't. They also found out from an islander, who had been taught English by missionaries, that October and November got six to seven inches of rain. After two weeks of rain, Matt fully believed it.

It was two weeks before they got any mail. Most everyone on the 48 boat got at least one letter. Matt was lucky and got three, one each from his mom, dad, and sister. His dad told him that his recruiter in Eufaula, Alabama, had called the house to make sure that he had been taken care of. Matt thought that the recruiter was planting the seed. He was sure his dad would get a call on some future date by the recruiter asking if his dad could help him out of a ticket. Matt had to remember to let his dad know not to do any favors for the guy because of him.

RM2 Tony Brown got a battered box in the mail. Inside the cardboard box was a wooden box with fifty 'Have-a-Tampa' cigars, also known as 'Tampa Jewels'. The entire boat smelled of cigar smoke by nightfall.

The skipper even had one, and one in his pocket also. Sidney took out the cigar that was in his pocket and handed it to Matt. "You've tried brandy, now for a cigar." He leaned in close then and whispered, "Don't inhale it. I don't want my executive officer getting sick in front of the crew. If you walk off the boat I'll know why, just don't run. Get out of sight before you puke."

Matt knew that he had to go through the initiation so he took the cigar, thinking the smell was already bad enough. However, when lighting up, he found the smell to be not as bad as it had been. QM2 Hall had a camera and he took a picture of Sidney with his arm around Matt with the cigars in their mouths.

Later, Matt heard Al Ross telling GM2 Byhre, "The XO is still a kid but he don't show it none, like some."

"Aye," Byhre replied, "he's a good sort alright. He risked getting sick to be a part of us."

Al Ross nodded, "Aye, he has my respect."

"Mine too," Byhre answered.

Those guys will never know what they did for my self –esteem, Matt thought. He was suddenly glad all over again that he'd chosen to go along with Sidney and put in for PT school. Later, Matt pulled Ross aside and said, "My mom and dad better not ever see those pictures."

"Why, Mr. Blue, I don't know a soul on this boat who would do such a thing," Ross said, raising his eyelids as he spoke.

CHAPTER FIVE

THAT PATROL WAS THE FIRST of many. Patrols when the sky was so black that you could hardly see the bow of the boat. To make things worse and to add to the confusion was the weather. Rain tended to make uncertainties more uncertain. The rain made the crews uncomfortable and often ill. Every last one of them pulled their duty, though. No matter how many patrols went out, the Tokyo Express kept coming. While they did their best, they couldn't prevent the Japanese from sending more and more cruisers, destroyers, and airplanes down the slot.

One evening a storm came through and, without being ordered, they took the PT boats out of the basin to ride out the storm. The 46 boat was right behind them, with Frank throwing up his hand while Ted was putting on a tarpaulin.

"Thirty minutes and it will be worthless, if that long," Sidney muttered, speaking about Ted's tarpaulin.

It was a rough sea and, at times, Matt was worried that they were going to be capsized or pooped. They survived, though, without damage to the boat or the loss of any of their crew. When they got back in the basin, some of the docks were in shambles. Had they stayed tied up in port, the boats would have been smashed to pieces. Frank with the 46 boat followed Matt in, as did the 60 boat. The 38 boat had escort duty and Matt wondered how she was making out.

The next day, Lieutenant Commander Montgomery applauded them for taking the initiative to get their boats to safety. "We are in a shooting war," he said. "so we need to take care of all our weapons." He had already given the speech that their mission had multiple facets. They were to help the marines and keep Henderson Field in operation, as well as prevent the Tokyo Express from re-supplying Japanese held islands and also block the escape by sea of the Japanese infantry when the marines routed them. The PT boats' crews weren't sure that they'd done much of a job at any of those, though it wasn't for the lack of trying. Their ammunition and fuel use would support that.

***

SLEEPING ON BOARD THE BOATS was a living hell. The smell of wet bodies, uniforms, and wet boots, along with that of fuel, oils, and lubricants were beyond tolerable. So between night patrol, boat and gun maintenance and trying to catch a little bit of sleep, they set about building accommodations. *I use that word very loosely,* Matt thought. Through hook and crook, they were able to build a hut for the officers of the four boats.

The sides of the huts were boards left over from when the Japanese had the island. The roof was made out of various pieces of tin screwed together in a manner so that any holes in it were not over their cots. The cots were made by local natives. Curtains hung over their door and both windows. The curtains were cut from old tarps and hung basically to keep out most of the rain. Several of the crew hooked a cook tent from a group of marines. When the tent was set up, it was better than their huts.

While the accommodations were better than being on board the 48 boat, they still had to contend with the damn mosquitoes and rats. Between their hut and the cook tent, a large lean-to was built with lots of hooks to hang up wet uniforms and boots. After a patrol, they got some barrels that were soon set up to catch rain water, and they paid a woman from the village to wash their clothes. She didn't want money, as it meant nothing to her, so they paid her in cigarettes, candy, and a can of Spam here and there. It was a good system.

A day rarely passed that Matt didn't curse those rich political men in Newport, living in those fine mansions, while he was stuck on this malaria-infested island fighting for their butts. Still, as bad as it was, it was better than what the marines had in the jungles on Guadalcanal and the other islands. They had it bad over there... real bad. Matt did his best to remember to pray every day when going to bed. When he prayed he always included the marines. He also prayed that his family would never have to live like this or face death almost every night.

The one thing that no one could complain about was the mail, Matt thought. Once it started coming, they got mail at least once a week. One day Matt noticed Frank going through what looked like a manual for PT boats. .

Frank looked at Ted and Matt, after a bit and said, "You know other than combat readiness and proper care of the engines, we don't do a damn thing like this manual says."

Ted was now looking over Frank's shoulder and reading. "It says here that you can't even throw cigarette butts over the side."

Matt replied, "That was written in case we were tied up at the Newport Yacht Club." His reply got a laugh from all of them, including Chris and Robbie, who'd walked in, just in time to hear the last of it.

A few minutes later, Sidney walked in and said, "Matt, round up the guys. We have to deliver a group of Alamo scouts tonight. I'm told to pick either the 46 or the 60 boat to escort us."

"Which one will it be?" Chris asked.

"Flip a coin," Sidney replied, and then added, "I was told to go slow so as to keep visibility down." What Sidney meant by the statement was so their wake wouldn't be so prominent. It could be a dead giveaway, especially if a Japanese plane was flying overhead.

Chris lost the coin toss, so the 60 boat would go with them on the mission. They left a little after 1800, which was six p.m.

The Alamo scouts rode up in the back of a six-by Army truck. An Alamo scout was a poor name to describe those fellows. They had the look of demons from hell. Some people even called them snake eaters, but didn't say this to their face. *If one of them came at me, I'd just go ahead and shoot myself,* Matt thought. *It would surely be a less painful death.*

Two of the scouts were chewing Beech Nut tobacco. Matt knew that they were bad asses when they swallowed and didn't spit. He wasn't certain, watching them, that his powdered eggs and Spam weren't about to come up.

A sergeant was in charge of the scouts. He asked who the commanding officer was and when Sidney walked over Matt followed. The sergeant had a map of Guadalcanal. He had marked a spot on the map where they wanted to get off. Al Ross walked up after seeing the skipper motion for him to come over.

"We'll have to be careful," Al cautioned. "Our charts showed a good size sandbar almost at the point where the Alamo scouts want to disembark."

"So what, we get wet going ashore," was all that the sergeant said in a no-nonsense manner.

Knowing the Japanese frequently monitored their radios, Sidney handed Matt the map so that he could walk over to the 60 boat and pass on the information, including where the sandbar lay.

When Matt got back to the boat, Sidney said, "Take her out, Matt. I'm going down to my rack. I feel dead beat."

Matt had noticed that Sidney had not seemed his jolly self lately, and he wondered if the stress of these patrols were getting to Sidney. Matt later found out that it was something much different.

Matt kept their speed down to patrol speed to limit the wake behind the boat. He heard Big Al telling Seaman Anderson, "We are in for rain."

The seaman was quick to ask, "How do you know?"

Big Al replied, "My knees are starting to ache real bad."

"Aw, that doesn't mean anything," Anderson said.

"I'll bet you a fiver that it'll rain inside of twenty to thirty minutes," Big Al said.

"I only have a dollar," Anderson said.

"We'll make it a dollar then," Big Al responded.

Matt just shook his head, he figured that eight out of ten nights they'd get rain. Miller's timing was about right. It wasn't long after that Matt felt the wind pick up and a gust nearly took his hat off. It wasn't another five minutes later that it started to rain. Big Al had won his bet.

The dark sky became black with the rain. The clouds blocked the moon so it was just the 48 and 60 boats on a vast sea of nothing. Al Ross came over and handed Matt a cup of warm coffee. "It was in my thermos" he said, explaining why it wasn't hot. Matt thanked Al and saw that he was looking aft.

"I see the 60 boat. She's about one hundred yards back," Ross volunteered.

"Good," Matt said, and then added, "I hope that you know where we are, Al, because I haven't a clue."

Ross smiled, "It's my job to know, XO."

Everything was quiet except for the constant hum of the engines below. *I'm glad that I am not an engine man*, Matt thought. *I'd go crazy down in the engine room, in its close confines.*

They had traveled at a steady rate and, looking at his watch, Matt figured that they were close. His thoughts proved accurate when he saw the orange flashes of gunfire. Matt nudged Al, who had been looking down at the control panel. As Ross rose up, the flashes lit up the night.

Matt called Anderson over and told him to go wake up the skipper and ask him to come topside. He then spotted Seaman Gill, "Pass the word for the Alamo scouts' sergeant to come forward," he ordered.

"Aye, aye , sir." Gill's response made Matt recall that Anderson had not responded at all. Hopefully he understood his instructions.

When Sidney came up, Matt reported, "Gunfire off the starboard bow. You can see the orange flashes."

The sergeant, who one of his men had called Belk, come up by then. "That's on top of where we want to land," Belk said. "I think we may need to shift south a mile," he added.

Ross spoke up. "I'll make the changes."

CHAPTER SIX

THE ISLAND WAS SOON IN front of them, a dark blob rising out of the water. The gunfire to the north of them continued.

"I think that's a destroyer," Sidney volunteered. "They're firing at the marines on the island."

"Why are they using machine guns instead of the big guns?" Matt asked.

"They are likely only firing at the flashes," the sergeant said. "They may be doing the same thing we are. A flash from the big guns will light up the sky and possibly give away the position of the landing craft," the sergeant responded. Matt thought, *that sergeant has once again impressed me with his combat savvy.*

As the crew was well-trained and now experienced, there was no need to pass the word, 'man your battle stations'. Most of the crew had been there since the flashes from the gunfire had been seen. Matt still liked to walk around the boat to each station and speak to the men, if time permitted. Byhre was at his twenty mm telling

Morales that he'd got a care package from home earlier that day with two cans of Sir Walter Raleigh pipe tobacco.

Byhre said, "When we get back to base, bring your pipe over and I'll give you a bowl. I bet that you'll like it better than that Granger you smoke."

Morales saw Matt and said, "We're locked and loaded, XO."

Matt smiled; it was the same thing that he said every time. He finished his rounds and reported to the skipper, "Battle stations manned and ready."

They were now about five hundred yards off the beach and moving at idle speed. "The Alamo scouts have their backpacks on and their gear is ready," Matt told the skipper.

Sidney looked at the chart they had and felt that they could get within one-hundred and fifty yards of the island, which would lessen the distance that the scouts would have to paddle their rubber raft. But that was not to be.

"We've run aground on a sandbar," Matt muttered.

The scouts put their raft over and started to row toward the island. The PT boat was still stuck, even with their weight gone. They rocked the boat and felt it move slightly but it didn't break free, so they tried again. All of the crew got on one side and ran to the other side. They kept this up for several minutes.

"Do you want Chris to give us a tow?" Matt asked.

Before Sidney could answer, machine gun fire erupted, first on the port side, and then both sides were under fire. The bow was the only part of the boat still stuck. The rear of boat was clear and the propeller was not in the sand or mud.

Sidney put the boat in reverse and put the boat in full throttle. The boat moved a few feet. All about them, tracers lit up the night. The 60 boat had moved so as to bring his guns to bear. The .50 calibers were talking, answering the fire from the shore. Sidney repeated his reverse full throttle and this time the boat came loose and shot back. The 48's gunners could now fully engage the shore. The Japanese had set up crossfire, but they were now facing more than they had bargained for.

"Radio the 60 boat," Sidney shouted to the radioman. "Let's get the hell out of here."

Sidney turned the boat to the right, away from the 60 boat, and gave it full throttle. Matt wasn't sure the radio message got delivered with all the machine gun noise but Chris Duncklee didn't hang around and followed them out.

The PT boats had just gotten out of range of the guns on shore when the night lit up like daytime. A Japanese destroyer was now on them. The two boats split apart and tried to get away. For some reason, the Japanese concentrated on the 60 boat. Chris was zigzagging and was laying out a smoke screen. The Japanese were firing with their machine guns, but suddenly they let go with the big five inch gun. The shell missed the 60, but came so close the splash drenched the crew

Sidney came about with every gun firing. The Japanese, though, seemed to ignore the guns firing from the 48 boat, and concentrated their fire on the 60 boat. Sidney had a determined look. The 48 boat was closing in fast. Sidney fired the first two torpedoes at four hundred yards. The first one hit the destroyer just forward of the bridge and bounced up in the air without exploding. The second torpedo, not a second or two later, hit and exploded. They were now at two hundred yards from the destroyer. When they fired the two aft torpedoes, they both hit close to the bridge with flames leaping into the sky. The Japanese stopped firing at Chris's boat. Sidney turned hard right and opened the throttles.

The destroyer was dead in the water but the aft guns still could be fired, so the 48 boat got out of the area. A fire started on the destroyer at some point, but the ship was still floating when Sidney, Matt and the crew lost sight of it.

Chris came alongside and said, "They riddled me good aft and I'm taking on water. Hopefully, when I get the boat planed the water intake will slow."

"We'll stay with you," Matt said and waved at Robbie.

Thankfully, none of the bullets hit the engine or gas tanks. They followed the 60 boat back to the basin. Robbie got off the boat and ran over to the tender. After fifteen minutes or so, the 60 boat moved over next to the tender and large lines were tossed over to the secure the boat so that it wouldn't sink. They decided to drain the gas out of the 60 boat, so hoses were passed down. They only had a quarter of a tank of gas, but gas was gas when your boat sucked five-hundred gallons of high octane fuel per hour at top speed. It was 0600 when they finished transferring the fuel.

Matt set the men to finish cleaning up the boat and then hit the rack. None of the crew put powdered eggs, Spam, and toast ahead of sleep. Sidney and Matt had an officer's call at 0800. They would have to give a report of the previous night's action before they could get any shut eye.

Matt suddenly thought of the Alamo scouts and wondered if they had evaded the Japanese. He couldn't help but think that they did.

CHAPTER SEVEN

THE PLEASANT SMELL OF PIPE tobacco filled the air, and Matt wondered if that was what woke him up. He looked at his watch and it was 2:30 p.m., or as the military said, 14:30. They had left the officer's call at 0900 that morning so he'd slept a good five hours. He sat up on the cot and put on his boots. He could hear voices outside and the tobacco smell had to be coming from the crew.

Matt was concerned, thinking about the news that Lieutenant Commander Montgomery had released at the officer's call. The Japanese had landed thousands of troops on Guadalcanal. There would have been more but the Navy, Marines, and Army planes had destroyed three of the six Japanese transports.

Outside, the lady from the village was washing clothes. She had two daughters with her. One of them was about ten years old, and her other daughter was in her late teens. It was easy to see that she was well developed. In fact, Matt didn't know that he'd ever seen a more beautiful creature. Her skin was almost a cream color compared to the other natives, including her mother, making Matt think that she may be the daughter of a Japanese or European. What struck him strange, however, was all the natives had blonde hair. This was much different than anything he'd ever seen. He went back into their hut and got four chocolate bars and a couple packs of Camel cigarettes. It was his way of payment and keeping a happy relationship going. The woman would give the Camels to her husband. The girls tore into the chocolate bars.

Matt found himself staring at the older girl and felt himself becoming aroused, seeing her topless breasts. He bid them good day and walked off before he embarrassed himself. At officer's call, the Ron3 commanding officer gave them the day off, so Matt walked over to tell the crew. Most of the crew was up and a poker game was going on.

Matt was not surprised to see Big Al with a large stack of chips in front of him. Pappy and Preacher were playing cribbage. Tony Brown had Big AL's guitar and was trying to make cords by looking at a piece of paper where someone had drawn a diagram. Matt could see one diagram labeled G, another one labeled C, and a third one labeled D. There was another page but he didn't look at it.

Matt could see the men were taking it easy and his news of an evening off was well received. QM1 Ross said, "You made their day, XO."

Ross and QM2 David Hall had a compass that they were calibrating. Matt suddenly heard his name being called. It was an ensign from the squadron office. He suddenly hoped the ensign hadn't come to tell him that things had changed and they had to go out tonight. Thankfully, that wasn't the case. He had a message in his hand. Sidney's wife had given birth to a baby girl, his second one.

Matt went to their hut and woke Sidney. He handed him the message and said, "Congratulations, Daddy." The news quickly spread, and everyone came by to congratulate the skipper.

Later, that afternoon the 48's scavengers came back with a case of Schlitz. It wasn't long before somebody added a bucket of Torpedo Juice. Torpedoes had 180 proof grain alcohol as fuel. The squadron had some old torpedoes that were surplus so 'somebody' drained the alcohol out and mixed it with orange juice. A cup was dipped in the bucket and handed to the skipper.

He took a pull, smacked his lips and declared, "Our TM's have improved on their recipe. I declare it fit for consumption and the smoking lamp is lit."

The crew gave a cheer and their cups appeared like magic and each man dipped up a cupful. *I will admit that rank has its privileges*, Matt thought, so he dipped his cup after Sidney got his.

Pappy and Preacher, the 48's torpedomen, related that they 'found' a case of canned orange juice on the dock and used it and a bag of sugar to mix the Torpedo Juice. What they meant was the tender was minus a case of orange juice and the mess hall had lost a pound of sugar. Matt was just glad that it wasn't grapefruit juice, since he didn't like it.

The crew had a grand time with the Schlitz and Torpedo Juice. Cigars were soon being passed out. A poker game got started and Miller won a big hand right off. As he raked in his stack of chips, he declared, "At home, I have the fastest horse, the fastest car, the prettiest girl, and the ugliest dog in three counties. I also have the best luck on the island now." The crew broke out laughing.

Matt was glad that they didn't get called for a patrol. He wasn't sure that they could have found the boat. Sadly, he woke up the next morning with a cigar nub in his mouth and a headache from hell, and not to mention the awful cigar taste in his mouth. It wasn't the type of thing that you'd write home about.

There was not a single member of the crew that, when they woke up that morning, didn't expect to go on patrol that night. They'd make sure the boat was ready, something A1 Ross was already sure of. They'd lounge about the rest of the day after that.

The smell of pipe tobacco alerted Matt that some of the crew was already up. Byhre held up his pipe in a salute of sorts as Matt walked out of the hut.

***

THE TOKYO EXPRESS HAD INCREASED the number of cruisers, destroyers, and transports coming down the slot. The Devil Boats, as the Japanese called the PT boats, were often the only force preventing some of the landings. Nobody ever said the Japanese were not smart. Since the PT boats had wreaked so much havoc on the Japanese landings, they devised another way of getting needed supplies to their troops.

The Japanese learned to rely on the speed of their destroyers to get them to the coast of Guadalcanal, dropping the supplies over the side in water proof drums, as they cruised down the slot, and then getting the devil out of there. If five or six destroyers came down the slot, three, maybe four would be carrying the supplies while the other destroyers would act as escorts or guard ships. To get the supplies to their troops on land without actually stopping, they'd travel down the coast as close to shore as the depth would allow and toss the supplies off the fantail.

The Japanese would clean fifty gallon drums and then pack them with supplies, but leaving enough room for an air pocket in each drum. They'd then tie them in clusters of up to ten drums. As they would get near a prearranged drop off point, they'd push the cluster of drums over the side.

Japanese troops on shore would watch and wait. When the drums were sighted they'd latch onto the drums and pull them to shore using long sticks and ropes. On occasion, small boats were used to get a hold of the drums. It was not uncommon for a single destroyer to have between two-hundred and two-hundred forty drums.

There were a few times that Matt and the crew prevented the destroyers from dropping off supplies to the Japanese. At other times, they were lucky enough to see the drums floating after the destroyers had made their retreat back up the slot.

The first time that they saw the drums floating, Sidney had Matt go aft and man the .50 caliber with Morales giving instructions on how to fire the guns. After a quick refresher, Matt blasted the drums, sinking the entire cluster. When the last drum sank out of sight, the hands all cheered. Matt was glad that he'd sunk the drums, but more importantly he felt if called upon he would be able to use the .50 caliber if necessary. He did hope and pray that day wouldn't come; yet knowing deep inside that in all probability it would...*WE WERE AT WAR!!!!*

Once the PT crews knew what to look for, the clusters of drums would frequently be spotted. If action permitted they'd sink them. Sidney felt that everyone needed to know the other person's job, so each time they came across drums, one of the crew who was not a gunner would take a turn.

QM2 Hall did such a thorough job of it, the crew all kidded him, saying he was in the wrong rating.

***

THE CREWS FREQUENTLY GOT ALERTS from scout planes that spotted Japanese convoys before they got to the slot. Montgomery would then send out numerous boats. With time, Ron 3 had gotten several more boats assigned to their squadron. With the new additions to Ron 3, in theory, it gave them a better advantage. Unfortunately, with more boats, the more aggressive the missions got, as did the risk...and with risk comes losses.

Ensign Padgette came to the officer's hut at 1300 hours one day looking for the skipper. "He's at the boat," Matt told the ensign, adding, "Which is where I'm headed too."

The 39 boat had gotten some bad gas, which almost got the boat in trouble the previous night while on patrol. It seemed that they'd refueled from drums and not the tender. The 48 boat hadn't used any gas from drums but Sidney was a stickler when it came to operational readiness of the boat. When investigated, a waxy substance was found in several of the drums filled with gas. That meant the drums hadn't been checked well initially or they had a saboteur. The gas would be thoroughly strained in the future.

Padgette, who had been silent while they walked, saluted Sidney and said, "We have a downed pilot. They're sending the 48 boat to pick him up."

The entire crew was suddenly all ears. Night patrols were dangerous. The men expected those missions and accepted them without grumbling...but a daytime mission. PT boats were easy targets for enemy aircraft. You could usually dodge a bomb from a single aircraft, but if there were several planes...if they were strafing and a bullet hit the gas tank, you were a cooked goose. No one wanted to leave a downed pilot in the drink...no one. But sending a PT boat out in the daytime meant fourteen to sixteen lives were in jeopardy instead of just one. That wasn't counting the PT boat either. Yet, the pilots risked their lives for them all the time, so there wasn't any such thing as not going to pick the pilot up.

Sidney went to Headquarters to get the coordinates while Matt got the boat ready for sea. They sent a runner for Steffey, their boatswain's mate, who'd been sent on an errand.

Frank was on the 46 boat, which was alongside the 48 boat. Matt looked over at Frank and said, "There is a letter in my foot locker." Frank nodded and saluted Matt. When they first got to Tulagi, they had made a pact, to mail a prewritten letter home to their parents should something happen to them.

The rumor mill is fast. Every hand on the 46 boat knew that the 48 boat was going to pick up a downed pilot. Friends wished friends good luck, and a couple of them even offered prayers for a safe return.

Sidney had just got back and the engines fired up when up when Pappy said, "Here comes Gill and Steffey."

Matt looked up to see the two men trotting toward the boat and then jumping on board as Sidney put the 48 boat in reverse. As the boat turned to head out of the harbor, Sidney gave the coordinates to Matt so that he could go over them with Al Ross.

They were memorizing the chart when QM2 Hall, who was looking over Ross' shoulder, spoke the words that Matt and Ross were both thinking. "We will have to conserve fuel if we want to make it back without having to find more."

They would have to travel at twenty to twenty-five knots, and even then they'd use two hundred gallons per hour. But it was best to save as much fuel as possible, so that if they had to fight or try to evade the enemy, they would still make it back home. If they got into a skirmish with a Japanese plane, you could bet they would have to use full throttle at times, and that would cause double fuel consumption. *To run out of fuel would mean that they were sitting ducks for the Japanese.* Matt shuddered when the thought crossed his mind.

CHAPTER EIGHT

THEY POSITIONED LOOKOUTS FORWARD, AFT, port, and starboard, changing the men every hour. No matter how good the crew was, after an hour or so, their vigilance started to slip. Something that Sidney realized when he was on board minesweepers. A sister ship had been sunk due to inattention of her lookouts. The crew of PT 48 was exhausted. They'd been on patrol every night for nearly a month, until last night.

MOMM2 Clark, chief engineer of the 48 boat, had already informed the skipper that the engines needed maintenance. "We're actually past due, according to the hours logged," he said.

As soon as they got out of the basin, the 48 boat passed two supply ships headed in. The men whistled and waved, getting waves back from the ships.

Ross, the observant one, said, "Did you see the bullet holes and shattered glass on the bridge?" Hopefully, the supply ships had had escorts until they had gotten to the bay.

"Well boys, it looks like we'll lose out on any fresh beer." This came from Ruby, who'd come on deck from the engine room and seen the battered ship.

Preacher spoke up, "The way that you were laughing and rolling on the ground last night, Rob, I'd think that you'd want to steer clear of alcohol, until you dry out."

"Awe, Preacher, I was dry this morning," Rob replied. Everyone laughed at his reply. Rob Ruby could certainly hold his beverage.

They had been underway for nearly four hours and should be at or close to their coordinates. The crew was betting that unless the pilot had a Mae West on, or some other type of flotation, he'd probably drowned.

Matt looked at the crew and said, "How about thinking of something positive."

Pappy spoke up, "Well, we should know pretty soon."

The wind had been picking up for the last several minutes and the sea was getting rougher. Dark clouds were scudding across the sky. In the distance, they could see the rain.

"Two at a time, go get your tarps," Matt ordered.

Some of the men went, while others didn't even bother since you still got fairly soaked even with a tarp on when at sea. The tarp did keep some of the wind chill at bay, though. The rain didn't last but ten to twelve minutes, just long enough to make everyone miserable.

The forward lookout called out, "There's wreckage just to starboard, Skipper."

"Good eyes, Phagans," the skipper replied.

They picked up a lot of wreckage and finally Gill saw the pilot hanging on to a piece of the tail section. The crew got him on board the 48 boat. They got his wet boots and flight suit off. He was half delirious and dehydrated. He had been in the water long enough to have hypothermia. After getting some fresh water down him, Matt opened the medical kit and took out the brandy and poured him some in a cup.

Matt had just got the brandy down the pilot when somebody, on deck, yelled out, "Enemy aircraft." Matt told Seaman Anderson to keep the pilot comfortable and rushed topside. There were two Japanese planes attacking them. *Damn!!!* Matt thought. *One would have been bad enough!*

The crew had both .50 calibers firing, as well as the 20mm gun aft. Each gun had a loader by the gun. Sidney had the throttle full forward and was zigzagging as best as he could. The planes were coming in from both port and starboard. The plane on the starboard side dropped a bomb. Sidney came hard to port and the bomb passed over.

Big Al yelled, "Damn, I could've touched that thing!"

Steffy added, "And lost a hand."

The planes were past the 48 boat, but in a minute, Pappy yelled, "Here they come again."

Both planes were coming up aft. You could see the damn bullets hitting the water but Byhre didn't panic and kept the 20mm firing. Just before the planes' guns hit the boat, Sidney spun the wheel and they made a hard left turn.

One I won't ever forget, Matt thought. It was so sudden that he was surprised the 48 boat didn't flip. But to Sidney's credit, not a single shell hit the boat.

The enemy was not so lucky. Black smoke was coming from the lead plane. It was losing altitude but it exploded before it hit the ocean. Morales had fired an entire belt from his .50 caliber gun and Preacher was helping reload the gun. The belt for a .50 caliber was nine yards long.

"You gave them the whole nine yards, Joe," Preacher joked.

Ross, who was standing by Matt, yelled out, "He's coming in off the bow."

"Not for long," Sidney responded, watching the plane come in.

The zero suddenly banked left, anticipating Sidney's move. Sidney had made two left turns previously, but this time he went right. This made the plane a prime target.

Morales, Byhre, and Big AL filled the air with a barrage of .50 caliber and 20 mm fire. They could see the bullets punching holes in the plane, it was so low, and then the plane exploded. The crew yelled out in joy. They had survived their first focused air attack.

"Anyone hurt?" Matt asked. No one answered, so he reported, "No casualties, Skipper."

"Thank you, XO," Sidney replied.

Matt waited a minute to let his emotions calm down, and then said, "I've never seen such boat handling, Sidney. You saved our bacon today."

"Thank you, XO. It's just knowing what your boat will do," Sidney said.

***

THE SUN HAD SET AND as usual the sky was black. Sidney had let the guys take a break and get something to eat and drink. He even let them have a smoke before it got dark. The pilot was feeling better and came topside, thanking them for picking him up and saving his life. After a few minutes, he went back down to his rack.

As soon as they started back to Tulagi, Sidney turned the boat over to Matt with, "XO, you got the boat."

For the next four hours, it was QM1 Ross and Matt in the cockpit with QM2 Hall relieving Ross at one point. The sky hadn't changed any and so far they hadn't run into any ships, theirs or the enemies. The weather had held, and with a little luck they'd be in port in an hour.

Sidney said, coming on deck, "As dark as it is, I wouldn't be surprised if we didn't meet up with some Japanese ships or our patrols."

They were not yet near the slot when the boat wobbled suddenly and then wobbled again. Someone yelled, "Man overboard." Sidney pulled the throttles back.

"What was that?" Matt asked.

Sidney glared at him, "The wake of a destroyer or a cruiser, maybe two." He then asked, "Who went over?"

"Morales," someone answered.

"Can you see him?" Sidney asked.

"No," was the reply.

Sidney said, "Watch the water and see if the light on his vest comes on." He came about with the boat and had two men lay on each side of the bow.

"Keep your eyes open," Matt said. "We don't want to run over him."

"There's a flash, more to starboard," Byhre said.

The current was pulling him toward an island. Sidney had to come around again but they got him. Big Al had a long pole and he held it over the side. Morales grabbed it and Al pulled him up and alongside the boat. He then grabbed Morales with one hand and set him in the boat.

"What the hell were you doing?" Sidney hissed.

"I had a loose flash suppressor," Morales answered. "I was trying to fix it when you hit whatever you hit."

"Get back to your station," Sidney growled. "Everybody get back to your stations."

***

THE CREW WAS STILL SETTLING into their stations when the unexpected happened again. Overhead, a scout plane came in low and dropped a flare on the deck of a destroyer. They had no idea that the ship was around. Matt thought, in *another minute the ship would have rammed us*. The destroyer's searchlight came on, but it was seeking the plane and not the 48 boat.

"Knock out that searchlight," Sidney yelled as he rammed the throttles forward.

The 48's guns went into action. The ship was firing and turning toward the plane when the searchlight was knocked out. Someone on the destroyer saw the 48's wake or the boat itself and realized that it hadn't been the plane firing at them. The destroyer's captain had the ship coming towards the 48 boat at flank speed. The destroyer was soon firing on them, at times, getting too close in spite of Sidney zigzagging.

The crew got the smoke machine going but they couldn't lose the destroyer. Matt sent out a message for help over the radio. He recognized Frank's voice responding.

The Japanese captain must have had all of his guns manned. The 48 boat got away from his bow with a hard turn but the guns along the side opened up. Somebody screamed and fell on the deck.

The words that Matt never wanted to hear came at him. "I'm hit, XO, take over."

Hall and Ross helped Sidney to his quarters and Hall did first aid and applied pressure dressings.

Matt took the helm and came around, and then he headed to cross the stern of the Japanese ship. "Preacher," he yelled, "stand by the torpedoes."

The destroyer captain had the ship turning, but Matt stayed right with him. It was a miracle, but while they were taking machine gunfire, the big guns didn't bear to fire. Matt didn't know if they could depress the big guns low enough to hit a small target at two hundred yards.

Matt reached over and pushed the control for the port side torpedo and then for the starboard side. Once the fish were running, Matt made a hard turn to port. The first torpedo hit and exploded and then the second hit with an explosion.

"You got her buggered now," Big Al said. He then made a gasp, "I'm hit, XO."

Matt ordered Ross to take control of the wheel, while he checked on Big Al. He was bleeding from both legs and he couldn't stand up.

"When did you get hit?" Matt asked, trying to consider the amount of blood loss.

"The first blast got me," Big Al answered.

"You were hit and continued to man the .50 caliber," Matt said.

"We don't have a lot of extra men, XO."

"Who else has been hit?" Matt asked.

Gill spoke up. "Anderson was, XO. He's dead."

They got Big Al bandaged up and Steffy pulled Anderson to one side and covered him with a blanket.

The Japanese destroyer was busy limping away, trying to keep from sinking. *I guess they decided to leave us alone*, Matt thought, **thank God**. They had no other action that night, which was a godsend. Headed back to base, they stayed at half speed so as to conserve their precious fuel supply. They had expended a dangerous amount during battle. Everyone would breathe a sigh of relief when they reached the base.

As the 48 boat neared the harbor, Matt radioed and asked for an ambulance and corpsman to meet them with a stretcher and a body bag. He was whipped and the crew was totally exhausted, but something else weighed on everyone's heart. They'd lost a shipmate. The skipper and Big Al would be shipped off to a hospital. They were not a complete crew anymore.

Once the medical people got there, Matt took a moment to speak with Sidney. "I'm sure they'll give you the 48, Matt," Sidney said. "I know that you'll take good care of her and the crew."

"Aye, Skipper."

"I hope to see you before too long, Matt," Sidney said.

Matt could see the emotion in Sidney's eyes. "If I can get away, I'll come see you, Sidney." He didn't. The next time Matt saw Sidney would be when he went home on leave. Sidney had been temporarily discharged and was waiting on a medical board. At least he was alive.

PART II

CHAPTER NINE

T HE CORPSMAN AND MEDICAL PERSONNEL were all around and Matt didn't notice Lieutenant Commander Montgomery until the ambulance drove away. Matt, seeing him, thought to himself, dang he should have gone with the ambulance. It was easy to see that the man had malaria, he looked drained out.

Matt saluted Montgomery and he returned it. "You've had a bad night of it, Matt."

Matt quickly summarized everything from the time they escaped the planes. Montgomery said nothing until Matt finished and then he asked, "Is she taking on water?"

"No sir!" Matt replied.

Montgomery nodded his head. "It was luck with that scout plane," he finally said after a long moment of silence. "Take care of your guns and wash away the blood. Tomorrow we'll get her over to the repair shop and turn the carpenters loose on her. How are the engines?"

"They are due their routine overhaul, but we've had no failures," Matt said.

Montgomery nodded and said, "I'm sorry about Sidney. I know that you were both from the same hometown. Well, the 48 boat is yours now, Matt. I'll see you at nine in the morning." He ambled off then. Matt called Al Ross over and filled him in on Montgomery's comments.

"Let me be the first to congratulate you on your first command," Ross said, saluting Matt and then shaking his hand.

An hour later, they secured the boat and Matt went to their hut, scattering a couple of rats. He'd written home asking for some rat traps, like his granddad used in the barn. Anything smaller and the rats would just tote them off. Matt was not sure how long he'd kept going over the events of the night. He did know that he was dozing off when he heard Frank and Ted come in. He sat up and shined a flashlight with a red filter on it.

Both men turned around. "We thought that you'd be dead to the world," Frank said.

"I'd just dozed," Matt replied. He motioned them to sit down on Sidney's rack. It dawned on them then that not all was well. They talked for nearly an hour. When Matt lay back down, it was five minutes until four a.m. He'd not get much more sleep. He set his internal clock for 7:15 a.m. and went to sleep. He woke up at seven o'clock so he quietly got up.

Chris and Robbie had come in at some point. Matt grabbed his douche kit and went to the showers and then came back to dress. When he got to headquarters, he could hear them talking of sending Lieutenant Commander Montgomery to Pearl Harbor and probably back to the states.

Ensign Padgett saw Matt and told him to have a seat. A few minutes later, Matt was shown into Lieutenant Hugh Robinson's office. On the way, Padgett whispered that Lieutenant Robinson had just taken over as the squadron commander. Sidney had felt that Robinson was a bit stiff-necked for a PT squadron XO. He was the commanding officer now.

When Robinson walked in, he shook Matt's hand and then said, "Have a seat, Lieutenant."

Matt thought that he'd made a mistake, but after shuffling through some folders on his deck, Robinson found what he was looking for. Opening the folder, he leafed through several papers and then took one out and handed it to Matt. It was his promotion to lieutenant (j.g.). It was effective 30July1942. The order for promotion had been sent to Melville, and then to Panama, and finally to Tulagi and Sesapi.

"It took them a while to get the paper work to you, but I'll make sure your pay will be adjusted," Robinson said. He then surprised Matt as he reached in his drawer and pulled out a pair of silver bars, which were collar devices for the khaki uniform or summer whites.

Matt had four sets of whites packed up in moth balls. He wore dungaree bottoms, a t-shirt and his officer's hat, just like everyone else. Lieutenant Robinson didn't say anything about Matt's dress.

Robinson asked about Matt's report, which he gave to him. Robinson sat down reading it. When he was finished, he leaned back and said, "A good report. Last night was a total disaster. We gave them all that we had, but they landed more Japanese troops." He then stood up and continued, "I know that you want to get back to the 48 boat and get the repairs started. You'll be glad to hear that your Gunners Mate Miller only got splinters in his leg, and he should be back to duty in a few months. We have gotten some replacements that will be here when the supply ships come in. I'll send a couple of the replacements, seamen or petty officers, over to you, to replace Anderson and Miller. We also have three officers coming, with two of them being ensigns. I'll send you one to be your XO."

"Thank you, sir," Matt replied. Matt thought that this Lieutenant Robinson might not be as bad as he had been led to believe. When Matt got back to the boat, the crew was waiting for him.

"I talked to the people at the repair facility, Skipper. They are ready when we are to start on the boat. Clark and I went over the repairs needed, and they agreed to pull the heads on the engines and see what kind of shape they're in. By-the-way, Skipper, con-gratulations of your promotion."

Matt smiled and thought to himself, *is there anything that Ross doesn't know*?

***

THEY HEARD A KNOCK ON the hut later that evening. Not once since the hut had been built had anyone ever knocked. They usually would shove the curtain aside and enter the room. Ted looked at Frank and Matt. "Is everyone decent?" he asked. Frank and Matt nodded their heads. Chris and Robbie were not there.

"Come in," Ted said.

A tall, skinny ensign walked in. "I'm Paul Turner," he said. "Is Lieutenant (j.g.) Blue here?"

"That's me," Matt said, getting up off of his cot.

"Open the curtain and let in some more light," Frank said.

"Sure, but you better warn him about the rats," Ted responded.

With the curtain open to let in more light, Matt could see the new officer was taking in their opulent quarters. At least, there weren't any rats scurrying about at that time.

"It'll grow on you," Matt said. "It's mostly dry on nights when the rains come and you're not on patrol. The roof does a fair job of reflecting the sun, so it's cooler inside during the day. Also, with the curtains open, you can catch a bit of a breeze when the wind stirs."

Paul's response let them all know that he would fit in great. "Well hell, what else could I ask for?"

"Make sure all your clothes are stenciled," Frank said. "We have a basket that we throw our clothes into and a native woman washes them for us. There isn't any starching or ironing but a good wash job. She will fold the clothes and lay them on your bunk. We pay her with cans of Spam, eggs, cigarettes, and chocolate. We tip her, occasionally, with a t-shirt or bug juice. Money means nothing to them. One more thing...and this is the most important thing...stay away from their daughters and the native women, if you value your life."

"Do you have any dungarees or t-shirts?" Matt asked when Frank was finished.

"No, just some work khakis," Paul replied.

"How about some boots?" Matt inquired.

"No," Paul said, shaking his head.

"You'll need the boots," Matt said, and then he added, "You'll meet the crew tomorrow. Our chief of the boat is QM1 Al Ross. Give him your sizes and he'll get you fixed up with uniforms. One last thing, Paul, we are a small crew. We depend on each other. Things are a bit relaxed, so don't expect to be treated like an officer at Newport. The crew acts correctly when the brass is around, but other times you'll probably be called "Ensign" until you're accepted. Then it will be XO."

Paul smiled, "I've never been one to stand on a lot of protocol, Skipper."

Matt gave Paul a slap on the back. "That's your cot," he said, pointing to where Frank and Ted were sitting. They both stood and shook Paul's hand.

"We have two more who bunk in here, Chris Duncklee and Robbie Turner," Ted said. They have the 60 boat. Frank and I have the 46 boat. It's the best boat in Ron 3." Matt threw his pillow at Ted.

***

PAUL'S KHAKIS WERE SO NEW that they still had the tags on them. He dressed and was ready as Matt was getting up. Matt dressed and they stopped at the mess hall. Paul scarfed up the corn beef in gravy that was poured over toast. In Navy slang, it was referred to as "shit on a shingle." He drank orange juice poured out of a can.

Matt stuck with the Navy coffee. He'd been told that they never tossed the grounds away. They just added more coffee to the pot. He did know that a spoon would stand straight up in a cup. But, a thermos full of coffee came in handy on patrol nights. This was something else that Ross made sure of...that they had coffee on board before they pulled out on patrol.

After eating, Matt and Paul walked to the repair facility. Ross was there before them, making sure the repairs were done right. "They are repairing the holes with mahogany," Ross said.

Matt knew that mahogany was hard wood and was used on the high dollar boats at Newport. He smiled, and said, "Well then, if it's good enough for the Newport yachts." Everyone laughed and Matt introduced Paul to everyone.

"We have replacements for Big Al and Anderson," Ross said. "They're about somewhere." He yelled out, "Gray! Gray, come here."

Gray walked up and Matt was surprised. He had on his blues. He was a GM3 with a red stripe across his sleeve. The stripe meant that he had been in the Navy for four years, yet was only a 3rd class.

"Skipper, this is GM3 L.Z. Gray. He has been a 2nd class, a time or two, but can't stay out of fights," Ross said.

"How come?" Paul asked.

Gray answered with the thickest accent Matt had ever heard. "I never got the hang of turning the cheek," he replied. Matt nodded and figured that Gray came from hill people or the mountains.

Byhre spoke up, "He knows his guns, Skipper."

Matt nodded and said, "Well, Gray, none of our men have done any fighting outside of with the Japanese. I'd like to keep it that way."

Before Matt could say more, MOMM2 Clark walked up. "We checked the engine. We were about to lose a couple of valves."

"Can you get them fixed?" Matt asked.

"The engine man says that they don't have any, but he's got an engine that they took out of the old 32 boat. We will check and see if we can use its valves and a piston," Clark replied.

Matt nodded and asked, "When will you know?"

"I'd guess within the hour," Clark replied.

Matt nodded his head again and spoke, "If they do have workable parts, when will the engine be ready?"

"I'd say tomorrow morning, Skipper."

"Thanks, Tom," Matt said, using Clark's first name. "I appreciate your efforts."

As Clark left, Ross brought the second replacement over. "This is Petty Officer Arthur Frongello, Skipper. Most of us have known him since MTB School. His nickname is "Wheels" and he's a true sailor. His first question on coming on board was, where's the coffee mess?"

Matt welcomed Wheels on board, using his nickname as he wasn't 100% sure he could pronounce his last name yet.

"Wheels can spell us at the wheel if need be," Ross said.

It was good to have another qualified crewman on board.

CHAPTER TEN

THE SKY WAS AS BLACK as navy ink. They'd already had a burst of rain, but instead of the sky clearing a little bit, it got darker. The wind was blowing enough to make the seas rough. The crew was being bounced about the boat. Recalling the recent 'man overboard,' the crew had secured themselves as they encountered one large wave after another. Looking to port, Matt could see GM3 Gray, and it was hard not to think of Big Al at the fifty caliber gun. *If Gray handles his gun like he's handled his fist, he'll get no complaints from the men,* Matt thought.

They'd been notified by scout planes that the Tokyo Express was on the move. Matt explained to Paul how the Japanese convoy got the name Tokyo Express, and how they'd named the PT boats, Devil Boats. Their job tonight was to lie to between Esperance and Savo and watch for the Japanese approach from the west. Once they spotted the Japanese, they'd notify their boats lying in wait. Paul was telling Matt how some of the boats at Melville were now equipped with radar. Thinking of their last mission, Matt thought, radar would have been a big help and likely would have saved a life. The lack of radar had certainly handicapped their boats and operations. Had they had radar, they could have made it harder for the Japanese to supply and land reinforcements on Guadalcanal.

Matt explained to Paul that often the first hint of a Japanese ship or submarine was when you were about to be run over or picked out by a searchlight. "I guarantee you, when that happens, your butt will pucker," he said.

***

THEY GOT TO THEIR POSITION a bit early which allowed them time, hopefully, for the crew to have a cup of coffee, or as the Navy called kool-aid, 'bug juice.' Where the name 'bug juice' came from, Matt had yet to find out.

They'd been in position for nearly an hour. The sea seemed to be empty...black and empty. They had been sitting in the eerie blackness long enough for the crew to get antsy. Matt could see L.Z. was restless. He must have been in another world when Paul nudged Matt and pointed to L.Z. Gray.

Matt, stepping over to see what the gunner wanted, was surprised by what Gray said. "Listen, Skipper," L.Z. whispered. "You can hear tiny waves slap against the hull. At times, they'll rock the boat slightly."

Dang, Matt thought, where had my mind drifted off to. As soon as L.Z. said it, Matt felt the boat rock and heard the waves lapping against the hull. "Spread the word," Matt ordered Wheels, "Japanese ships." He then had Sparks radio the patrol.

They then sat tight and watched and waited for the fireworks to begin. Ten minutes later, a Japanese destroyer passed not two hundred yards in front of them. Chris Duncklee, in the PT 60, had heard the message and moved out to intercept the destroyer. Hopefully, he'd put a fish in its belly. Chris later reported that the first two torpedoes were duds. The only purpose they served was to alert the Japanese of his presence. Amid fire from the Japanese, Chris made another run and the two aft torpedoes hit true. The explosions could be heard at the 48 boat and orange flames leaped up between the bridge and aft gun mounts.

"That will flood the boiler room," Hall remarked. Having served on board a destroyer, he knew where the boilers would be.

Searchlights from the Japanese destroyer lit up the sky. It swept over the 48 boat but didn't stop, finally finding the 60 boat. Chris was retreating but was still in range of the Japanese guns.

Matt told Morales, who was in the best position, to shoot out the searchlight. He'd not fired a dozen rounds when the sky was suddenly dark again. The darkness didn't last as another Japanese ship illuminated the night with her lights. They'd also located the 60 boat.

When the second ship passed the burning destroyer, she was lit up clearly by the fire. It was a cruiser, of all the rotten luck. Every man on board Matt's boat knew that they had to help the 60 boat, if possible.

Thinking of the cowboy matinees at their little theater in Union Springs, Matt shouted, "Saddle up, boys. Don't fire on the destroyer." He wanted to sneak up on the cruiser. "Hopefully, we can shoot out the searchlights to give Chris and Robbie a break, and then put a fish into the cruiser," Matt said to Paul.

The 60 boat was doing all it could, zigzagging and laying out smoke. The cruiser fired its forward guns. They overshot the 60 but it looked like the boat jumped up in the air.

"We don't have time for a torpedo run," Matt called to Gray. "It's your turn, L.Z., shoot out the lights."

L.Z. had the best position so it was time to see how good he was in action. A moment later, a single burst was heard and the light was out. He had shown his marksmanship. Had he failed, they would have turned all their guns on the damn light.

The 60 boat could escape now, barring another ship taking up the chase. But could Matt and the crew escape? The cruiser's guns were firing on them now. They came about, trying to get out of the cruiser's line of fire.

"Cease fire," Matt yelled as they made their turn and headed into the protection of the black night. The cruiser continued on by with her guns silent. "Preacher, Papa," Matt called over to their two torpedomen. "I'm going to attempt to go around the port side of the cruiser. We'll fire the forward fish at five hundred yards and get out of town. If we miss, we'll try again at four hundred yards."

"I'll pray for the fish to swim true," Preacher said.

"You do that, Preacher, with my thanks," Matt said and then added, "I'll pray with you."

***

SEARCHLIGHTS FROM HENDERSON FIELD FLASHED across the night sky. Further down the slot, orange flames leaped out of the big guns on the Japanese ships.

"Looks like a fireworks show," Paul commented.

"Aye, a deadly one, XO, " Ross responded.

They all knew that with each flash of the guns, men were getting killed. Hopefully, they could help the men on Guadalcanal in some small way. Matt did pray that their fish would run true. He had hoped that they would make their own run unnoticed, but apparently the boat's wake had given them away, even at slow speed.

"Well, Paul, welcome to PT boats," Matt said. "I hope you enjoyed your first experience. Just remember, if I fall, it's up to you. It'll be your job to get the boat and our people safely home."

"Aye, Skipper," Paul replied.

"Trust Ross," Matt added. "He's a pro." Paul nodded and Matt adjusted the course slightly and eased the throttle forward a touch.

Sidney had never used the torpedo sighting instrument, saying the accuracy was no better than pointing the bow at the target and letting go. As the 48 boat made her run, Paul gripped the side of the cockpit until his hands ached and turned white. Ross noticed and motioned to Matt, and they both smiled.

The cruiser had its port side guns blazing. Matt could see tracers flash by and, at times, he could hear a thud where the hull was punctured. *Please God, don't let them hit the gas tanks,* Matt prayed.

"If they break the coffee pot, I'll kick some Japanese butt," Wheels cursed, making Paul and Matt laugh.

"Ready to fire, XO?" Matt inquired.

"Yes, sir."

"Ready with the torpedos?"

"Aye," both Preacher and Pappy responded.

Matt stood at ready...wait...wait...fire! Both forward fish launched. Matt made a hard right and then under half throttle they moved away from the cruiser. When the twin explosions came, Matt was tempted to make another run but decided they'd done their job with no loss of life.

The torpedoes hit amidships, and that would stop the Japanese. *Would it sink them?* Matt questioned himself. Not likely, but they had a hell of a fire to put out. *Another run, no...we've been lucky and we're all alive.* They'd helped the 60 boat, and it was a good night.

Matt turned to Paul, "Walk around and check on everyone, XO."

"Yes, sir."

Seeing Wheels, Matt asked him the same question that he'd asked Paul. "How do you like the PT service now?"

Wheels smiled, "It'll do for me, Skipper, it'll do for me."

CHAPTER ELEVEN

T HE FOLLOWING MORNING THEY WOKE up in time for officer's call. Last night, Chris had walked by Matt and with a gentle slap on the shoulder he said, "Thanks Matt."

"Anytime, Chris," Matt replied.

The men on the 60 boat knew that the 48 boat had saved their bacon, but they would have done the same for Matt and his crew, and may have to yet.

Lieutenant Robinson told Matt at the officer's call that coastal watchers had seen both of the attacks on the destroyer and the cruiser. After they had retreated from the cruiser, fire from the torpedoes caused a series of explosions. This morning an oil slick and debris were sighted but there was no conclusive evidence that they had sunk the cruiser, or even hit it for that matter.

Frank, always one to speak out, said, "Well, it was conclusive enough for the 48 and 60 boats. Hell, I guess we need to have a man taking pictures or a movie camera attached to the cockpit recording the action."

When Frank hushed the room was quiet for a minute, and then Lieutenant Robinson spoke, "No one doubts you men, least of all me." It was quiet again for a minute, then Lieutenant Robinson took a sip of his coffee and started the meeting again.

"The commander of the Advance Naval Base Guadalcanal has ordered all available PT boats to intercept a force of five destroyers and one transport headed toward Guadalcanal. The force was sighted by scout planes who radioed in the sighting."

Frank, Chris, and Matt all looked at one another. 'All available PT boats' meant them, as the 46, 48, and 60 boats were the only ones operational. All the other PT boats were being repaired. They didn't say anything. Lieutenant Robinson wished them well as the men walked out. A few of the other skippers spoke to them. They were all sympathetic that they were the only operational boats in Ron 3. Matt, Frank, and Chris held no ill will towards the others. The reason they couldn't go on patrol was that they'd faced the enemy too often. The PT boats could only take so much. The wear and tear on the men and the boats was starting to show. Matt and the others had been out three nights in a row and each time they faced planes, destroyers, and a cruiser.

It was Chris who joked, "Hell, Frank, Matt attacked a dang cruiser. These destroyers ain't got a chance." Everybody laughed.

When they got down to the boat, Ross and Hall were there to meet them. "The holes have been patched, Skipper."

"Thanks," Matt replied. "Have you heard what our orders are for tonight?"

They both nodded with Hall saying, "Looks like we'll have our hands full."

Steffey, the lone boatswain's mate, had overheard the conversation, "I hope they don't shoot up any of my patches."

Morales laughed. "It would be hard to miss one, Charlie. She's a lucky lady alright, but she's floating on patches."

Ross set the men to checking out everything from the firing mechanism on the guns to checking the torpedoes, while he and Hall checked the cockpit controls and Brown the radio. As soon as he was satisfied, the men were set free until 1630 when they'd meet and go over any concerns and discuss the patrol. Between now and then, the men were free to do as they pleased. Some of them wrote letters, and Matt was one of them. Paul went running, and everyone thought that maybe he had a loose screw in his head. Somebody was picking a guitar while others played cards. Tony Brown was reading a western by Zane Gray titled "Wildfire." Matt thought in all likelihood they'd see real wildfire that night.

Someone had lit a pipe, which smelled good. The smell got Matt to wondering if the tobacco tasted as good as it smelled. If it did, he might take up pipe smoking.

Matt started down to the boat at 1600. The first thing he noticed was 'lucky lady' had been painted on the cockpit. It was a very good job. Seeing the name showed how the crew felt about the boat. What surprised Matt was it had been gunner's mate L.Z. Gray who'd done the lettering.

Gray saw Matt and walked over. "Like it, Skipper?"

"Sure thing," Matt replied. Pausing a minute, he said to L.Z., "I'm glad to have you on board. I'll try to get your second chevron back."

"Thank you, sir," he responded.

Then out of the blue, Matt asked, "What's L.Z. stand for?"

"Well sir, my mama wanted me named Leroy after her daddy. My dad said no son of his would be stuck with Leroy as his handle. No, I'd be named Zane, so I'd be Zane Gray, like the man who writes cowboy books. Mom said if she couldn't have her son named Leroy, he dang sure wouldn't be named Zane. Dad left mad and while he was gone the nurse came in to fill out the birth certificate. For my name, mama compromised and said, 'L.Z. Gray. When dad found out he was pissed but it was 'done and did' as they say."

***

FRANK, AS THE SENIOR MAN, led them out at 1800. He had checked at headquarters and no changes had been reported so they fired up the engines and fell in line behind the 46 boat. Matt noticed that Ted was at the helm of the 46 boat, so he called Paul over and let him take the 48 boat out.

The obligatory weather showed its contrary self before they got out of the harbor. Matt felt the mist on his face as dark clouds hovered above. The good thing was there was little wind so the ocean was calm, which meant a smooth ride as they headed to their destiny. They had reached the assigned area and idled in a curtain of black. Matt could barely see Frank's boat and Chris's boat was not visible.

The radioman stuck his head up and whispered, "I was going down the frequency and hit one where I picked up Japanese talking. It didn't last thirty seconds, and I've tried to pick it up again but no luck. I do feel that they are close by, Skipper."

Matt nodded and told him to get back to his radio. Fifteen minutes later the dark tuned to day and all hell broke loose. The destroyers had seen them somehow. The boats thought that they were alone when at least three searchlights blinded them. Matt, not knowing where Chris was, had to go forward and to starboard, hoping that Frank would turn to the left and port side. He'd just pushed the throttle when the leading ship fired their forward mount. The 48 boat was rocked by the concussion of the shell. Paul fell down and Ross grabbed him. They turned on the smoke generator and then zigzagged at half throttle, trying to limit the wake. They were still unable to shake the damn Japanese, though.

The Japanese fired the forward mounts again and Matt heard a scream above the engines. He hoped that the man would get some care from his mates, since he didn't have the time. Morales, Byhre, and Gray were keeping a steady rate of fire going.

"Paul!" Matt shouted. "Get Preacher and Papa to stand by the depth charges. Maybe we can get the Japanese off our butts with one."

Instead of zigzagging, Matt turned in a circle. As he did so one of the gunners took out the Japanese searchlight. They continued turning and then Matt straightened up directly in front of the Japanese bow.

"Now," Matt yelled.

It was either Preacher or Papa who had set the depth charge really shallow. When it went off, the bow of the destroyer jumped in the air. They could hear their alarms going off, and the firing stopped.

"Let's set her up for a torpedo run," Matt shouted.

It was not to be, however. Frank's boat passed in front of the 48 boat, with a Japanese destroyer firing at him.

CHAPTER TWELVE

THE JAPANESE MISSION THAT NIGHT must have been seek out and destroy the devil boats, as they found themselves in the thick of it.

"Turn your fire on the destroyer chasing Frank," Matt ordered his gunners.

The Japanese made themselves a good target, which Matt felt sure that they could have sunk, but the destroyer chasing Frank was a greater need. Matt had not seen the 60 boat for some time. Guns along the starboard side of the destroyer picked the 48 boat out and began firing at them.

"Damn," Wheels yelled. "That's an anti-aircraft gun."

Byhre turned his 20mm on the enemy cannon. For a minute, it was a duel to the death. Matt and everyone else were praying that their gas tank and engines wouldn't get hit. Matt knew that he'd never forget the duel if he lived to be one hundred. Most of the enemy fire was either over them or in the water. The sound of bullets over their heads left a lasting impression.

A bright flash and a small explosion came from the Japanese cannon. Matt's gunners had won one more time. While the battle seemed like it went on for several minutes, it only lasted thirty seconds or so. They were now up to the Japanese bridge, pouring lead at it and trying to shoot out the searchlight. They could no longer see Frank's boat. Matt just prayed that they were alive.

They were firing at the Japanese bridge and searchlight when Ross said to Matt, "I believe they are taking fire from the other side, Skipper."

Had Frank gotten away from the searchlight and was now firing or was it Chris. Matt wished it was a damn battleship so it could take care of the entire lot of destroyers.

"We must have killed people on the bridge, the helmsman anyway," Paul shouted, as the ship skewed making a sudden starboard turn.

Thank God the blasted searchlight was out. The destroyer seemed to cant as it continued to turn.

"Train your fire below the waterline," Matt yelled.

Matt and the crew could see holes being punched into the hull from their guns. He said to Paul and Ross, "Let's get out of here." They turned away from the destroyer.

Once away, they could see Frank's boat firing at another destroyer. He was making a torpedo run at the Japanese. He fired his first two torpedoes at five hundred yards or less and made a hard left after firing. It would be a close thing as the destroyer was turning, but it was too late for the Japanese. The first torpedo hit about the aft gun mount with the second one close behind. The explosions lit up the night. *The Japanese would be busy for a while trying to save the ship,* Matt thought.

Brown poked his head up from the radio room, "The 46 boat says head home. We've done enough!"

They finally found Chris. His port side engine was out after the Japanese fired on them. The middle engine sounded like it would go any minute. Frank told Chris to set the speed and they would follow along. Hopefully, the night's action would please the big brass, with the five destroyers turning back. There weren't any destroyers sunk but the coast watcher reported visible damage and one ship was being towed.

When they got back to port and Matt hit his rack he didn't really care what the high brass thought. They'd done all they could against superior forces. Matt was thanking God that none of his men were hurt and they'd made it home one more night when sleep overtook him.

***

MATT WOKE UP THE NEXT morning at the sound of Ross dropping mail on the little table by his rack. He rubbed his eyes and looked at his watch to see that it was 0720...0720, damn, he'd slept past his usual get up time. He saw, looking around, that Paul was sitting up and yawning. Frank and Ted were still sleeping, while Chris and Robbie were up and gone. He was not surprised. They'd want to get over to the maintenance and repair facility early. Matt dressed and went through the mail. He handed one letter to Paul, and stuck two letters in his back pocket and headed to the chow hall.

They had fried bologna, powdered eggs that didn't look runny, and oatmeal that did. Sugar was available for the oatmeal but no raisins. There was toast, coffee, and green bug juice which Matt took to be lime Kool Aid. He took two slices of bologna, two pieces of toast and made a sandwich and got a cup of coffee. A first class cook walked up as he was getting his coffee.

"We got some syrup in this morning, sir, if you would like some," the cook said.

"No thanks, Cookie, maybe in the morning," Matt replied. He opened the letter from his mom as he ate his breakfast.

Everything was fine at home, his mom wrote. One tidbit of bad news, though. Mr. Will Crompton had died at the age of eighty-four. He had liked Matt and used to let the boys play in his hayloft, and camp out in the barn. Mr. Will and his wife used to sit on the porch every evening and drink a NuGrape soda. Matt couldn't imagine what Mrs. Ada would do now. Of course, Mr. Will had hired a man named Otis, to work the farm. Matt figured, at least in the short term, that Otis would still keep on as he'd been doing for years. They didn't have any close family, it was always just the two of them. Mom had said that Mrs. Ada had told her that Mr. Will and she had started their life together in that house and that's where it would end.

Matt finished the letter and put it back in his pocket. He sure wished that he could have seen Mr. Will and Mrs. Ada one more time. The second letter was from his sister. It was almost the same as his mom's. Katie left out the part about Mr. Will, but what she did say surprised him. Lieutenant Sidney Hinson was home. Katie had talked to Dianne but it wasn't clear if he was home for convalescence or was he awaiting medical discharge from the Navy. He didn't know if Sidney could do well in the civilian world after putting ten years in the military. Matt, after re-reading Katie's letter, made his way over to where Paul sat, taking his coffee with him.

Paul, seeing that Matt was reading his mail, hadn't wanted to interrupt him so he'd sat down at another table. He was eating his breakfast, when Matt came over and sat down. After taking a bite, he asked Matt, "What is Iron Bottom Sound?"

Matt took a sip of his coffee and formed his reply. "It's an area between Guadalcanal and Florida Island where a large naval battle was fought against the Japanese, during the battle for Guadalcanal.

In the battle, dozens of ships were sunk, ours and the Japanese. So it was named Iron Bottom Sound." Thinking of all the men on those ships at the bottom of the sea gave Matt a shiver.

"Is there any wooden boats down there?" Paul asked.

"I don't know," Matt said truthfully.

"Well, let's not be the first," Paul said.

❉❉❉

OFFICER'S CALL THAT MORNING HAD a bit of good news. A supply ship had come in with cases of parts. Hopefully, they would be for the PT boats. It also had six sets of radar to be installed in various boats. The whole squadron were all happy with this news, taken at face value.

A chief petty officer would oversee the installation of the radar and train a petty officer on each boat on how to operate it. The next bit of good news, which Matt considered the best news, was the PT boats 37, 28, and 61, were all ready to go. It was then that they got the bad news. Gas was short and so was fifty-caliber ammunition. Matt couldn't believe his ears...short on ammunition and gas. *How are we supposed to do our jobs fighting the Japanese?* For some reason, Matt looked at the calendar. He'd lost track of what day and month it was. It was November 9th. They had no way of knowing it, but hell was about to get hotter.

CHAPTER THIRTEEN

IT WAS STRIKE TWO. FRANK'S XO, Ted Walters, had a good arm. He took a sign from Chris Duncklee, who was their team's coach. The score was three to two in their favor. It was two outs and Matt had two strikes with a man on second. If only Matt could just get a hit. Sweat from the heat of the afternoon sun and pressure to win this game made him call time and step back. Matt thought as he stepped out of the batter's box and wiped his eyes and face on his tee shirt, which was already wet with sweat. *I can hit off Ted*, he thought.

"Don't let Ted get you, Matt," Paul called out.

Humph...Matt thought. *He just struck Paul out with three fast balls.* Matt stepped back up to the plate expecting Ted to change his pitch. He did, but Matt got enough of it to sail over the outfielder's head and into the water, which was our fence for homerun purposes. Everyone on Matt's team was laughing and shouting, but above the shouts an ominous sound arose.

Matt didn't want to hear it, neither did anyone else. Air raid... They dropped everything and ran to the boats. They had to get underway before the Japanese bombed them into kindling. They made their way out just as the enemy planes showed up. It had proven to be a close call, but they were able to get the boats safely out of the harbor.

Looking up at the sky, Matt figured there had to be at least fifty planes overhead. They were apparently going after bigger fish than the PT boats, though. Matt thought that maybe he was wrong to feel relieved, or maybe it just wasn't their time. Either way, he was thankful that they all survived. They found out more at the next few officer's call.

The Japanese had chosen the middle of November to reinforce their troops and regain complete control of Guadalcanal. Matt and the other officers were told that Rear Admiral R.K. Turner and Rear Admiral T.C. Kinkaid had a total force of one aircraft carrier, two battleships, eight cruisers, and twenty-two destroyers. It sounded to Matt like a sizable force. What stood out to Matt and his friends was that there was no mention of PT boats. *Maybe we could sit out this dance*, Matt hoped, but inside he knew it was a fallacy. He also wondered how many of those ships would end up at the bottom of Iron Bottom Sound, the ship graveyard at the end of the slot between Guadalcanal, Savo, and Florida Islands. Matt shuddered to think of his men, the enemies and others that lay beneath the sea in a watery grave. This was something that Paul and Matt had just talked about.

They soon learned that all of their planes were ordered to attack every Japanese airfield in range of Guadalcanal. *Well, that's one place where we will likely be used*, Matt thought. They would be picking up downed pilots, and in the daytime. Their recent experience was still clear in everyone's mind.

On the night of the 12th of November, the American forces met a larger Japanese force and a ferocious battle took place. The results were devastating, the American forces lost five ships and several were damaged. Matt later learned that the battle only lasted thirty-four minutes. In that time, Admiral Callaghan was killed on board his flagship, the *San Francisco*. The Japanese battleship, *Hiei*, had taken many hits on its topside but still floated. Planes from the carrier, *Enterprise*, as well as planes from Henderson Field attacked the enemy all day. Finally, the big battleship sank. That night the Japanese were able to bring cruisers and destroyers into Iron Bottom Bay to shell Henderson Field once again.

Frank and Matt had been given orders to go out and escort the heavy cruiser, *Portland*, back to Tulagi. They completed this mission and were secured. Matt looked at his watch and it was 12:30 a.m. or thirty minutes past midnight. As the *Portland* made its way into the harbor, Matt asked Paul if he knew where the 46 boat was.

"Sorry, Skipper, I haven't seen her," was Paul's reply.

Matt called down to Sparks, the radioman, and he denied any messages from Frank. *Damnation*, Matt thought. Frank and Ted must have found something and couldn't risk a radio transmission.

While Matt and his crew were trying to locate the 46 boat, the Japanese opened up and were shelling Henderson Field again. From the sound of the guns, they knew that there had to be at least one big boy out there.

"Look at that flare," Paul shouted.

It turned night into day while it lasted. It served its purpose, lighting up Henderson Field as it had done. Matt decided to try and put some torpedoes into the big cruiser. The Japanese also had destroyers scouting the entire area, sending up one flare after another. At one point, Ross saw a Japanese destroyer pass down their starboard side. Thankfully, the PT boats were much smaller and closer to the water, so the destroyer didn't see them.

Matt knew that with all the scout destroyers all about, it would be suicide to try to get within four hundred yards of the heavy cruiser. So he did something that Sidney had never done as skipper of the 48 boat. Matt used the torpedo director. He moved the helm slightly until he had a perfect line on the Japanese ship. It was the first time that he'd fired a fish from over four or five hundred yards. The torpedomen were ready, with Preacher on Matt's side, and Pappy on the other. They were now inside of nine hundred yards. Matt fired the two front fish, and then the rear two. He then made his turn and got the devil away from this hellhole as quietly as possible.

The men were watching the fish. Pappy cursed, as the starboard fish ran to port, but the port torpedo ran true, as did the two aft torpedoes. They had fired at an extreme distance for them. So everyone quickly became impatient waiting on an explosion. They didn't have to wait long, as they finally heard a loud explosion, and then a second one. Two out of four fish had found their marks. That was a fifty percent success rate, but that could get you killed.

They still hadn't found Frank, but after those explosions they were sure to have some mad nips, as L.Z. Gray called them. They hadn't fired any of their other guns and Morales, speaking to Byher said, "Well, the brass can't complain about our ammunition usage tonight."

BM2 Steffey laughed at Morales' comment and then added, "We won't need any new hull patches either."

"They're talkative tonight," Paul remarked.

Ross responded, "XO, that's what you call releasing tension." Paul nodded his head. *He was learning*, Ross thought.

Tom Clark, MOMM2, the senior man in charge of the three big engines came on deck, and Matt's heart skipped a beat. Clark rarely came on deck until they had reached home. As Clark walked towards him, Matt feared the worst.

"What is it, Tom?" Matt inquired.

"We've got a bit of a problem, Skipper. First you need to throttle down."

Matt didn't ask why, he just did as Tom recommended. Matt knew to not do so could cost them an engine and maybe their lives.

"We have a ruptured oil line, Skipper," Clark advised. "We put a good patch over it, but it's still leaking. I've got a bucket to catch the oil and pour it back in the reservoir and I've got new oil if we need it. But the faster we run the more she spews. We have to shut the engines down to fix the leak, which I know we can't do right now. So," Clark continued, "I'd keep her around fifteen knots until we get home."

Word quickly spread as to why they slowed down. The men's tension was back now, and this was especially true when they heard an aircraft coming in. Their wake was much smaller than a wake at their usual speed of twenty-three to twenty-five knots, but it was still there. A general sigh of relief was heard when the plane passed over them.

"Maybe he's too tired to mess with such a small fish," Steffey said.

"Or maybe it was one of ours," Hall responded.

"Who cares?" Preacher threw out

"He's gone," Wheels, who had been unusually quiet, spoke up.

"Well, Skipper, ammunition won't be the only thing we've saved tonight, that will please the brass. We've saved them some gas."

"I wonder if we'll get a good boy badge," Pappy then responded. "I for one wish that all four of those damn torpedoes had hit their target," he added. "I'd love to see L.Z. paint a cruiser below those Japanese planes."

Preacher said, "Above it, not below it. When we get a big boy like that, it's got to go on top."

Paul turned to Ross, "I believe the tension is gone again."

Ross smiled and said, "Thankfully."

They made it to their slip around daylight. The first thing that Matt noticed was the 46 boat. It was back, thank God. It was too late to try to sleep before officer's call, so Matt decided to write up his report and get a shower; then he'd sleep.

Matt spoke with Clark before he left the boat. "I can fix the leak easy, Skipper. We'll go eat first while the engines are cooling down." Matt nodded and thought, *Clark knows his job*.

At officer's call, Matt found out that after they'd torpedoed the big cruiser, the Japanese broke off action and sailed away. *We did some good besides making a flash*, Matt thought.

CHAPTER FOURTEEN

S LEEP DIDN'T COME, SO MATT got up and started reviewing his journal. Shaking his head, Matt thought, *this is boring*. Other than dates and times, most entries were nearly all the same. Repetitive actions with little difference from night to night. The actions hadn't felt the same but the reading of them soon became boring. Especially the number of times that they felt they'd sunk a ship only to be told there was no conclusive evidence. If they were given torpedoes that weren't defective there might be more evidence.

Matt gave a sigh. There was no doubt the 48 boat had made the heavy cruiser tuck its tail and run last night, which certainly gave Henderson Field a bit of a reprieve from the shelling.

Outside, Matt could hear a commotion, "Where's the Skipper?"

"In his hut," was the reply Matt heard. He recognized the voice as MM3 Phagans.

"Come in, Phagans," Matt said.

"Skipper, you have got to come quickly. They are discussing sending three nurses to Vanuatu on board a PT boat."

Matt smiled, and slipped on his shirt and hat, and then he wiggled his feet into his boots. "Let's go, Phagans."

As it was rare to show up at headquarters without a specific reason, Matt tried to think of a reason to go. When they neared headquarters, Matt saw the HQ chief, who was the radar specialist. *That's it, I'm checking to see when we might get radar*, he thought.

Two of the three nurses were in the little waiting area. The supply ship that was supposed to have left yesterday did in fact leave. However, it was attacked by Japanese planes before they made it into the open sea, so they limped back into port with one boiler out and only one working. Because there was a critical need for the nurses on Vanuatu, they were seeking transportation.

"I have the boats," Lieutenant Robinson was saying to the supply ship's captain. "It's gas that I'm short on."

Captain Best of the supply ship spoke up, "I'll give you the damn gas." Lieutenant Robinson agreed to go then.

Ensign Padgett spoke up, "Sir, I believe the 48's skipper is here."

"What for?" Robinson asked.

"I believe that he wanted to speak with Chief Peckham about the radar."

"Go get him then," Robinson ordered.

"Aye, sir."

When Padgett told Matt the commander wanted to see him, he also leaned in and said, "You owe me one, Matt."

***

THE 48 BOAT WAS REFUELED and then fifty gallon drums filled with gas were rolled on board. Matt had misgivings about the gas. They'd blow up like a bomb if attacked by a Japanese plane. However, if Lieutenant Bulkley did it with General MacArthur on board, so could Matt. Al Ross said, "The Santa Cruz Islands are about two hundred and fifty miles southeast and roughly between Tulagi and Vanuatu. If we needed to we could pull into one of these, and maybe refuel and layover during the day."

"Sounds good," Matt replied. He told the nurses to go get their gear and be back at 1800. He then checked with MOMM2 Clark about the best way to conserve gas.

"We could shut down an engine," Clark said. "That would give us extra mileage but if hell broke loose, we might find ourselves in a pinch for getaway speed. I'd just run them as we usually do, Skipper," Clark said, his eyes on the nurses' figures, as they walked away.

The nurses were back to the boat, with their gear, at 1800. They were introduced to the crew using their navy ranks first, Lieutenant Kricia Morris, Lieutenant Karen Hamby, and Lieutenant Haley Stanford.

Paul spoke to the nurses, as they got underway, "You may want to take those hats off. A gust of wind comes along and they're gone. Once the hats are in the wake, they're beyond using them again."

"I'll take them," Radioman Brown volunteered. The nurses quickly took off their hats and passed them to him.

"You are welcome to stay on deck as long as you like," Matt told the nurses. "However, we usually have bad weather every evening without much warning. If the wind picks up, you might want to take that ladder below decks. XO, if you will, take the nurses for a tour around the boat." Paul was glad to oblige.

For the next half hour, the men put on a dog and pony show. L.Z. even helped each nurse up into the fifty caliber turret. Pappy and Preacher showed off the torpedoes.

Byhre said, "You've seen the fifty calibers, now look at a real gun." He then explained about the 20mm."

The nurses were then taken down to the engine room and were impressed at the size of the three power plants. They were soon back on the deck where Ross and Hall explained the navigation and Paul went over the controls in the cockpit. Each nurse had to take the wheel for a few minutes.

"You guys seem like one big family," Morris said.

Matt replied, without thinking, "We feel like a family. We feel it when we lose somebody too." As if to drive home the words, it thundered.

Wheels was quick to usher the nurses down below deck. However, the rain came down suddenly with such force, that Nurse Stanford's back was soaked before she made it below. Paul pulled a towel out of his locker for the nurse, and then went back on deck.

The sea was rougher than usual. The crew had a hard enough time of it, but it was hell on the women. Matt sent QM2 Hall down to lend a hand where he could. As usual, the squall only lasted about thirty minutes. The sea calmed down, and the ride through the rough seas wasn't nearly as bad as it had been. It wasn't long before one of the nurses came on deck. In a few minutes, the other two nurses followed her up.

"It's so dark up here," Karen said.

"Aye, that's why we pretty much stay at our stations," Matt responded. "Finding a man overboard is a touchy thing."

Hall spoke to Morris, "It's like this most nights. You have no idea who may be lurking out there, very often, the first hint is when they fire on you or turn a searchlight on. You then grab a hold of something and pray you get away. Of course, we all have faith in the skipper. He hasn't let us down yet. Sometimes, he's so cool; I think he's got ice water in his veins."

"Knock it off, Hall," Matt ordered. "You'll upset the women."

"It's the truth, Skipper, we all know it."

Thankfully, Lieutenant Hamby asked, "Does the moon ever come out?"

"Sure it does, you just can't see it half the time."

***

THEY MADE IT TO SANTA Cruz about an hour before sunrise. The biggest island, according to the charts, was Nendo. It had a decent bay, so they pulled in. Matt got off the boat with a side arm and walked on shore. It was obvious by the cookfires that there were islanders there. Would they give them a problem, God only knew?

Matt got back to the boat and set up a watch schedule...two men at a time, standing two hours on watch. Wheels made a big pot of coffee. Ross, Paul, and Matt would take turns staying awake, and the coffee would help. Matt, more tired than sleepy, took the first watch.

Before long, Byhre called down, "Company coming, Skipper."

Matt walked to the port side and saw three people standing there. Two of them were island women and the other one was a white man. The white man turned out to be Father Murphy, a British missionary. They talked a bit and Matt invited him on board. The native women handed trays of cooked meat, bread, and fruit to the crew, but they wouldn't step on board the boat. The crew sent the food down to the galley, after Matt had taken a piece of meat and a slice of bread.

"That's pork," Father Murphy said. "It's a suckling pig."

The pork tasted very good and Matt ate it all. He then asked about the Japanese.

"We see their planes and ships, but they've only stopped once and that was in early 1942," the good Father said. "There's not enough here to interest them. If you are planning on laying over today, I'd like to show you a better place to tie up. There is more tree coverage, and it would be better for us and you. If you're spotted by a plane you can bet they'll be back."

"I'll get her cranked up," Matt said.

"You don't need to do that," Father Murphy said. He then spoke to a girl, who ran off.

A few minutes later several able looking men trotted up. Matt had the crew pass them a bow line, and walking along the shore, the men pulled the boat into a thicket. Matt wanted the bow pointed out as a precaution, so by using long bamboo poles, the boat was pushed around to where they were in the position to make a quick escape if needed.

The nurses followed Father Murphy ashore to visit the village. They were soon back to get some medical supplies. Preacher, Pappy, and L.Z. volunteered to carry the articles ashore for the nurses. By the time it was getting dark, Matt couldn't help but wonder if they were treating every person on the island, shanghaiing his crew along the way.

Matt called over to Paul, "Let's go see what's keeping the nurses and our men."

Paul strapped on his side arm and told Ross that they would be back soon.

Over a small rise, they could see a small fire, and sitting around it were their missing sailors. The nurses appeared to be finishing up with the villagers, with Father Murphy being used as a interpreter. What surprised Matt was that most of the villagers had gathered around his men and listened to them play a guitar and sing. He later found out that Father Murphy had given the guitar to Preacher.

Preacher was picking out an old gospel song, and L.Z. with Pappy was harmonizing at times. *Dang, their pretty good*, Matt thought.

"Our very own gospel trio," Paul said.

It was soon time to head back to the boat. The crew and the nurses came back smiling and wearing straw hats and shell necklaces made for them by the women and children. Preacher had that old guitar and Father Murphy brought several letters that he wished to be mailed.

The moon was up when they left the village. The sound of laughter drifted up from below the main deck as the nurses rehashed their experience. One of the nurses had caught Matt's attention as she was bending over treating a child. He chided himself for having impure thoughts of the lady. He gulped when he realized she had turned her head and caught him eyeing her derriere. Matt turned around, but had to admit to himself that it was one fine butt.

They made Vanuatu the next morning just before six a.m. or 0600 military time. They had one fifty gallon drum of gas that hadn't been used.

"That's cutting it close," Clark complained.

"We made it," Matt responded. "That's all that counts."

It took until noon that day to get permission to fuel up and fill the drums with enough gas to get back to their base. The brass didn't want to share their gas. Finally, it was the nurses that settled it.

"We'd still be on Tulagi had they not brought us here." That comment did the trick.

When they said their good-byes to the nurses, Karen whispered to Matt, "I saw you staring."

"God gave me eyes and an appreciation for beauty," Matt responded. He was proud that he'd thought of something witty.

The return trip was uneventful. It didn't even rain on them one time.

CHAPTER FIFTEEN

LUCK CAN, BY ITS VERY nature, be a fickle proposition. Since the battle of the big boys, now being called the Battle of Tassafaronga, the Tokyo Express resumed their run. The navy's small PT boat squadron went out nearly every night. The squadron had some successful actions but looking at the available boats, it didn't take much imagination to realize there had been some very grim times as well.

However, the Lord smiled on them and they got an early Christmas present…Navy scout planes! Several cruisers were damaged in a big battle and could no longer carry their scout planes, so they were given to the PT boat squadron to help with their patrols.

Matt became friends with one of the SOC (scout observation planes) pilots, Keith Pearson from Tallahassee, Florida. The two men made a deal. Matt would go flying in the Kingfisher with Keith up the slot on a scouting mission and then Keith would go with Matt on one of the 48's boat patrols. Frank and Ted thought that Matt was crazy, and that the commanding officer would never allow it, so they didn't tell him.

Matt thoroughly enjoyed the first part of the flight. Flying down the slot and having an aerial view put a different perspective on things. They had made it to the end of the slot and in the distance could see dark clouds.

"I bet there's a bunch of Japanese hiding in that bad weather," Keith volunteered.

The ride had gotten a bit rougher and as far as Matt was concerned it was time to head back. Keith was not of the same opinion, and he was the pilot. Keith seemed to turn and Matt thought they were headed home. No sir, Keith was just going around a few clouds.

"The light is starting to go on us," Keith said, which was obvious to Matt. "We'll give it ten more minutes and then head back."

It didn't take ten or even five more minutes. As soon as, they got through the cloud coverage they were in, they saw the ships. There were seven Japanese destroyers. It was not the biggest force that they'd engaged, but it was big enough. Keith banked the opposite way and headed for the slot. On the way back, Keith reported the ships and pushed the throttles forward. Matt could feel the plane picking up speed.

"I have to get you back in time for us to go out tonight," Keith advised.

They landed and Matt went to the hut. He was pleasantly surprised to learn that the 48 boat wasn't going out that night and neither were the 46 or the 60 boats.

**

WORD SOON CAME DOWN THAT on the first of January, they were to get a present…a full squadron of PBY's. The Navy Patrol Bombers that were also called Catalinas. For the first time since becoming a part of Ron 3, Matt felt like they might be getting the upper hand. The next night he questioned his thought process. A scout plane reported twelve destroyers were headed for the slot.

Their PT force had been reinforced by Squadron 2. With the arrival of these new boats, the decision was to send out eight boats in three groups to deal with this new threat. Frank and Matt had been assigned just to the north-northwest of Guadalcanal. Two boats were off of Cape Esperance. The rest of them would patrol off Savo Island. They'd been waiting for what seemed like a long time for the Japanese to close with them from where they had been sighted. Matt began to wonder if they were headed their way after all. He'd just looked at his watch and it was near 12:30 a.m. L.Z. Gray who Matt had come to think of as 'Hawkeye' from the book, 'Last of the Mohicans,' was on target again.

"There they are, Skipper, a damn slew of the Japanese," L.Z. said.

They advised the other group of PT boats of the sighting and then they got into position for a torpedo run. With guns blazing, they started their run. Everyone was ready and in place with Preacher and Pappy as torpedomen. They had just made it to five hundred yards and had a good target before them. Matt hit the switch for the first two fish. They swam true, and as he turned they exploded amidships of the destroyer. She was far from sunk, however. The ship's searchlight came on and they quickly had the 48 boat in the beam of light. Matt pushed the throttle forward to get away from the searchlight and guns, only to become sickened. An engine had failed. It seemed like the power was coming back and then the second engine failed. There wasn't a man on the boat who thought that they had a chance.

Frank then put the 46 boat right across the bow of the destroyer. They were firing for all they were worth and somebody got the searchlight. Frank had his smoker going and that helped.

The 48 boat only had one engine left, but they couldn't fight with one engine. Matt turned tail and headed back to Tulagi and their base, with a stop at Savo Island. Frank stayed with them until they made it around Savo Island, where they anchored.

"We'll come back for you," Ted shouted as they pulled away.

It seemed the darkness closed in on them. They could smell the stench of battle smoke as it drifted their way now and again. Being on the leeward side of the island afforded them some protection from the wake of the destroyers and PT boats but they could still feel the boat bob up and down.

The sound of battle raged, so somebody was making progress, as one explosion after another was heard. At one point, a burning destroyer sailed by, lighting up the night.

MOMM2 Tom Clark came topside and spoke, "I have no idea what caused the engines to go, Skipper. To have it happen like it did makes me wonder if we don't have a saboteur. They have been running too good and now this. I'll help the maintenance guys tear the plants down and see what we can find."

"Do they have any extra engines?" Paul asked.

"They don't even have any extra parts, XO, but I'll make sure we do all that we can," Clark said and went back below.

For an engine to fail was like a personal insult to Clark, so Matt had no doubt that he'd do all he could to repair the engines.

"The fighting seems to have slowed down a lot," Wheels volunteered.

Matt had noticed that as well. He just hoped that nothing had happened to the 46 and 60 boats.

Brown had been listening to the radio. "We've sent the Japanese packing, Skipper."

Matt nodded his head, and heard a boat coming...a PT boat. "We only have one engine," Matt yelled to Frank as they came alongside.

"Let's rig a tow, and use some gas," Frank said. "I'd rather do that now than be here tomorrow trying to get home."

Matt smiled and thought... *it is tomorrow*.

***

CLARK WAS AS GOOD AS his word. By the time, Paul and Matt had breakfast; Clark had the oil pans and the heads off.

"See that, Skipper, its grit and sand. Somebody definitely put it to us. They probably dumped a can of sand down the oil spout."

Matt reported that they'd been the victim of sabotage, at officer's call that day. The decision was made to assign a watch over the boats at night. The thinking was that some native was promised a lot by the Japanese to sabotage the boats.

Paul had a different thought. "I'm thinking that some sailor has had his way with one of the natives' wife or daughter."

Thinking of the wash woman's daughter, Matt didn't doubt it possible. On the way back to the hut, Matt bought a carton of Camels and a dozen Hershey bars. It didn't hurt to show a little appreciation to their wash woman. Rumors on the island were the natives used to be headhunters!

CHAPTER SIXTEEN

DIRT DOES AN AWFUL JOB on engines," Tom Clark explained as he showed them the damage on their left wing engine. "When sand or dirt enters the cylinders it will grind between the pistons and cylinder walls. That will screw up the piston rings and walls themselves. When the rings wear down, they will not seal. This allows combustion gas to leak into the crank case. It's what we call blow-by. You soon have engine failure."

"You didn't mention the valves," the machine ship guy added.

"Yeah, they're shot as well," Clark said.

Matt stood there looking over at Paul. He often acted like he understood every word that Clark was saying. What did hit home was it would be later than sooner before the engines were fixed. That hit Matt hard. To be knocked out of patrol duty due to enemy fire was one thing. For it to happen because of sabotage was a bitter pill to swallow.

Paul asked, as they walked away, "Do you think it was one of our guys?"

That had never occurred to Matt. "Round the men up, Paul," Matt said. "It's time to have a meeting."

Word was passed around and they all met in front of the crew's tent. The guys gathered around, with some of them sitting on tree stumps, cans, crates, a few of them had chairs, while some of the men were just standing or leaning against trees.

QM1 Ross set the tone of the meeting by calling, "Attention on deck," as Matt and Paul walked up.

It was the first such meeting since Matt had become skipper and Sidney had had only one. "At ease," Matt said. "Guys, you all know that we had double engine failure last night. Were it not for the 46 boat, a lot of us and maybe all of us wouldn't be here today. Engine failure is a risk that we live with…" Matt let that sink in a minute, and then added, "But not when it is sabotage." Disbelief filled the faces of the crew, and anger was rampant with men cursing.

"Attention on deck," Ross called again.

The men became quiet, but the anger remained. Matt didn't suspect, not for a minute, that a single one of the crew would commit such a deed, and he told them so. They went over the possibilities then, including enraged fathers, Japanese sympathizers, and even someone with a grudge against one of them.

Preacher spoke up and said, "I don't know of a single man who is dallying with the natives, from our crew or any other." The men all agreed and everyone had pals on other boats.

"We might need to assign someone to be on the boat at all times," Morales threw out.

"Headquarters mentioned putting a watch on the boats," Matt related.

Pappy spoke up then, "When we find out who did it, Skipper, we'll take his butt on patrol with us and strap him to a torpedo." Everyone liked that idea.

A FEW NIGHTS LATER, CHRIS and Robbie were on patrol when a destroyer got after them. They made their escape but ran aground on a coral reef. They were able to pull her off, but the bottom of the boat was gone. It was pure luck that they made it back to the basin. The boat was condemned as a total loss, but the good thing was that the 48 boat got her engines.

Once the engines were out of the 60 boat, the shop, with Clark watching over every move, took the engines apart and, finding nothing wrong with them, they put them in the 48 boat.

Matt felt bad for Chris and Robbie until he learned that they were headed back to the states as instructors at Melville. Everyone wrote letters and gave them to Chris, knowing that they would get home faster traveling with Chris and Robbie than by putting them in the mail on the island.

Two days later, the 48 boat was ready for a trial. Every crew member went to their station and inspected everything, not leaving anything to chance. Chief Peckham had been busy installing a radar unit in the boat once he found out that we were going out on patrol. He spent a lot of time with their radio man Tony Brown and QM2 David Hall, who would be acting as Brown's backup, and David Gill was also looking on.

They took the 48 boat out of the harbor and the chief, with Brown and Hall looking over his shoulder, made a couple of adjustments. The chief then pronounced the unit was working well.

Headquarters must have felt that they'd taken it easy long enough, so they assigned the 48 boat patrol duty for that night. The PBY's had spotted a group of ten destroyers headed in the direction of the slot. The planes were able to sink one of the destroyers but they lost a plane and pilot doing it.

***

THE 48 BOAT DEPARTED ON patrol, with the engines purring along just the way that MOMM2 Clark liked for them to do. They had been assigned a spot just off Iron Bottom Bay. The theory was their radar would alert them of the Japanese ships approaching. The night was jet black...so black that you couldn't really see the men sitting at their guns aft. No one was making a sound. Every man was deep in his own thoughts.

Matt was thinking about his sister. Had she found the 'right man' yet? A man that she would want to spend the rest of her life with. He thought of the girls who he'd taken to parties and the high school prom. They had all been very attractive, and there was one that he'd looked at more like a sister than a sweetheart. They'd done some heavy petting or necking, as they called it down south, but good girls didn't go all the way.

A sudden explosion jarred Matt's mind back to the job at hand. There was another explosion, and then another one. This was followed by a bright flash of light. Off to starboard, torpedoes were exploding as they hit a Japanese cargo ship, causing fire to light up the night.

"Hard right, Skipper," called out Al Ross.

Trusting Ross, Matt asked no questions. He cut the wheel to starboard and gunned the throttles. The boat shot forward as a Japanese destroyer nearly swamped them with its bow wash. They kept turning until they'd made a full 360 degree turn, but much slower than when they'd started.

"Where is she?" Matt asked.

"Just to port," Ross replied.

The 48 boat had just managed to keep from being run over by a damn destroyer. The Japanese were firing on them with their aft guns, now that they'd spied the boat. The 48 boat crew was returning fire. So far, the Japanese hadn't brought the big guns to bear on them.

Paul yelled down to Brown, "You didn't pick up that destroyer on radar?"

"No sir, it still shows clear," Brown replied.

"That's the truth," QM2 Hall added.

They got the smoke generator working and somehow got away from the destroyer's guns. Under the cover of the smoke, they circled around and came up on the destroyers again. The Japanese had forgotten about the 48 boat and were after the 110 boat now.

Matt, taking advantage of the situation, set up a torpedo run right at the stern. Somebody on the Japanese ship saw them as they released the two forward torpedoes. The Japanese were too late. The 48's fish ran true, lifting the back of the destroyer as they exploded. The ship was now dead in the water. The 48 boat came in again on the port side, and at two hundred yards, they fired the last two torpedoes. The torpedoes ran true and hit the Japanese ship and exploded. The destroyer bucked up in the air and split in two. As the 48 boat came around, they fired into the burning cargo ship.

"To port, to port," Paul was yelling.

It was as if the ocean was lifting up. A Japanese submarine's conning tower was breaking water. The 48 boat was out of torpedoes. *Damn*, Matt thought, the gunner's were pouring all they had into the Japanese submarine, but her captain must have realized the danger and submerged. They dropped both depth charges but no debris surfaced. The fight was over, so they secured and headed for home. The engines, the guns, and the torpedoes had all worked well, thank God. The radar...not worth a damn!

***

THE NEXT MORNING AT OFFICER'S call, Matt told everyone how they'd almost got run over by the destroyer because the damn radar hadn't worked.

"I'd say that it was working fine," Chief Peckham said. "Your man either wasn't paying attention or wasn't listening to my instructions."

It was as if someone had spit in Matt's face. Without thinking, he was out of his chair and in the chief's face with Paul grabbing his shoulder. "I'll be damned if that's so, Chief! It didn't work." Matt was totally pissed at the chief's accusations. Everyone knew the chief was lucky that Matt didn't floor him.

"Have you been in combat, Chief?" Matt asked. "I mean actual shooting combat where you lay your life on the line night after night."

"Ere...no," the chief replied.

"You need to go out with us then on our next patrol," Matt said. "We face the enemy damn near every night. If there's anything, anything at all, that will give us an edge, even a tiny advantage; I assure you we would embrace it and give it our fullest attention. So, don't give me any crap about it was my man, I won't hear it. Furthermore, it was two men who checked the radar. Fact is, I invite you to go out and check the radar yourself."

Paul and Frank had gotten between Matt and Peckham by this time, trying to cool down the situation.

Matt paused to catch his breath and calm his nerves. He then added, "I'll guarantee you that there's not a man on the boat that won't let you take his spot, Chief."

Lieutenant Robinson spoke up at that point, "I think that you've made your point, Matt." He then turned to Peckham, "If Matt said that it didn't work, Chief, you can take that as gospel. Both PT 61 and PT 110 have reported trouble with their radar units as well."

Peckham was red faced but said that he'd check out the systems. "It may be the PT boats are too rough for these units," he said as officer's call was dismissed.

Matt was never surprised at how fast scuttlebutt could get passed through the enlisted ranks. By the time he and Paul got back to the hut, the crew had all gathered and someone had come up with a case of Pabst beer.

"To the best damn PT skipper there is," they sang out as they offered Matt and Paul a beer.

When they all had a can of beer, Byhre proposed a toast. "To a skipper who cares for his men." Aye, ayes went up.

L. Z. then spoke up, "We all heard that when the chief tried to shift the blame to Brown, you jumped up ready to whoop some butt and gave him an ole time arse chewing. That's why we all trust you and respect you and love ya, Skipper. You take up for your men and we all know it."

Preacher spoke up and said, "God bless Matt Blue. He's second to none." The guys cheered again.

Matt waved them down. "Folks are trying to sleep."

When Matt hit the rack after finishing off two Pabst beers, the last thing he thought about before drifting off to sleep was the commanding officer's interest in their spotting the submarine. *Is this a new twist, or one that they'd just not identified until now?*

CHAPTER SEVENTEEN

HE 48 BOAT HAD GONE out four of the next six nights. The previous night, however, would live in Matt's mind forever. It was the 12th day of December. The 44 boat had fired its torpedoes, cut right and opened up her engines. She'd then suddenly slowed down, almost to a stop. Why...they'd never know. Matt had thought maybe it was to come around for another torpedo run. She never made it, though. A Japanese gunner on the destroyer had her in his sights. The shell hit the 44 boat aft, right over the engine room and fuel tanks.

Matt and the crew all stared in disbelief. One minute, the 44 boat was doing her job and the next she was a ball of flames.

"I didn't see anybody jump before it was hit," Paul said.

"Me either," Al Ross said, echoing the XO.

The destroyer was turning now, thinking they'd done their job. Matt was tempted to attack the destroyer.

Paul read Matt's mind and said, "Survivors first, Skipper. It's what the men expect."

The leaking gas from the 44 was burning on top of the water. Someone on PT 48 cried out, "To port, Skipper."

Matt saw the arm then. They pulled up next to the arm, but it was too late and the body sank into the sea. They looked about for survivors for several minutes.

"If anyone made it, they'll head for Savo," Matt said to Paul and Ross. "We'll idle that way."

The men were looking all around the boat. Most of the men looked dumbfounded as the reality registered to each of them. Each man was thinking of all the close calls they'd had.

Matt didn't remember seeing Radioman Brown come topside, but he approached and asked, "Do we radio it in, Skipper?"

"No!" Matt snapped. "Let the Japanese find another way to get confirmation."

"Yes, sir," Brown replied.

They made it back to base, fighting a heavy rain and strong winds. The weather was so bad, Matt was not sure that they'd be able to tie up the 48 boat when they got there. But the squall passed them, just before they entered the bay.

"I'll drop by Headquarters and let them know about the 44 boat, XO," Matt said. "I'll see you at the hut afterwards."

Half an hour later, as Matt approached the hut, his mind was still trying to deal with the loss of some good friends that they'd made on the 44 boat. As he walked up he saw the men standing or walking about. It dawned on him then that the canvas tent top had been torn apart in the gale. It looked awkward, the sides were still standing but there was no top.

Matt called Ross over and said, "Have the men sleep on the boat. You can rig a canopy if you're a mind to."

"Aye, aye, Skipper," Ross replied.

By the time Matt hit the rack, he immediately fell into a deep sleep. He was mentally and physically exhausted, as were the rest of the men. Matt slept until eight the next morning and he fought the fog that filled his brain as he got up, and went to the chow hall.

Paul was talking to Frank and Ted, filling them in on the loss of the 44 boat. Matt sat down across from a Seabee officer.

"Do you have any large tarps or canvas?" Matt asked.

The Seabee shook his head no, but wanted to know why Matt asked. Matt told him and the Seabee then asked, "Were you out with Turner last night?"

Matt nodded his head yes and then added, "He's my XO."

"It's a hell of a mess that you guys go through every night," the Seabee said and then he added, "I'll see what we can do for your men's tent."

"I'd appreciate it," Matt told him. "If you ever want to ride a PT boat, I'll fix you up."

The Seabee smiled and responded, "Not on one of your night patrols." They both smiled at his response.

At Headquarters, everyone wanted to hear the story of the 44 boat again. Several boats had already secured or were in a different area of the base when the story was first told. The commanding officer said that he'd send a boat to Savo Island to check on any survivors.

After officer's call, Matt went straight back to bed. He stripped down to his skivvies, telling himself that he'd shower later, but his work uniform reeked. The old adage his aunt was so fond of, 'when you smell yourself, others have been smelling you for three days,' came to his mind. Well, it would have to wait this time.

A loud squeaking noise woke Matt up. He looked at his watch, blinked, rubbed his eyes, and looked at his watch again. It was 1300 hours, he'd not had but three hours sleep. He heard a motor revving up then...a big motor, like a big caterpillar motor. He walked out of the hut in his skivvies and saw a frame had already been built around the top of the crew's tent. A caterpillar was lifting up sheets of corrugated metal. It wasn't scrap tin but nearly new corrugated metal. The Seabees fixed it in such a way that the metal came down over the top of the tent canvas.

I bet that wouldn't come down with anything less than a bad storm, Matt thought. He went back in the hut, grabbed a towel, and headed for the shower. He'd get no more sleep today, and he knew it

Later that day, they learned that a few survivors were picked up on Savo Island. The loss of lives was worse than expected, though. Of the crew, two officers and seven of the enlisted crew were known to be lost. This was not something Matt would put in the letter for home that he was writing.

QM2 Hall knocked and stuck his head through the door. "Hey, Skipper, we are going to play some ball with the Seabees. You want to come?"

Matt hadn't played ball in a while so he was all up for it. They marked off bases and a field of sorts. A home run was if you knocked a ball past the palm trees and into the water. Matt was the pitcher for his team and a big First Class Seabee for their team. Matt's team had the Seabees going into the ninth inning by two runs. The Seabees' next guy at bat kept rubbing his eyes and struck out; his swings were not even close. The strikeout ended the inning and the game.

When Matt walked toward the home plate, the guy staggered a few steps and fell down. Matt helped him up, smelling his breath. "You guys make some torpedo juice?" Matt asked, knowing the wallop it packed. No one answered. He looked about and hadn't seen any of his guys drinking the juice. "Preacher," Matt called.

"Yes, Skipper," Preacher replied.

"Did you make up a batch of torpedo juice and give it to the Seabees?" Matt asked.

"Aye, Skipper, it was a "thank you" for the roof. We told them it was powerful stuff and to take it slow."

The Seabee lieutenant walked up. He'd heard the last comments and said, "Don't worry about it, Matt. He told 'em like he said. But I've yet to see a Seabee take it slow with anything."

Matt looked over to where his guys were and he could see that they had two cases of beer. Matt smiled and said, "We have some beer left. You guys come on over and help us finish it up."

"Free beer," the lieutenant called. The lieutenant's guys were all smiles, while a few of Matt's guys shook their heads.

Wheels said, "Awe Skipper, we gave them the torpedo juice."

Matt responded, "That's why I'm offering them some beer. We need to show some appreciation for their efforts."

An hour later, the beer was gone. The Seabee lieutenant walked up again and said, "I don't think I've actually introduced myself. I'm Ray Gamble."

They shook hands and the Seabee stuck the stub of a cigar in his mouth. After a few not too steady steps, he stopped. Turning toward Matt, he said, "We had a real good time, Matt. The best since we've been on the island."

Frank and Ted walked up then. "He's in such a good mood, Matt, you should have had him build us a new hut."

Matt smiled, "When the hangover from the beer and torpedo juice hits, he might not be as charitable as he is now."

"No," Ted agreed. "We might even need to hunt up a way to keep us halfway hid."

They all laughed but Matt thought, *Ted may have hit upon an excellent point.*

CHAPTER EIGHTEEN

A HAZY SUN DESCENDED OVER THE harbor on Tulagi. As Matt glanced across the waters there were some places where the water gave off a glimmering orange glow. He reached into his pocket and took out a pair of aviator's sunglasses. They were a gift from a thankful pilot for rescuing him when his plane went down. The wind picked up a bit and you could hear water lapping at the wooden hulls of the PT boats. *The remaining boats*, he thought.

Scuttlebutt had it that a big change was coming down the pipe. One that would improve supplies, food, even housing for the PT boat crews. This brought other thoughts to his head. The brass said that Guadalcanal was about to be completely in the American hands. When that happened, all services would likely pull up stakes and follow the war. The PT boats would surely relocate if for no other reason than the cost of gas going from the base to where the action was taking place. Gas and ammunition were both reported to be low.

Morales, Gray, and Byhre were going through old, partially used belts of ammunition. They were removing the unused rounds, cleaning them up and making new belts for the guns. In the past, that would have been unheard of. Some of those belts had shells that had been fired but didn't go off. The Brass wanted them put in an empty ammunition box.

Mike Phagans voiced what they all thought about that idea. "That makes no damn sense. If one round goes off, it's likely to set the entire box off and cause holy hell."

"And that from the mouth of a machinist," Byhre quipped.

Matt, therefore, broke all the rules and told his men to throw them over the side. Eventually, the saltwater would get to the primers.

Paul Turner, PT boat 48's XO, walked down to speak to his skipper. "There might be a change in orders, Matt. We've just got word that eight Japanese destroyers are headed toward Iron Bottom Bay with an ETA of midnight."

At that time, there were only seven boats ready for patrol. One of which was leaking, but the source of the leak hadn't been found yet. In reality, there were only six boats that could go out. *Would they send out all six?* Matt didn't think so, probably they would send three...possibly four at the most. He needed to walk up to Headquarters to see what, if any, changes were in the making. He still didn't move, though. He watched the distant sun dip over the horizon, and it was a beautiful sight to see.

Paul watched his skipper. They needed to get on up to Headquarters, but he felt inclined to give Matt his moment of solitude. Who knew when he'd get another chance to sit and think?

Their orders had changed; it was to be Iron Bottom Bay. The moon seemed unusually bright that night. It was January 1943 already. Christmas, other than a bigger meal, had changed very little from any other day on the island. The Japanese didn't observe Christmas like the Americans did, the heathens.

If Matt was back home, he'd be heading back to college after the Christmas and New Years break for his masters degree. His dad would be warning him of the number of drunks on the road after a New Years party, so drive careful. A thought crossed Matt's mind. *We'd gotten Christmas off.* That was the usual comment made by the cotton mill employees back home in Alabama. If they had to face the enemy nightly like the PT boats' crew did, the cotton mill employees would never complain again.

Matt had an aunt and cousin who worked at the cotton mill. In fact, several hundred of Bullock County's people worked there to have spending money. A good number of the men had farms that they worked, in addition to, working at the mill. Most of the men liked the second shift as they worked the farm until time for their shift to start at the mill. They'd work their shift, then they would go home and to bed. A few of the men, though, would stop off for a beer or some shine.

Matt would never forget a teacher pulling him aside one day when he'd been a bit rowdy and cutting up in class. She said to him, "Matt Blue, you are one of my smartest students. But if you don't buckle down, you're going to end up working at the cotton mill for the rest of your life." That talk, along with her ear pulling, stuck in Matt's mind. Yet, here he was facing death most nights so that the good folks at home, who'd never heard of this part of the world, could work and sleep in peace.

One of his old girlfriends had written and said that she'd looked up the Solomon Islands, in their World Book Encyclopedia, and it looked like a beautiful area. Well that counted for something. He had written back and said, "Were it not for the war, it would be beautiful." He couldn't bring himself to tell her of the horrors of war.

***

WHEELS WENT ABOUT THE BOAT with a big thermos filling the men's coffee cups. Steffey carried a tray of Spam sandwiches, which the men gobbled up. The coffee was warm, not hot, but black and strong. "It's guaranteed to wake a dead man up, if he hasn't been dead over three days," Hall swore.

Patrolling with Frank and Ted, as they frequently did, gave a sense of security. They knew that each of them would be alert and ready. At the present time, they idled along, clouds now covering the moon for minutes at a time. This was the nerve-racking part, the waiting, under the sky's blacker-than-death look.

The other two boats, on patrol, were positioned about a half mile away. The moon broke through the clouds, for a moment, showing a slight chop to the sea. The men already knew that from the way the boat bounced in the water.

At 00:30, or 12:30 am, as most of them would say, the Japanese were sighted about a mile off Savo Island and Guadalcanal.

"Yonder, Skipper," L Z said, pointing, "Three destroyers!"

Matt wondered to himself, had the Japanese got past the lookout boats or had they come in from a different direction, which would not surprise anyone, as they always did the unexpected.

Frank signaled for Matt to go port as he'd go to starboard. To the north, orange flames lit up the night sky as the other two PT boats were attacking the Japanese.

"Well, they know that we're around," Paul mused.

"I doubt they had any thoughts otherwise," Matt responded.

Matt and PT 48's target was turning and heading towards the action.

"Frank's already drawing fire," Ross shouted.

Frank would have to hold on for a moment as Matt started a run on their destroyer. A flare went up.

"Eyes inboard," Ross shouted, not wanting the men to lose their night vision, staring up at the flare.

Matt wondered, as they began their run, if another Japanese destroyer hadn't come on the scene and was focusing on Frank's boat. He hardly had time to set up his run on the original target, so he couldn't help Frank right then.

As the 48 boat got into firing position, all the Japanese seemed to focus on Frank's boat. Did no one see them? Not that Matt was complaining. But they did need to finish this run and lend Frank a hand. Someone mentioned that he had his smoke generator going, and hoped that it would help. They closed with their target and machine guns on the destroyer started to fire on the 48 boat.

"Well, they're not blind," Paul said.

"It's too late," Ross responded, as their forward fish was on the way.

"They must have seen the spark when the torpedoes were fired," Pappy said.

Both of the fish ran true, with one hitting the propeller and exploding, while the other one was almost a miss, but it tore a hole in the stern of the port side of the destroyer. The 48's guns continued to rake the stern of the destroyer.

"That'll take some damage control," Ross shouted.

While Matt zigzagged out of sight, the Japanese fired a salvo at them. The shells hit where they had just been.

"Their main battery is still working," Paul shouted as he wiped his face.

A splash so big that it could have swamped the boat had come on board. They were able to get away while the Japanese sat dead in the water. The third destroyer had changed his focus and now directed it at the 48 boat, allowing no time for them to fire their other torpedoes into the Japanese ship sitting dead in the water.

The 48 boat was taking a lot of machine gunfire as Matt continued to zigzag and they got the smoke generator going. Matt prayed, all the while, that the engines and gas tanks didn't get hit. They could all hear bullets tearing into the wooden hull. The 48 boat could turn a lot faster than the destroyer, and it was their speed that saved them. As Matt shoved the throttles to full speed, he couldn't help but think "who cares about a wake right now." They had to get away from those guns, and damn quick.

Matt changed directions and told Preacher and Pappy to be ready with the aft torpedoes. They were getting very close to the destroyer, under three hundred yards, when they fired the aft torpedoes. Instead of a hard right, Matt went hard left, zigzagging every other breath or so, praying it was not their night to die.

Matt heard, and the gunners saw, the explosion when the torpedoes hit the destroyer...but there was only one. They'd either missed with one torpedo or it was a dud. Either way, the Japanese captain's attention left them to look after his ship.

The other destroyer had come about and was headed out of Iron Bottom Bay, towing two of the ships. They'd only seen three destroyers, and the other boats only saw two, so they had not met eight destroyers, only five. All Matt could think of was, 'Thank you Lord.'

The 48 boat soon picked up Frank and the 46 boat. They didn't see the others but Brown said that there had been messages passed to head home.

They were only a few miles from home when LZ Gray shouted, "Planes, I hear planes!"

Matt throttled back and changed course. They could soon see the plane coming in their direction flying low. It was a Japanese plane all right, but it must have been out of bombs and ammunition, or felt charitable. It dipped its wings and kept going.

A sigh of relief came over the 48's crew.

PART III

CHAPTER NINETEEN

THE JAPANESE WERE CUTTING THEIR losses and pulling away from Guadalcanal. What the Navy had thought was an all out push to gain control of the area was, in reality, the Japanese trying to take men off of the island. A pilot said that when the destroyers would turn tail without a fight, it was because they'd loaded all the troops that they could. It sounded reasonable to Matt, but they had lost a lot of boats and, more importantly, a lot of good friends.

Thinking otherwise, command still sent out patrols. PT 48 had only made two more patrols before the engines that they had borrowed from the 60 boat, *"gave up the ghost,"* as Matt's dad's friend had been so fond of saying.

Therefore, Matt was not surprised when he got orders back to Melville. It was not surprising that Paul, Frank, and Ted got orders as well.

"I guess they're getting shy of real combat veterans to teach," Ted volunteered at chow after getting the news.

What did surprise Matt is the next day most of the crews were also ordered back.

Again Ted volunteered, "It sounds like they need crews for new boats." Matt didn't dispute Ted, since he was generally right.

They got back to the states in late February, and reported in to Melville after the work day had finished. They, as usual, had twelve hours to do as they pleased, so they walked down to the waterfront.

"Damn," Frank said.

The trainer boat was covered in ice. They had all traveled in blues, but this New England weather meant it was time to hunt a heavy coat. A part of Matt's uniform that he had never bought. They went over to the exchange and all four of them bought peacoats.

Seeing their tans, the lady helping them smiled. "I bet that you've just got back from the South Pacific." They nodded their heads 'yes'. She went on to tell them that her husband had been a marine over there but was sent back wounded. "He lost an arm, but at least, he was alive," she said.

Matt didn't know what to say so he smiled and nodded. He knew several people who would have been glad to give an arm or a leg to come back. The lady thanked them for their service and they donned their coats and left.

The next morning, they got a bigger and better surprise. They were given two weeks leave. They took a bus to New York and then each of them headed in their own direction. Paul and Matt rode the train to Montgomery, where each of their families were waiting. Introductions were made all around and before they went their separate ways, they stopped in a diner and ate supper.

When they got home, Matt knew that, being in his old bed, he'd go right to sleep. He was wrong. It was past two in the morning when sleep finally overtook him. The smell of breakfast, 'real breakfast,' woke Matt the next morning.

His mother had bacon, eggs, grits, biscuits, and honey sitting on the table when Matt walked in. He was suddenly ravenous. After breakfast, he helped his mom clear off the table and washed the dishes.

Matt's dad was ready to go on patrol but said that he had the freedom to choose where in the county he patrolled. Matt decided to go ride with him. They drove by the high school, and later that morning they stopped in at Sidney's house. At first, it was like always, and then Sidney said he had to go before a medical board and prove that he was fit for active duty.

Matt said all the right things, but he wasn't sure that he'd improved Sidney's morale at all. It then occurred to Matt, "You want to talk about a combat vet to teach at Melville." Sidney would definitely be the right choice for the job. He didn't need full use of both arms to teach.

At noon that day, Matt called Melville and spoke with Commander Specht. Whether on active duty or just as a vet, he'd get Sidney back to the school, Specht promised. He would also have the medical board changed from Montgomery to Newport, where he had a bit of influence.

Matt went by to see Sidney again as he left to catch the train to New York. Sidney's uniform was a bit loose, but the fire was in his eyes and he had a big smile on his face. Sidney's wife gave Matt a kiss on the cheek, and whispered, "Thank you."

While on leave and feeling brave, Matt asked for and got a dinner date with Sidney's sister, Dianne. Just being around a woman makes a man feel different. He couldn't remember ever having a better time than he did with Dianne. There was nothing romantic about it. It was just two young people making the best of what was offered when your country is at war.

They went to the Lilfred Theater at the end of Prairie Street. They watched the Three Stooges, Dizzy Detectives and Pony Express. The short movies made Matt's eyes water, as he laughed so much. While Matt was using his shirt sleeve to dry his eyes, Dianne had a hanky. The main movie was Tarzan Triumphs. It was about Tarzan battling Nazi paratroopers. It had Boy, Cheetah, the chimpanzee, and enough elephants. Cheetah was full of antics, which was the best part of the movie, Matt decided, along with having a beautiful woman with him.

When Matt took her back home after the show, she thanked him, and gave him a kiss on the lips. She looked at Matt a moment and then rushed in the house. That kiss on the lips could have led to something much more had he pushed it, but then that would have complicated things. It did create a stirring inside Matt that didn't easily go away. He thought about stopping at the Ballerina, a tavern on the Montgomery Highway. He had no doubt that he could find a willing lady to relieve his pent-up desires at the tavern, but his conscience wouldn't allow him to do that, so he decided to go home.

Matt was glad that he did as his mom and dad were on the front porch swing. "Waiting up for me?" he asked.

"No, I had to work a wreck," his dad said. Matt's mom always waited up for his dad when he had to go out at night. "Moonshine and driving don't mix," his dad said. Matt didn't know why but the mention of moonshine made him think of the men's 'torp juice.'

Matt and his parents carried on a degree of small talk for a while, but they were all in bed before midnight. After breakfast, the next morning, they rode down to Western Auto. They had one of the new televisions there. Mr. Gilbert said the thing cost two hundred dollars. Way *too much money*, Matt's dad thought. Matt knew that on a highway patrol's salary it was. But if he survived the war, he'd get his mom one of those televisions.

Those two weeks of leave flew by. Matt rode horses with a friend and went to the show again with Dianne. He tagged along with his mom and dad as they went to visit ailing relatives. He stopped by Lamar's house to visit his mom and dad. They were both cordial but their eyes seemed distant and their thoughts appeared to be a long way off. *Maybe I shouldn't have worn my uniform*, Matt thought.

Matt and his parents ate at Holmes Café one night, and they went to a Bullock County football game another night. The coach told the boys that Matt was one of the best he'd ever coached. They both knew that wasn't true, but Matt wouldn't dispute the coach. Each of the players came by and shook Matt's hand. He went out on the field for the coin toss, and even the team captains from the other side shook his hand.

Matt's dad bought him a box of popcorn, which he ate, and then he finished off his mom's box. It was the first popcorn that he'd had since leaving for the South Pacific, and he made up his mind to take some back with him. He'd find a way to pop it.

The Thursday before Matt had to leave, his dad and he went fishing. They caught a mess of catfish. As they headed back to the truck, his dad mentioned that the fish were just right, the right size for frying. Matt didn't mention it, but it had dawned on him, and this was one fish fry he'd miss.

Suddenly the two weeks had gone by. Matt's leave was over and he found himself getting back on a train. Paul and his family met them at the train station, only this time when they left, instead of smiles, their mothers were teary-eyed. Their fathers put up a stoic, brave front but Matt could hear the tremble in his dad's voice as he said goodbye.

Back at Melville, they found out that the seventy-seven foot boats were no more. Something that had been rumored back on Tulagi, but nobody had seen a new one. Now, it was gospel. Elco was making eighty footers these days, and the Higgins Company down in New Orleans was making seventy-eight footers. Both were improvements to the old boats.

The officer who was driving home the improvements and advances in the new boats was...Lieutenant Sidney Hinson, a true combat skipper. Commander Specht had called and convinced the medical board that he needed Lieutenant Hinson. His value as an experienced combat instructor far outweighed any disability. So Sidney was assigned to Specht Tech.

Before long, Frank and Matt were reunited with their old crews. They found out that same day, that they'd been given new boats and would be traveling back to the South Pacific on them. Matt wasn't sure that he liked the news. But, at least they were going to be familiar with the area. They'd survived it once, so he saw no reason that they couldn't do it again...Lord willing.

Another change was sprung on them. Each boat would now have three officers. When Matt saw a list of available officers, he immediately put in for Ensign Robbie Turner. Matt was a bit surprised as he couldn't find Chris Duncklee's name anywhere. Sidney told him that usually meant that he'd been sent to a ship or was in operations somewhere.

The following day they were given their assignments. Matt was given the PT 174 boat and Frank was given the PT 172 boat. The boats' armament had vastly changed and was very impressive. Each boat had a 40 mm mount, two torpedo tubes, two twin .50 caliber machine guns, one 37 mm forward mount and a 20 mm mount, a .30 caliber machine gun was also mounted on the bow, and on the starboard side.

Matt never figured out why, but the 174 boat carried radar, a SO-A radar unit. Three of their men, Radioman Brown, now a second class petty officer, David Gill, now a petty officer also, and QM2 Hall were trained in the operation and use of the unit while they were at Melville.

Matt was glad that they'd gotten the proper training on the radar. Hopefully, this new radar would prove to be an improvement over the unit that was on the 48 boat. He just hoped the new one worked as well in the South Pacific as it did at Melville.

Another surprise came their way, also. Instead of taking the boats to Brooklyn to be loaded on a ship for transport, they'd take them to Panama under their own power. They saw nothing wrong with that. Matt wondered if this had to do with Ron 10's new commanding officer...Lieutenant Commander Roy West Singleton. His XO was another surprise for Matt, proving life is full of surprises. Chris Duncklee, now a full lieutenant, was the squadron XO. It was good seeing him again.

At their last meeting before departure, the route was laid out for them, taking full advantage of places where they could refuel. Morales and Byhre had ridden a bus to Newport on one of their liberties and visited a tobacco store. They brought back with them tins of various tobaccos...Three nuns, old Holborn, Alexander Flake, Barneys and more. Every day they got a different aroma, at times, it was almost like a pleasure cruise. It was good to hear the men laugh and joke. They'd motor down the east coast of the United States and into the Caribbean Sea, and on to Balboa in Panama.

Sidney had stopped by to see them off. "I hope you like the boat, Matt. I had your name on her from the day I knew you'd be getting one."

Another surprise!! Matt always figured it was Sidney's way to say 'thank you.'

CHAPTER TWENTY

They made it to Panama without incident and went through their required training. Having an experienced crew made a lot of difference, but nothing could prepare them for what was headed their way. They just didn't know it yet.

The facilities at Panama's Taboga Island had been improved greatly. It had all the comforts of home... well, not quite...but better than before.

In May, they were all loaded on board the tanker SS *Stanvac Manila* for transport to their new home. The six boats traveling to their new base included the PT 165, 167, 171, 172, 173, and Matt's boat, the PT 174.

While in Panama, L.Z. Gray got promoted back to second class gunners mate. Matt had written the recommendation, requesting that he be promoted again. In truth, he should have been a first class. When Gray was thanking Matt for the promotion, he asked Matt if he liked to read. When Matt replied yes, he pulled out a book titled *"The Gun"* by C.S. Forrester.

Matt had long ago noticed that Gray always had a book in his back pocket. He'd often read a pocket size paperback a day. Matt read the back cover of "The Gun" and told Gray that he'd love to read it, thinking that he'd have time while they were being transported on the *Stanvac Manila*.

The weather from Balboa to the Pacific was mostly clear, and the seas were smooth. Matt read the book, "*The Gun*." When he gave it back to Gray, he handed Matt three more books. One was by the same author and the other two were by Zane Grey.

"You sure read a lot," Matt said, speaking to Gray and thanking him for the new books.

Gray smiled, "I've found that there's an element of truth and a bit of history in most books, Skipper. So by reading, I'm passing time in an enjoyable manner for me, and learning something new in doing so."

Matt was impressed with L.Z.'s words. He had suddenly discovered that Gray could, when he desired, speak perfect English. Something he didn't do around the crew. He'd just seen a side of the man that most folks would never know was there.

A gale came upon them two weeks after leaving Balboa. The seas got up but the crews from each boat made sure everything was secure and fastened down tightly. They'd left their belongings on board their individual boats, deciding not to haul it to lockers on board the tanker and then back again to their boats when they unloaded. As events took place, Matt was glad that they'd made the decision.

***

IT WAS 0409 ON THE 24th day of May, 1943. Matt had been awakened by a bladder screaming to be emptied. He'd just gotten back in his rack and looked at his watch, thinking he had a few more hours that he could sleep. That's when the explosion occurred. A tremendous explosion that threw Matt out of his rack. He'd suddenly found out what it was like to be torpedoed. As he picked himself up off the deck, he could hear the bells clanging and men shouting. The sea was heavy and choppy so he had to hold onto his rack to stand and get dressed. Someone was yelling, "Abandon ship."

Matt called to Paul, Robbie and Chief Ross to round up the crew and meet at their boat. Once they were out on the deck, they could see that the aft part of the ship was down. The ship was sitting still in the water and had no lights on. The crew met Matt at the 174 boat and they started working to free her from her cradle. Other officers and men were working on their boats as well. Matt had his gunners man their guns in case they had more uninvited guests.

At dawn or a little after, the stern of the tanker had settled down to the point that the PT 174 had water under her and was pounding against the cradle. An officer, Ensign Falvey, made his way to the bridge to release the 174's anchor cable.

She was now taking a beating, still pounding in her cradle. At one point, everyone at the boat heaved to get her off the cradle. They managed that, but the bow was hard against the tanker's super structure. MOMM2 Tom Clark climbed on board and, even though the smell of gas was strong, got the engines started. They backed the 174 boat clear then, and that helped the morale as everyone began to cheer.

The good cheers didn't last long as a wave picked up the 173 boat and slammed her down on some boat davits. It was soon discovered the gas tanks and bottom of the boat were ruptured. As the bow of the *Stanvac Manila* rose in the swell, PT 173 broke loose and sank.

PT 171 boat broke loose and floated clear for a moment and then sank. The tanker started going down. It was just after 1200, eight hours after the torpedo had struck.

PT 167 boat went down with the ship but somehow got loose from her bindings and shot clear. Her hull was the least damaged of all the PT boats. At 1300, a destroyer showed up and lines were passed to the 167, 171, and the 174. They were taken in tow by the destroyer. Frank's boat, PT 172, was able to make Noumea, New Caledonia under her own power.

Matt couldn't help but think how lucky they were, as they neared Noumea. They had lost PT 165 and 173, and one man was lost. However, had the Japanese submarine fired another torpedo, they may have all gone down. Of their crew, BM2 Steffey snagged himself on a nail from a cradle, and MM2 Phagans got a nasty burn as he fell against a hot exhaust when they were trying to save survivors who'd jumped in the water. The corpsman dressed both wounds and told them to have both men checked out once they reached Noumea.

***

THEY MADE IT TO NOUMEA, New Caledonia without mishap. The repair facilities went to work right away. On the boats, there was a beehive of activity as workers swarmed over the PT boats. Even Frank's 172 was checked out from stem to stern.

RON 10's commanding officer, Lieutenant Commander Singleton was everywhere, getting progress reports on each boat and then reporting to the brass. Matt went with Steffey and Phagans to the hospital, thinking his presence may get them treated and out of there sooner than later. As they sat waiting, Matt kept seeing a nurse who looked familiar, but all that he could see was her back and side.

Matt, never being overly shy, walked up to the nurse's station and spoke, "Is that you, Nurse Morris?"

"Who's asking?"

"Your old PT boat friend," Matt replied.

Morris was writing down some numbers that must have been important. She said, "Hold on a moment," without ever looking up.

Matt waited a moment and was about to go back to his seat, when she told the corpsman that it was right, and then she looked at Matt.

"Matt...Matt Blue! Come around here," she said. He stepped around the petition and got a big hug. "What are you doing here?"

"The short answer is to get two of my men treated and then back to the boat. The long answer is our transport ship was hit by a torpedo. Our boats were damaged and we were towed here for repairs," Matt replied.

"Call your men over," Morris said, which Matt did.

They walked back to a treatment room where she called a corpsman over to take off the bandages and then she called a doctor over to treat them, after their wounds had been cleaned.

Matt followed Kricia to a break room and there were Karen Hamby and Haley Stanford. They all hugged and chatted for ten minutes. They then set up a time to meet for dinner at the officer's club at seven p.m. that evening. He was impressed that they actually had an "O" Club.

Steffey and Phagans were both getting shots when Matt came back by. "If we are still here in three days, we are to come back for a dressing change," Phagans volunteered.

Matt laughed. They all knew that in three days they'd be long gone.

***

MATT, PAUL, AND ROBBIE MET Kricia, Karen, and Haley that night at the "O" Club. While enjoying a real steak, fries, and a cold beer, Matt had the nurses in a trance as he told them of the torpedo attack on the *Stanvac Manila* and the frenzy to get the PT boats free and away from sinking ship.

Karen asked if on the way back they thought they might be able to stop by Santa Cruz.

"It's possible," Matt answered.

"Good," Haley responded. "We'll get a care package together and we'll each write a letter to Father Murphy."

Kricia then looked Matt's way. "When you guys get settled in, send us your address."

Karen took a napkin and wrote her address down. "This is the same address for all of us, just change the name."

Matt took the napkin and tucked it away. Late the next afternoon, they left Noumea. Matt felt a sense of loneliness as they left. Saying goodbye was not one of his strong points and he'd come to like the nurses a lot, one in particular. But he didn't mention that, not with a war going on.

As they put the shore behind them, Matt looked at the stack of boxes filled with medical supplies. It would make Father Murphy happy to know the nurses still thought of him. He'd certainly enjoy the letters that each nurse had sent. In fact, Matt had three letters himself, and he couldn't wait to read them.

They were very thoughtful women. They had also written a letter to the crew, which Matt gave to Chief Ross to read to the men. It wished each man all the luck in the world. The last line read, "We'll never forget the brave men of PT 48."

It's PT 174 now, but I won't forget the PT 48 boat either, Matt thought.

CHAPTER TWENTY ONE

MATT WAS NOT SURE WHAT he was expecting of their new home at Lumbari Island, but compared to Tulagi it was certainly lacking. They beached their boats beside a row of boats already beached. As Matt jumped off the boat, he looked at Frank, who shook his head.

Lieutenant Commander Singleton said, "I'll go announce to the brass that Ron 10 is here, and hopefully find out what I can about quarters."

From the look of all the boats with canopies over the bow, Matt wondered if some hadn't decided the boats actually were the best quarters to be found.

Two sailors walking by paused and asked the crews if their boats were the new Elco 80 Footer's. Frank answered, confirming that they were.

"Are you the guys that were riding the tanker that the Japanese slipped a fish into?"

"Yes, that's us," Chief Ross, who'd gotten off the boat, replied.

"Welcome to Todd City," one of the sailors said. "We're on the 162 boat." The chief thanked the guys for stopping by and welcoming them to the island.

"You didn't ask about quarters," Matt said to Ross. Ross just shrugged his shoulders in reply.

They all wandered down the beach and into Todd City. The first thing they saw were mud holes every few feet. There was an abundance of tents and several huts, some with thatch roofs, while the others had tin. Most of them were open on each end to take advantage of any breeze blowing. They found the mess hall where several seamen were getting the place cleaned up and ready for lunch.

"This is one more crowded place," Frank swore. Matt had to agree.

They finally saw the Headquarters building. It was not built any different than the other places they'd seen, just bigger.

They sighted Lieutenant Commander Singleton, so they walked over. He looked at them and muttered, "It's a mess, nothing but a dang mess. One person, who I asked about quarters for the boat crew, said pick a spot. Just let us know where you settle. Some ensign then said, 'Don't get too comfortable anywhere as several boats are going over to Rendova. It's only ten miles or so, but you'd have to start all over.'"

Matt decided that they'd send Chief Ross and Hall out when they got back to the boat. They'd get the real skinny. Paul and Robbie were sitting on the bow of the boat with their legs dangling over the side when Matt returned. The chief had the men cleaning and checking the equipment and the guns.

Matt saw their engineer, MOMM2 Clark, on deck and he was smiling. He saw Matt and said, "Those new engines are built well. We didn't use one drop of oil from Noumea to here."

Matt was pleased with that. He figured the trip to Panama and the trip from Noumea to here had been enough to, as his dad would say, break them in right. He called the chief over and told him to pick someone to go with him and find out what he could about Todd City, specifically about quarters.

Ross called over to QM2 David Hall and said, "Let's go for a walk."

Ross and Hall were back an hour later. "We are in the thick of the base now, Skipper. We did talk to a guy from PT 157, who said that they were about to move out so we could move into their place."

Lieutenant Commander Singleton was back before dark. "Squadron 6 is moving to Lever Harbor," he said.

Frank nodded, "We know. We are going to move into PT 156 and 157's huts."

"The 161's will be open as well," Ross volunteered.

Singleton nodded, "We'll have to make do with it. It seems there's a lot of ships nearby and plenty of PT boats about. What they don't have an abundance of is gas."

"Or ammunition," Chris Duncklee added as he walked up.

Matt had not felt good about this move since they left Noumea. Was it intuition, homesickness, or as his aunt used to say 'you got the mulligrubs' which meant that Matt was in an ill-tempered mood.

They spent an hour talking to Chris. He said that he had a good job but he missed the boats and the closeness of the crew. Being around the brass all day didn't strike Matt as something he wanted. Before he left, Chris told them if they needed anything, to see him. *He need not worry*, Matt thought, *I will*.

Later that afternoon, Matt told the guys to rig a tarpaulin or canvas over the bow and anyone who wanted to sack out there was welcome. He even slept on board in his rack that night. It was hot, but mosquito free.

It was near noon the next day when Lieutenant Commander Singleton sent for the RON 10 skippers and XO's. "We've gotten word that the Tokyo Express is headed our way."

Matt thought to himself, *may as well break the ice now as later.*

It was August 1, 1943. They would see how these new eighty footers did in real combat. Clark and his mate had just fired up the engines and they were backing out of their space when the air raid siren went off.

"Let's get out of here," Matt yelled to his guys.

It was almost dusk but the sky quickly darkened with enemy planes. They were motoring out of the harbor with Frank right behind them. Bombs were falling now, and some went into the trees where they heard a blast but couldn't see what had been had hit.

The damn Japanese struck pay dirt then. A bomb hit both PT 117 and PT 164. The blasted boats leapt up in the air. Two torpedoes came loose from the 164 boat and ran around the bay. They ran up on the beach then and got stuck in the sand. Neither of them exploded, thank the Lord.

The PT boats filled the air with all sorts of gunfire, .50 caliber machine guns and 20mm Oerlikons.

Byher and Morales were shouting, they'd scored a hit. Smoke was coming from one of the bombers and it was losing altitude, but they didn't see it splash.

Once the planes were gone, third officer Robbie Turner made us laugh when he said, "I reckon they thought that they'd soften us up before tonight's play."

It wasn't the first time the men under Matt's command had been targeted by Japanese planes.

L.Z. summed up what most of the men felt. "They better not have screwed up our new quarters dropping those bombs over the base like they did." Several of the men echoed L.Z.'s remarks.

They motored back to their slip, such as it was, and waited until the word was passed to pull out. They'd been told that four Japanese destroyers were bound for the Blackett Strait on the west side of Kolombangara to Vila at the southern tip of the island. They also found out that they were sending out fifteen boats, in total, to deal with the four destroyers.

"We'll be running into each other at every turn," Chief Ross swore.

Neither Frank nor Matt had ever in their experience seen so many boats being sent out.

"It's a damn mess is what it is," Paul volunteered. "We told Lieutenant Commander Roy West Singleton our feelings when he came for us to get underway." However, there was little he could do.

Singleton climbed on board the 172 boat, since Frank was the senior officer. They filed out of Rendova Harbor and then headed towards each boat's assigned location.

CHAPTER TWENTY TWO

I T WAS NEAR MIDNIGHT WHEN Radioman Brown called up that he had radar contact.

"We know it works, at least," Paul said.

The destroyers were approaching the PT boat's position from the north.

"They'll be along the Kolombangara coast before long," Brown advised.

Matt was torn between using the radio to alert Frank, who was idling not twenty yards away. It all suddenly became a moot point. Two PT boats had started firing on the destroyers.

"I don't know what they're thinking," Ross said. "I've never seen .50 calibers sink a destroyer yet."

Brown said, "From the radio chatter, they thought that they were firing on landing craft."

"God help them," Robbie muttered, more a prayer than otherwise.

The Japanese turned on searchlights and opened fire with their big guns.

"They know, by now, that they aren't dealing with landing craft," Ross threw out.

Eagle-eye Gray spoke then, "Someone is making a run at them, Skipper. A proper run."

Frank moved forward and waved for the 174 to follow. A few minutes later, Frank was making a run when a PT boat crossed right in front of him. Frank cut hard to port and avoided the collision. One of the destroyers turned on its searchlight but they were tracking down the boat that had crossed Frank's path.

"Alright boys, let's see what we can do," Matt said adding, "L.Z., that spotlight is yours."

As they started their run, a ship aft of their target fired up a star shell to light up the PT boats on his quarter. The effect was that it gave a good view of the target. Pappy and Preacher were standing by the tubes. At six hundred yards, they turned their fish loose. Knowing that Frank had cut to port, Matt went to starboard. L.Z. had knocked out the searchlight, thank the Lord. The 174 made a half circle and then slowed down. Two explosions were heard.

"We hit her, Skipper."

There were more star shells going up and Matt's man, L.Z., who could hear a flea fart at forty yards yelled, "Planes, Skipper."

Matt could hear the planes. "Cut our engines back to idle," he ordered.

The planes could easily see a wake. More star shells went up.

"They are doing that so that they can find targets for the planes," Robbie said.

Matt didn't disagree and a moment later the big guns on a destroyer were firing.

"Hopefully, his smoke generator is working," Matt said, thinking aloud of the unknown PT boat.

"Whose, Skipper?" Paul asked.

"Whoever they are firing at," Matt responded. "If he guns it, the wake will give him away to the planes."

Ross spoke up then, "This night has cluster you know what written all over it."

They lay idle with every man listening, and then Morales shouted, "Damn, look over

there."

They had all heard the crash and saw a ball of flame leap into the air.

"Damn, some PT boat has just bought the farm," Hall swore.

They watched for a few more minutes, and then Brown stuck his head up and said, "Boats headed home, Skipper."

"Should we go investigate that explosion?" Robbie asked.

Paul answered him, "We were too far away to get a good location. We can't turn on the lights so we're as likely to run over some poor soul as to save him."

"Let's head for home, guys," Matt said. "We got our licks in. Hopefully, they'll learn that you can't put but so many fish in a pond before they start in on one another."

"Breaking philosophical, Skipper?" the chief asked.

"Shut up, Chief, or you can drive us home."

***

ONCE THEY GOT BACK TO base and more boats came in, the picture was pieced together. They found out a Japanese destroyer rammed PT 109. The gas tanks ruptured and fire broke out immediately. Matt was thinking that was probably the flash that they had seen towards the north. The brass said that the night was the least effective PT action ever executed.

"Hell, I could have told them that," Frank said. "They didn't appoint a leader, and there was no communication unless somebody's butt was in a fix and they called for help."

Thirty torpedoes had been fired with no confirmed hits.

"We know that we hit our destroyer," Preacher said.

"Damn straight," Pappy seconded. "Twice," he added.

Lieutenant Commander Roy West Singleton made his argument to the brass that the crew saw their fish hit the destroyer.

Their response was that they didn't doubt their word, but they had nothing to confirm the hit.

"Same old crap," L.Z. said. It was what was on everyone's mind.

"We shoot one up the commodore's arse, you think he'd confirm it?" Morales asked.

"Now, Joe," Preacher began.

Morales held up his hand, "I got you, Preacher, but I could have said worse."

"There's nothing planned for tomorrow night," Frank said to everyone. "Maybe we can get situated on our quarters."

It was several days later that they got word that there were survivors from PT 109. Two boats, PT 157 and 171 got the task of picking, up the men from the 109 boat. They were a happy bunch when they made it back to an American base, after being on an uninhabited island by themselves for a week. They were, however, in pretty good shape for shipwrecked sailors.

***

FOR THE BASE, THE WAR changed again. But such is the way with war. Matt felt that they were doing more damage to the Japanese ships than either the Japanese or the American brass wanted to admit.

Their new job became barge hunting...barges with thick armor and shallow drafts. Their armor plating and guns matched, and in some cases exceeded the fire power of the PT boats. They found that they were suddenly in a different type of war, facing a tough adversary. The barges were so shallow drafted that the torpedoes were useless against them.

The first sighting of a Japanese barge came when the 174 boat was ferrying some officers and a coastal watcher to do a reconnaissance of an island to check out its usefulness for an airfield. They had off loaded their passengers and were taking it easy. A couple of men were basking in the sun, two were fishing, and L.Z. Gray was reading. Two of the guys had broken out a pipe and cigar. Matt enjoyed the pipe aroma, but he could have done without the cigar stench.

Matt had three men on lookout duty. One of them was to port, one to starboard, and the other one was keeping his eyes on the land. Matt knew that L.Z. would hear a plane before anyone else, even when reading as he was now doing. This had so far been the easy assignment that they'd been promised.

It was after lunchtime and the men had just finished with their fried bologna sandwiches when L.Z. said, "I think our passengers are coming back."

The coastal watcher and his native assistant made it back. The man had been singing, which was what L.Z. had picked up on. It was another hour before the officers all made it back. They loaded up the PT boat and were headed back to Lumbari, when they rounded a point of land and there she was…a Japanese barge with a flag blowing in the wind. The PT boat was doing about twenty knots and so swept by her and had to come about to engage.

Matt's crew reacted without a word from him, Paul, or Robbie. Ross spoke to their guests and asked them to go below or get down, out of the way. They obeyed without question.

Preacher fired a torpedo, only to see it go underneath the barge and hit a palm tree at the water's edge. Preacher just looked at

Matt. They took fire from the barge as they went by at near full throttle. On the second pass, they had every gun that could bear firing at the barge. It was disheartening to see their .50 caliber shells ricochet off the side of the barge. The larger caliber guns, the 37 mm forward mount and the 40 mm aft mount seemed to be earning their pay.

The Japanese gun, at one point, was silenced and right after there was an explosion. The barge must have been carrying heavy duty ammunition to some place. The barge had turned to face the 174 boat as they made that last attack. A tarpaulin covered stack, which must have been ammunition, had to have been hit by one of their shells. After the initial explosion, it looked like a fireworks display. As a rocket went off, Matt put some distance between them and the barge in case there were more. They'd just got out of range when another explosion went up. Even at their distance the percussion rocked the 174.

PT 174 started back towards the barge, using caution, checking for survivors before leaving the area. There were none, Paul reported as they started for home.

"Your report just got a bit more exciting, Skipper," Morales called out. "Wait a moment, please, before we head home." Even with all the witnesses, he wanted a picture.

Matt gave him a minute to get his camera and snap a few shots of their first barge kill. Matt knew by tomorrow morning they'd have a barge painted among their kills. None of the brass had said anything about kills after they'd started taking pictures. He'd let them know they had copies.

The coastal watcher, seeing Joe's camera, smiled and gave a brief nod and a wink. He knew the scoop of getting credit from the brass as well as they did.

CHAPTER TWENTY THREE

F IGHTING BARGES BECAME THE GAME. They found out the Japanese were using a metal hulled craft that was fifty feet long. It could carry up to one hundred twenty troops or fifteen tons of cargo. They were slow but had armor plating over the important parts, meaning the engine and helmsman or coxswain or whatever the Japanese called the man at the wheel. They were also more often than not well armed.

Most of the barges had a 40 mm gun mounted. This would tear a wooden boat apart in minutes. The barges also had the firepower of the individual troops, when they carried them. Matt and his crew found that the best way to neutralize these guns was to feed them more lead that they could handle. As long as they were firing at the barge, the enemy kept their heads down. Matt didn't blame them, but in doing so, it allowed the PT boats to get out of range.

The Japanese were very ingenious people. They would call in aircraft to help protect them at times. They also set up shore batteries along the routes the barges took. Some of these machine gun nests were spotted by marines on shore, and a few by US aircraft, but more often they found out about them when they were fired on.

They had been on several barge hunting trips and had sunk one barge and left another beaching itself. GM2 Joseph Morales decided to show the brass their victories, for lack of a better word. He kept a camera with him at all times when on patrol, and took more pictures than ever. Joseph didn't smoke cigarettes so he'd give a guy at Headquarters his government ration cigarettes to develop his film. Since none of the officers smoked, they chipped in as well.

Matt was not exactly sure when or how it started but one afternoon Lieutenant Commander Singleton came over to their boat with papers in his hand. Handing them to Matt, he said, "Here is a map with a spot marked on it, and here are the coordinates. You will pick up a squad of soldiers who will go on patrol with you. A little extra firepower never hurts." He also made every one of the crew happy. "When the 172 boat gets back, you guys are slotted for R&R in New Zealand." Everyone heard this and gave a cheer.

They picked up the soldiers exactly where they said they'd be. Sergeant John E. Belk was the man in charge. He was a mean looking cuss. But looks can be deceiving. He was a friendly soul from South Georgia. That's not to say that in battle he couldn't become as mean as he needed to be. There was another big man with him, who was carrying a light machine gun, a Browning BAR. The way he toted it, they could tell he was very comfortable with it.

Another man who boarded had no guns, but he had two cameras hung around his neck. He was a journalist named Hollis Walker. He shook each of the officer's hands and said that he was excited to be on this patrol.

Robbie, of all people responded, "Well, keep your head down if shooting starts. A bullet in the head will end that excitement."

"Thank you, that's good advice," Hollis replied.

They were to patrol that night near Bairoko Harbor off the north shore of New Georgia. The Japanese were trying to move troops away from New Georgia to their stronghold on Kolombargara.

As they headed towards their position, Radioman Striker Gill called to Morales, "You can put your camera up tonight, Joe. This man has plenty of them."

"Pictures from two different sources helps prove the point, doesn't it," Morales responded.

***

IT WAS NEARLY 1 A.M. when Brown's head appeared at the top of the ladder. "We've got positive radar contacts, Skipper. "

They passed the word and the lookouts grew even more vigilant. Pappy was the first one to spot the enemy.

"To starboard, Skipper. Looks like a barge out front with two auxiliary ships behind."

Matt was sure that the auxiliary ships were there to take off the troops. "We can get one of the auxiliary ships with torpedoes," Matt said to Paul, Robbie, and Chief Ross. "The 40 mm gun will have to handle the other auxiliary ship. We'll hit the last auxiliary ship first."

They sat where they were idling so as to make no wake or present a target for enemy aircraft or some lurking destroyer. Everyone was quiet.

Ross carried the word to Dale Byhre. "Concentrate the 40 mm gunfire on the second auxiliary ship. Punch a few holes in her bottom if you can," Ross said.

The barges moved slowly at one knot. So the 174 crew was getting impatient by the time Matt was ready to make their run. They eased in, to less than five hundred yards from the barge.

Paul asked, "Why not use one torpedo each for the auxiliary ships?"

"If I knew they'd run true and we were certain that one of them wasn't a dud, I would," Matt replied.

Paul smiled, "That's why you are the skipper, Matt."

They were less than four hundred yards when L.Z. hissed, "I hear planes."

Matt said, "Damn! Fire the torpedoes and let's ease out of here if we can."

"Why ease out?" the journalist asked.

"So that we don't make a wake the plane can spot," Matt replied. At that time, both torpedoes struck the first ship.

"They know that we're about now, Skipper," Robbie said.

Matt bit back the response that was on his lips.

"You hurt that one, Skipper, they are putting rafts over the side," Ross volunteered.

Sergeant Belk cursed, "Damn, I believe they're hauling troops somewhere rather than going to pick up some."

"Planes overhead," L.Z. volunteered.

Everyone sat still and waited. A flare was dropped but it drifted a bit as it lit up the night. They were just in the outer periphery. The sound of the plane started to fade and then it was gone.

"Byhre, the next auxiliary is yours," Matt said.

The 174 came in at regular attack speed. When the guns opened up, the soldier with the BAR was up on the bow of the boat. He started firing as the other guns did. The night lit up as orange flames jumped from the 40 mm gun, in spite of the suppressors. A blaze of tracer fire zipped through the night coming and going.

Matt worked around the aft part of the auxiliary ship as they poured more fire into it. "Cease fire, cease fire," Matt yelled.

The ship was a sieve. Whatever it was carrying was heavy, as water was pouring in. Matt looked at Paul and Robbie, "Now, for the hard part."

Walker had constantly been taking pictures, and Matt asked, "Got what you wanted?"

"So far, Matt, so far," Walker replied.

Sergeant Belk asked, "You not going to sink the rafts?"

"No! That's not a practice in the Navy," Matt responded.

They hadn't gone a mile before the man with the BAR on the bow shouted, "Yonder is your barge."

Matt maneuvered so as to give his gunners the best shot . Gill and Preacher were reloading for Byhre on the 40 mm. Steffey, Pappy, and Phagans kept the .50 caliber loaded. They kept up a constant fire until Morales' gun jammed. As hot as the gun was, he set to work clearing the jam.

L.Z.'s guns kept up the barrage, as did the BAR on the bow. Suddenly there was an explosion inside the barge. Flames jumped up into the black sky. Burning soldiers were jumping over the side. Most of Matt's crew sat by their silent guns and watched.

The barge must have been carrying gas, the way the flames continued billowing up like a roaring inferno. Matt shivered, watching, and praying that when it was his time, he wouldn't go like that. The journalist had even stopped taking pictures.

"Let's go home," Matt said. "Robbie, you have the helm."

CHAPTER TWENTY FOUR

T HEY'D HAD MAIL CALL WHILE Matt and the others were out on patrol. Matt had six letters on his pillow when they returned. As tired as he was, he still looked to see who they were from. The nurses Haley, Kricia, and Karen had each written to him. They had turned out to be great pen pals. His mom and dad had each written and he also had a letter from Sidney Hinson. He broke open Sidney's letter first. Sidney wrote that he was doing well and had been given command of PT 343 and was attached to RON 24, which was headed to the Southwest Pacific. His friend at Melville said the lieutenant commander promotions would be coming out before long and it was felt that he'd be on the list. This meant his days as a PT boat skipper were limited.

Sidney had taught Matt a lot. He was truly a man with ice water in his veins. A couple of times, Matt thought that he'd bitten off too much but he always pulled it off. Maybe that was the difference between a good PT boat skipper and a great one. Matt didn't think that he'd ever be a great one...maybe he cared too much for the men in the boat. They certainly didn't shirk their duties, and Matt tried to take on every task with his mind on taking the fewest possible chances.

Matt finished Sidney's letter, and then he put it with the others on his table that he would read later. He was too tired right then to read them. He pulled his sheet over his head and was asleep instantly. The next thing that he remembered was being woken up by Ross.

"Wake up, Skipper, or you'll be late for officer's call," Ross said.

Matt sat up on the bed, and Ross handed him a small envelope. "Pictures," he said. "Some of them are pretty good."

Matt opened the envelope as Ross walked out of the hut. A smile came over his face as he looked at Walker and Morales' handiwork. He got up and dressed and headed to officer's call. He was just outside the building when he met up with their squadron commander, Lieutenant Commander Singleton.

"Morning," Matt said as he saluted the commander. He handed him the envelope and said, "Pictures showing proof of our kill last night."

Singleton lifted his brow as he gave Matt the eye. Viewing the photos, he smiled and said, "I'd call this confirmation."

In the meeting, Matt was congratulated on doing a good job. The passengers had already related the events of the previous evening.

The base commander said, "We hope to get confirmation of the kill in my reports soon." He seemed taken aback a bit when Singleton showed him the pictures that Matt had given him.

"I believe, sir, we already have the confirmation," Singleton said. After he said this, the pictures were passed around to the other officers.

"Yes," the commander finally said. "Those do put an exclamation point on the report, don't they?"

Feeling that the commander wasn't happy at not being given a heads up, Matt volunteered, "We had a journalist embedded with the Army scouts, who rode with us." He just gave us the pictures. This seemed to appease the commander.

Someone asked, "Matt, did having the Army guys on board seem like help or were they a hindrance?"

"Help," Matt said automatically. "Yes, they contributed greatly to the firepower that we laid down, especially the man with the BAR, on the bow of the boat."

"Hmm, maybe that's something we can add," the commander said.

The meeting broke up then, and several of the officers gave Matt a slap on the back. Having a man with a ready camera was a focal point of the conversation for most of them. Matt went back towards their area, but he stopped by the mess tent with Lieutenant Commander Singleton and they got some lukewarm coffee.

Singleton said, after he doctored up the coffee with cream and sugar, "We leave for New Zealand at 1630 hours tomorrow." Taking a sip of the coffee, he peered over the cup at Matt. "Have your crew in ship shape order and mustered by Headquarters no later than 1600 hours."

"Yes sir," Matt replied. It dawned on him then that the commander had said we. Did that mean that he, their commanding officer, was going with them? *Well, so what*, Matt thought. Roy West Singleton, Lieutenant Commander, USNR, had proven to be a good commanding officer.

Matt saw, as he walked up to their area, that most of the guys were reading their mail and just lounging about. He was sure that the rumor mill had already made the crew aware of the departure tomorrow for a little R and R. The boat had already been made ready. Ross had seen to that.

When Matt looked about he saw Preacher talking to a man that Matt had seen before, but otherwise didn't know.

Preacher saw Matt looking his way as the seaman walked off. He gave Matt a quick wave and walked over to him. "One of Frank's crew," he said. "Tell me, Skipper, have you ever felt alone? I mean, a gut wrenching, deep in your soul alone, where you actually felt forsaken by God?"

"No..I can't ever recall being like that," Matt responded.

"Me either," Preacher replied. "But, Arch, that's the seaman's name, grew up never knowing who his mother or father was. He ran away from the orphanage when he was twelve. He lived by his wits until the war came along. He lied about his age and got in the Navy without a birth certificate. He bought a used Bible and had someone fill out the pages in the front. The authorities accepted the Bible entries as proof of his age."

Matt had heard of such stories, but they were at war and men were needed. After all, who would lie in the Bible?

Preacher took a deep breath and gave a sigh. "Arch feels the weight of the world riding on his shoulders. He gets no mail, and he feels out of place when the others talk of home, their moms and dads, brothers and sisters, or even ballgames. It's only since joining the Navy that he's eaten regularly and had clothes that didn't come from a thrift shop, the Salvation Army, or he stole them off a clothesline. He's never been to birthday party, had birthday cake, nor has he ever had a date with a girl. He's had sex with a prostitute old enough to be his mother. When we have mail call it is a depressing time for him. I've asked my wife's sister to write him a simple letter as a friend. He, at least, learned to read and write in the orphanage. I first saw him one day after a mail call and he seemed so dejected. I walk over an introduced myself."

Preacher continued, "I gave him a corn cob pipe and some tobacco. He asked me if I was a real preacher. I said no, but that I believed Christ was my Savior and that he rose from the cross. I told him also that once the war was over, I planned on becoming a real preacher. He said that when I got a church, he'd come to it. Skipper, it broke my heart when he said he used to watch church services through the windows. I asked why he didn't go in and he said that he was too dirty and smelly for genteel people. He also used to peep in windows when families had supper together. He almost got caught doing that and ran. But the mother left a plate of food on the back porch for him, so he must have been seen. Skipper, it broke my heart listening to him tell his story. Seeing families doing things together hurt him the most and he considered going back to the orphanage where he at least knew a couple of the kids."

Pappy called to Preacher, so he gave Matt something close to a salute and walked over to his friend.

Ted, Frank's XO, was in the hut when Matt walked in. For some reason, Matt asked Ted, "What sort of man is Arch?"

"The best," Ted responded. "A loner for sure, but otherwise he's the best. He's just a seaman but Frank and I would like to see him made a gunner's mate. He would soon become a petty officer, if he had a rating. Why do you ask?"

"Just curious, I've seen him talking to Preacher a lot," Matt said. "I think they've become friends."

"Who's not Preacher's friend?" Ted replied as he ducked and went out the door.

Matt sat down on his cot, alone in the hut, and he wondered how many more were like Arch? Men who need help in so many ways but would likely never get it as long as this war went on. This was something that he might mention to his dad the next time he was home. He usually had an answer.

He couldn't dwell on it right now, though; it was time to pack for their R&R trip to New Zealand.

✱✱✱

THE NEXT DAY, AFTER ARRIVING in New Zealand, Matt found out that Frank would be the acting commanding officer of RON 10 while they were gone. Matt was sure that Frank liked that and found himself smiling at the thought. Ted would be the acting skipper of the PT 172 boat. Matt would guarantee that Ted liked his change, even if it was a temporary one.

✱✱✱

AUCKLAND WAS A PRETTY PLACE even with a war going on. Rooms for the officers had been reserved at the Grand Hotel. The men were given rooms at the Hancocks. They had five days to put the war behind them and to rest and recuperate before they had to return to the Seagrove Aerodome for the trip back to the war. Matt could only hope and pray that it would go away while they were there. It was wishful thinking on his part.

Lieutenant Commander Singleton surprised Matt by telling him to call him Roy while they were away from the squadron. After they got checked in, Roy asked Matt if he had a list of what he wanted to do and see while they were in New Zealand.

Matt honestly told him that he'd not thought that far ahead. "Eat some decent food," Matt said, "and maybe see a few things that I've never seen before." Matt knew that that was a lame response, but it was the best he could come up with.

Roy nodded his head that he understood. "I'm a married man," he volunteered, "so I will not be partaking in tasting of the forbidden fruits offered by the ladies of the evening."

Matt smiled at Roy's comment. He could name a dozen or so horny sailors who would be scouting out the availability of the local ladies. The chief had passed out condoms before they left, which was a joke, Matt thought, but didn't say so.

"One condom per man and we are to be in Auckland for five days," Roy quipped. They both laughed at that. "I get your drift," he said, smiling.

The four officers went out that night and had steak. "The meat was very good, I've tasted none better," Matt volunteered.

"That's because of the clear air and lots of rain," the waiter said, when Matt praised the food.

"There are so many ration signs, I'm surprised that we got a steak," Robbie said.

"Had you not been in uniform, you would not have," the waiter responded.

Matt had had wine before, what college age kid hadn't. But the wine they had with their steak was of the finest wine he'd ever tasted.

"It's called Babich," the waiter said, smiling as he spoke. "It has been very popular with the Americans on rest and recuperation in Auckland." Matt made up his mind to get a bottle to take home if possible. He just wouldn't let his preacher know.

The next couple of days were spent sightseeing as a group. Then by mutual agreement, they all went out by themselves on the third day.

Matt, having forgotten which way the traffic flowed, nearly stepped out in front of an oncoming bus. A young woman let go of her bag of groceries and pulled him back in the nick of time. However, in saving his life, she lost her groceries.

Looking at her, with his heart pounding, Matt was finally able to get out a thank you. Two things he noticed at once were that she was trying to stand on one leg and he, in addition to ruining her groceries, had hurt her foot and ankle by stepping on her. They were in front of the market where she had shopped. Matt sat her down on a bench, and tore off a piece of the paper bag and wrote down everything that he saw. He then went back in the store after obtaining her promise to not move.

Matt asked the store clerk, "As an American officer, do I have to have any type of rationing stamp?" After the store clerk said no, Matt gathered up her groceries, and then he filled up a second bag with things he was sure she wasn't able to get.

She was on the bench when he came out. Thank God, he thought. They rode the bus to her apartment complex, where after a back and forth conversation, Matt persuaded her that he meant her no harm, and that after he took the two heavy bags up to her apartment, he would leave.

She finally gave in and asked, "What's your name?"

"Matt Blue," he replied. "I'm a Navy officer. What's your name?"

"Sheree," she said.

"It's nice to meet you," he said, holding out a couple of fingers to shake her hand, as he couldn't completely turn loose the bag he was holding.

Thank goodness her apartment was located on the first floor. It had a small kitchen, dining area, and sitting room, all out in the open. A doorway led to a bathroom that Matt could see, as the door was open. He assumed that on either side of the bathroom, bedrooms would be located.

Sheree asked to be excused for a minute, and limped to a bedroom. Mail was on the table where he had set the bags down. Matt saw a letter addressed to Sheree Scott. He took the grocery list out of his pocket and quickly scrawled down her address. He was tucking it in his pocket when she walked back in.

She had taken off her jacket. When it's summer in the United States, it is winter in New Zealand. She had also changed her shoes and didn't limp as bad with the flat shoes on.

"You were coming home from work?" Matt asked.

She gave a quick smile and said, "Yes."

"I again want to say thank you for saving my life," Matt said. "In the United States, there's an old Indian saying, 'If you save someone's life, you are then responsible for that person.'"

In truth, Matt didn't know if it was an old Indian saying or not, but he thought it sounded good. It got a smile out of her, though.

She started taking the items out of the bags. Matt noticed that she had a sniffle and a bit of a cough. She stopped and looked at Matt, when she came to the steaks and bottle of wine. Speaking to Matt, she said, "You expect me to cook this for you?"

Matt smiled then and responded, "They are for you to do with as you wish. I would like to take you out to dine."

She didn't say anything for a minute. "I'm not one of those good time girls that you G.I.'s look for when you come to Auckland," she finally said.

"I never thought you were," Matt responded, and then he added, "I'm not a G.I., I'm a naval officer and the skipper on a PT boat."

She sat there for a long moment, and then asked him, "What is a PT boat?"

He didn't realize it, but for the next forty-five minutes he talked about PT boats, and occasionally answered her questions. When he finished talking, two thoughts hit him. One was the big poster at Melville - *'Loose lips sink ships'*. He'd just had diarrhea of the mouth. The second thought was *Sheree Scott is a beautiful woman*. Her blond hair was pulled back in braids, and she had sparkling green eyes and a quick smile. He was instantly in love...or lust.

Finally, she said, "There's a drug store down the street to the left. Go get a bandage for my ankle and we'll see about going out."

It occurred to Matt that once he was out, she'd lock the door. However, she gave him a key and said, "I'm going to get a bath while you are gone."

Matt started to volunteer to stay and wash her back but he didn't think that she'd understand his humor. He walked down the street, realizing it had been much warmer in Sheree's apartment. Did she need that for her apparent cold?

The pharmacy was at the end of the block and was very appropriately named, 'The Drug Store'. A lady clerk quickly pointed him to the right section. The clerk asked what type of injury he was going to treat. Matt told her an ankle sprain. She pointed him to what she called an elastic bandage or ACE bandage. The term ACE came from it being an All Cotton Elastic bandage. Matt was impressed.

He paid the lady and as he walked out the door, she warned him, "Don't wrap it too tight. You'll cut off the circulation of the blood." He thanked her and left.

When Matt got back to the apartment, Sheree had a foot propped on the toilet drying it off. She had nothing on. She looked up and closed the door.

He suddenly felt short of breath.

CHAPTER TWENTY FIVE

EFORE MATT KNEW IT, IT was Sunday and time to meet at their hotel for the trip back to the war. Saying goodbye to Sheree was the hardest thing he'd ever done. He gave her his address and asked her to write.

She only said, "We'll see."

Sheree and Matt had previously stopped by his hotel to leave a note saying that he was alright and staying with a friend. When he came downstairs, Sheree was coughing but said it was nothing. The Thursday night dinner had been unbelievable. They didn't realize it, but looking around the restaurant, they saw that they were the last customers. Matt tipped the waiter well, who then asked them to wait a minute. He went into the restaurant and came back then with the bottle of wine that they'd opened but hadn't finished.

"Take this home," the waiter said with a wink.

Matt took Sheree home and they had one more glass of wine. When he made ready to go, she touched his arm and said, "Stay here with me tonight."

Matt went to bed in the second bedroom. An hour or so later, she came in wearing a gauzy peach colored nightgown. As she slid beneath the covers, she whispered, "Hold me, Matt, just hold me tonight."

Matt woke up as Sheree was climbing back into bed. As he looked at her, she said, "Go relieve yourself and come back to bed."

He went and did as he was told. When he got back in the bed, he caught a brief whiff of alcohol. Was it to relax her or for her cough? If it was for her cough, it was working well.

When Matt got back in bed, Sheree became a tigress. She proved to be everything a man could ask for and then some. She was all woman...a lover. The next day and a half, she took Matt to new heights, highs like he'd never experienced. There was no doubt that he was hopelessly in love with this beautiful creature.

Matt told her of his feelings, but she just smiled and put her finger to his lips to hush him. "We are living in a very magical time," she whispered. "When the war is over, and we are both alive, then it will be the time to speak of love and such things.

He knew that she was right, especially doing what he did in the war. Matt nodded and took out his money, giving her most of it. "This is to help with the food that I ate," he said. She nodded her head in assent.

He took her and crushed her to his chest as he kissed her long and hard. He had written his name and address down for her, and laid it on the table before he left. He made it back to the hotel a half hour before the bus got there.

Roy smiled when Matt walked into their room. "I was wondering if I needed to send out the shore patrol to find you," he said.

Matt smiled and replied, "Present and accounted for, Roy...I mean Commander."

Roy just smiled and said, "I sent word to the chief to check everyone for alcohol." Matt looked at Roy to see if he was serious. Roy continued, "They don't mind the candy and cookies the Red Cross gives out by the bucketful, but no alcohol. You'll have to sign a sheet attesting to the fact that you inspected their baggage."

Matt nodded but he doubted that there'd be more than one, possibly two bags that didn't have any whiskey in it. He even preferred they have it, rather than them drinking 'torp juice'.

When the bus came and they went to pick up the crew, Matt said to Chief Ross, "I hope if they have anything liquid, it's wrapped well to prevent breakage."

"Aye," Ross replied. "I personally checked every bag, Skipper."

The men stacked their bags on the back of the bus, and then they came around and got into the seats.

"You will never see a more tired looking bunch. I don't believe they could have stood another day, Chief," Matt said.

"You're right, Skipper," the chief responded. "They took full advantage of their time."

As the men passed by, Gill, who liked to cook, paused and said, "I got a great recipe for doughnuts, Skipper. I'll get the stuff together and make them on our next patrol."

"That's wonderful, David. I'm sure the crew will love them," Matt replied.

Gill smiled and as the guys went by the chief said, "The boy teamed up with a baker's daughter. I'm hoping that he didn't leave anything in her oven."

Matt laughed, but in truth, he hoped none of them, including himself, had left anything behind or, more importantly, were taking anything with them that they didn't want.

***

THE DAY THEY GOT BACK, Lieutenant Commander Singleton came to Matt and said, "Let Robbie handle the boat as much as you are comfortable with, Matt. We are going to send some guys back to the states to go through Melville. I put Robbie's name in as a skipper candidate."

"That's good, but what about Paul," Matt said.

"Robbie is actually senior by a few months. He'll actually be lieutenant (j.g.) before he finishes school. The way things are going, I'm hoping we'll have things in hand in another year," Lieutenant Commander Singleton said.

The next afternoon they cranked 174 up and took her out in the harbor to make sure everything was as it should be before their next patrol. What Ross would say is, 'just making sure she was ship shape'.

After Matt was certain that all was normal, he called Robbie over and said, "Take the helm." He then pointed out a partially submerged tanker. "That's a destroyer and you are going to torpedo it. Bring her around and make your run. Tell me why you are doing what you are, as we go."

"Aye, Skipper. Do we have two or four fish?"

Damn, Matt thought, *it was a great question.* The number of fish would make a big difference. "You have four."

"Aye, Skipper," Robbie replied.

"Chief, inform the men that we are having a drill and in the drill we have four fish," Matt said.

"Aye, aye Skipper," Ross replied, with a bit of a smile. He went even a bit further and said, "In this drill both the Commanding officer & XO are dead."

Robbie made his turn and started his run, making about twenty five to twenty eight knots. He had his gunners ready to return fire and had his torpedomen ready at the forward tubes.

"Why only twenty-five knots?" Matt asked Robbie.

"To keep from making any more of a wake than we have to, also, any faster and we'd outrun our torpedoes. You don't want to turn in front of your own torpedo," Robbie replied.

Robbie fired his first two fish. The chief said one went astray and one was a dud. This was something that had happened to them in reality. Robbie brought them around and started his second run, letting his fish go at around five hundred yards.

"Both hits," Chief Ross declared. Torpedo run exercise was over but drills weren't.

Matt walked over to L.Z. Gray and said, "Sing out that you hear a plane."

L.Z. did just that. They were already at a slow speed, and when L.Z. reported the aircraft, Robbie cut his engines and they drifted along, with no wake. It would have been hard for a plane to see them.

Matt finally said, "Take us in." Robbie did as ordered and they touched sand as gently and perfectly as could be done.

"Okay, Robbie, while the men secure the boat, I want you to explain to me the perfect torpedo attack," Matt said.

Robbie smiled, "I've read it, Skipper." He cleared his throat and leaning against the cockpit, one hand on the wheel, he smiled again and recited, "The perfect PT attack has the PT running slowly with silent engines by using the unique flapper exhaust system, moving quietly into position, firing torpedoes and then moving slowly and quietly away without detection."

Matt smiled, "I noticed your emphasis on unique." They both laughed at that.

"I know Captain Bulkley knows what he's talking about, Matt. But this isn't my first rodeo. More than half the time we've made a run, we're being shot at."

Matt nodded and said, "That's the times when you have to decide what the best action to take is. When you've been spotted and all hell is breaking loose, I'd not worry about a wake. They already know you're there. One rule holds fast. Don't turn until your torpedoes are away."

"Aye, Skipper."

***

THE 174 WENT BARGE HUNTING two nights later. They picked up the same Army guys minus the journalist at the assigned coordinates. Sergeant Belk smiled, when we asked about Walker.

"He got shot taking a dump," the sergeant said.

They all laughed and someone asked, "Did it kill him?"

"Naw, but when he farts, his butt cheeks whistle," the sergeant responded. The Army guys all laughed again.

"Lieutenant," Sergeant Belk said, becoming serious. "We cut a new trail making our way to meet you. It would surprise me if the Japanese haven't set up a new ambush area. I'd bet that we find a barge or plane waiting for us when we reach that area...maybe both."

"Maybe we can handle the barge before a plane arrives," Paul volunteered.

They backed off the coast a bit, but didn't leave sight of it. Sinking barges was the main objective for now, so if one was lurking about, they'd try to sink it and do it quickly. Hopefully, they could sink the barge before any planes showed up. And it would just be a single plane, hopefully.

One of the boats had recently come out on the losing end of two Japanese zeros. They dodged one's strafing, but the second plane got them. It killed both officers and four of the enlisted, including the chief of the boat. Two of the engines were knocked out. The boat was brought in by a second class gunner's mate at the helm and a good motor machinist that kept the one engine going. Fortunately, they shot down both planes. Losing so many shipmates at one time definitely had an effect on the rest of the boat's crew. The reality of how fragile life was hit home hard, but so did the desire for revenge.

Matt relayed to the crew what Sergeant Belk had said. "They'll expect us to come in from the north, but we'll go out of sight of land and circle around and come in from the south."

Sergeant Belk's BAR man went up and laid down on the bow, situating his gun on a sandbag. *I don't think that I've heard the man do more than grunt his responses since we first met him*, Matt thought. *If ever a man had the look of a killer, he does.* Matt was glad that he was on their side.

Calling Robbie to the helm, Matt said, "She's your baby. Just remember, this is one time that speed is our friend and wake be damned."

Robbie gave a big grin and said, "Gotcha, Skipper."

When Matt turned towards the stern, he saw one of Belk's soldiers with a long tube-like weapon. "What is that?" he asked.

"Give me that, Jonesy," Belk barked. "It's a stove pipe," he said in reply to Matt's question. "Otherwise, it's called a Bazooka. The Army nomenclature would be something like 'Antitank Rocket Launcher'. If it works on a tank, it ought to work on a barge." Belk then went through, with Jonesy's help, the operation of a bazooka.

When he was finished, Belk gave a sigh. "The problem is, we found this under a dead guy. He had a knapsack on his back, but there were only three rockets in it. When the rockets are gone, the damn thing is useless weight." Matt nodded his understanding.

Belk took the stub of a cigar from his pocket. He spit over the side and stuck the nub back in his mouth. "We'll try to come up with some more rockets."

The way he said it, Matt knew he meant by hook or crook. While it was not something that the Navy would normally stock, Matt said that he'd put his guys on it as well. Belk's response was a big grin.

CHAPTER TWENTY SIX

THEY HUGGED THE COAST AFTER circling around. It was only a couple of miles until they reached the spot where the scouts suspected a barge would be lying in wait. Nobody on the boat doubted that the Japanese had other guns set up for an ambush. The men had been given fried spam sandwiches and bug juice. Now they were at the battle stations locked and loaded.

The night was a little on the cool side. A brief shower was just enough to soak their uniforms. With the wind blowing, the men had to be cold. Matt would have liked to have been able to pass around coffee or hot chocolate, but time didn't permit it.

The sky was now clear and a quarter moon could be seen in the eastern sky. Robbie had the boat cruising at twenty to twenty five knots. The men's chatter had gone silent as they could feel the tension as they neared the target.

On the bow, the BAR man held up his hand. Belk leaned over and whispered, "Can you stop the engines?" They did, but the boat floated on, and the silence was eerie.

L.Z. hissed, "Skipper." Matt walked over to him. "I hear the Japanese talking. It sounds like someone is pissed."

The boat drifted a bit further and the Japanese voices grew louder. Then, the PT boat was on them. The barge gate had been dropped down too soon, or had malfunctioned and was tangled in trees and vegetation.

The BAR man must have seen something that everyone else didn't as he opened up his gun, not on the barge but into the trees behind the barge. Everyone heard the gun as it went off. The Japanese fired a field piece in response. It was high but was lucky enough to hit the radar dome. The PT boat crew began pouring fire into the barge and trees.

David Gill, who was acting as a loader for L.Z. cried out, "L.Z. is hit, Skipper."

Matt took over the fifty caliber gun. Thankfully, Robbie had shoved the throttle forward and gotten the boat out of small arms range. The field gun fired again but no one saw where the shot fell. Robbie brought the boat around and everyone cut loose with their weapons again.

Belk had knelt down in front of the cockpit with his bazooka. As the boat closed, he fired a round at the barge. It must have done some damage, as the firing from the barge stopped. The Japanese fired the field piece again, and Matt was sure that he felt the heat and heard the whistle of the shot as it went over his head.

Belk, aiming at the muzzle flash, fired the bazooka again. The PT crew weren't sure if he hit the field piece, or the ammunition for the field piece, but there was a chain reaction of explosions, one after the other. Everyone kept firing until the boat got out of range again.

"Are we going to make another pass, Skipper?" asked Morales.

"No!" Matt responded.

"Damn, I didn't get a picture," Morales said.

"I think that barge is done for anyway," Belk said. "We'll get a closer look after you put us off."

Matt nodded and said, "Just be careful."

Belk replied, "I think the bazooka did alright."

"Get a picture if you can," Morales called out.

Matt could see his hands shook a little bit. After battle jitters, something they all got at one time or another. As they continued on their patrol, Matt looked at L.Z. He had blood all down one side of his face and in his ear.

"Go get the first aid kit and some water," Matt told Gill.

Using the water to rinse the blood away from L.Z.'s wound, Matt was thankful to see it was a graze and not a penetrating wound. It would have to be stitched up once they were back at the base. Flushing the wound with the cold water caused L.Z. to come around.

"Is it bad, Skipper?" L.Z. asked.

"You'll need some stitches," Matt told hm.

L.Z. nodded and made to get up. Matt said to him, "Easy now, one step at a time." They sat him up and, after a bit, he stood up.

Pappy made everybody laugh when he said, "L.Z., I guess this means that I don't get your doughnuts." L.Z.'s response was not nice.

Matt then had Robbie take the boat to the extreme point of the patrol area, without seeing any more barges.

"We'll head back, I think," Matt said. He called Gill over and said, "Think you can get the doughnuts started? I'd like to give a few to the Army guys."

"Sure thing, Skipper. This recipe is for eighty doughnuts. We'll have more than enough to share."

Robbie brought the boat about and headed back to the rendez-vous point where they picked up the Army guys. Gill finished the first batch of doughnuts just a few minutes before the meet up. Matt's first thought was, *they don't look like any doughnut I ever saw.*

Gill was smiling as he passed the tray around and said, "They aren't pretty but they are sure tasty." The Army guys agreed as they inhaled three each in a minute or less. "Take one more," Gill said and then he went back down to the galley.

The Army guys gave their thanks. Chief Ross was passing out doughnuts but paused as Robbie slowly and cautiously eased the boat into shore and let the Army guys off. On the way home, Gill brought up more doughnuts and somebody brought coffee around.

Paul handed Matt a cup of coffee and spoke loud enough for the crew to hear, "I thought for a minute that we were about to have a revolt when Gill told the Army guys to take one more doughnut."

Everybody laughed and ate their doughnuts. Gill had done a good job with his first batch. Matt claimed three of them himself. After a time, Gill got better at making them, but stopped trying to make round doughnuts. Instead, he called them doughnut sticks.

***

AT THE BASE, L.Z. GOT stitched up and never missed a patrol. Matt made it to breakfast the next morning and sat by Lieutenant Commander Singleton. Matt told him that Robbie had it all down and going through Melville was a waste.

Singleton replied, "He has to go so that he can get his boat. We got a message that he's been promoted. I thought that you'd like to tell him."

Matt replied, without thinking, "Thanks, Roy."

At officer's call, there was a lot of conversation about the Army bazooka. Nobody could agree if it was better, overall, than the Bofors 40 mm gun that they had or not. Lieutenant Commander

Roy Singleton put the discussion to end by saying it was highly unlikely the Army had any to spare. After the general meeting, Matt was called in to discuss the readiness of the 174.

"She's ready to fight now," Matt said. "We have several holes forward that need to be patched and, of course, we need a new radar dome."

He was dismissed with the understanding that they'd see what could be done with the radar dome. As he walked over to the 174's tents, somebody was playing music. He immediately recognized the song. *That Silver Haired Daddy of Mine*," by Gene Autry. When they had left the states, Gene had Billboard's number one song for country.

Pappy saw Matt and called out, "I got a record in the mail today, Skipper. It got here without breaking." Matt nodded. The sound of the record playing stated the obvious.

Preacher walked over, "I put your mail on your cot, Skipper." Matt thanked him and asked if Robbie or the chief were about. "I'll go round them up," Preacher volunteered.

Matt went into the tent. He had a letter from his mom and dad, and one from his sister, but nothing from Sheree. He was a bit down, wondering why she hadn't written. He was worried about the worst possible scenario, but had heard nothing of New Zealand being attacked recently. His thoughts were interrupted when Robbie, Paul, and the chief walked in.

"You wanted us, Skipper?"

"Yes, Chief, have the troops gather outside," Matt replied.

"Yes, sir."

Matt took a Navy message that he'd tucked under his pillow out and, speaking to Robbie and Paul, he said, "Come on, guys."

They both looked at him but didn't ask any questions. Outside, the crew was all bunched up. Matt said, "I have here in my hand a copy of the Navy's promotion list for Lieutenant (j.g). It seems that our very own Ensign Robbie Turner has been promoted to Lieutenant (j.g)."

Everyone clapped and cheered. Matt quieted the crew down. "It seems that we are losing him next week as he's headed to the states to get his own boat."

As Matt said that, he looked at Paul. *Why had they not taken him?* As XO, he had the experience and was definitely qualified. This was something that Matt wanted to talk to Lieutenant Commander Singleton about again. He then thought of Frank's XO, Ted. He had been with Frank since the beginning, like Paul had been with Matt. *Why haven't Paul or Ted been sent back?* It was nothing against Robbie, but Paul and Ted were just as due…at least, in his mind.

The next morning, Robbie and Matt were called to Headquarters. This would be their parting, Matt knew. He was going to miss Robbie. He'd become a good friend. At Headquarters, Matt was given orders to take the 174 boat to Tulagi for repairs. It was a two hundred mile trip.

The clerk spoke up, "It is one hundred ninety-seven miles." *Smart ass,* Matt thought.

"Take a couple of extra drums of gas," the commanding officer said. "It's better to be on the safe side."

The Russell Islands were a little over halfway. It they got into any trouble, they could maybe pull into Pavuvu Island. During the push to take Guadalcanal, an airbase had been built there. Lieutenant Commander Singleton wasn't sure if it was still used or not.

The 174's orders had them leaving the next morning. Matt could see Robbie as he got up to leave. They had already said their good-byes so Matt threw up his hand. Robbie smiled, stood and saluted him. Matt felt a lump in his throat so he quickly left, not wanting anyone to see him getting emotional.

Matt called the guys together when he got back to their area. "We are headed back to Tulagi to get the boat repaired." He thought that he'd hear complaints about traveling in the daytime and being a target for the Japanese planes, but that was never mentioned. They all seemed excited to get back and see their old base.

PART IV

CHAPTER TWENTY SEVEN

HE 174 BOAT MADE THE trip without any incidences. There weren't any Japanese ships or planes. Luck and the Almighty was with them. Tulagi had definitely changed since they were there...a lot. The base facilities had been expanded and spread out all over our area. A tender was at the anchorage with two PT boats tied up to it.

The repair facilities had also been enlarged, providing more shops to perform various repairs. It looked as if they could handle major overhauls on the PT boats. Large storage areas could be seen, as could gun emplacements to defend against air raids. Though, as the war had moved on, Matt doubted that air raids were as much of a problem as when they were stationed there.

The clerk back at headquarters had said the service unit here on Tulagi could support forty PT boats and keep them in combat operational readiness. The max that they'd had was twelve and rarely were they all operational. But looking about now, Matt could believe the forty number. The Seabees had built three wharves for the PT boats.

At Macambo, a small island located in Tulagi harbor, was a place for torpedo overhaul and base housing. The housing was much different than their old hut and tent. The last thing they noticed was the tank farm. It looked like they had eight one-thousand barrel tanks set up. They also had a hospital of sorts at Blue Beach.

Paul bumped Matt's shoulder. "Look at that, Matt."

It was a derrick, built right down at the waterfront. By the end of the day, they found that RON 3 was still stationed there at Tulagi, but so were, RON 1 and 2, and 8. There were four squadrons in all.

They tied up and Matt went up to Headquarters to get directions. He didn't see anyone he knew, and it was a bit disappointing. He was told where to take the 174, where officer billets were, and if he'd send someone back in half an hour, they'd have billets for the crew. The base had grown so the officers and crews didn't camp together anymore.

Matt saw a familiar face, as he was leaving. It was one that he definitely recognized. "Padgett, Padgett, is that you?"

Padgett turned around and said, "Matt Blue, by all that's holy."

"I see that you are a lieutenant (j.g.) now," Matt said.

Padgett smiled and responded, "They don't keep us ensigns forever, you know."

They talked as they walked down to the boat. Padgett said hello to the crew, and then they cranked up the boat and started to motor over to the repair facility.

"Do me a favor, Matt. Let me take her over," Padgett asked.

Matt thought, *why not, I'm right here.* He had no need for concern as Padgett handled the 174 like a pro. Matt remembered then that Padgett came from a well-to-do New England family and had handled boats all his life.

We pulled up to the wharf and Padgett took my forms. He walked Paul and Matt up to the repair office.

"This is a personal friend of mine," Padgett said to the supervisor. "He was with the first RON 3."

The guy was friendly and said, "I hear that you used to beach the boats at night, plug the holes using flashlights for light and patching them with glue and plywood."

"We did whatever it took," Matt answered matter-of-factly.

Padgett added, "He was skipper of the 48."

"So you sunk a destroyer and put fish into a cruiser." He reached out and shook Matt's hand again.

"Do you have a truck that we can have the loan of?" Padgett asked.

"Sure thing, and I'll get you a driver, also."

The truck came down to the water and they loaded their gear on it. They were given rooms in a fifty man camp setup.

"You'll all be together here, Matt, which I think you'll like," Padgett said. Matt did like the idea of them all together in one place. "By the way, they're making this a base for seaplanes," Padgett said.

"Damn, that's impressive," Matt replied.

"If you need anything, I'll be at Headquarters," Padgett volunteered. As he was leaving, he stopped and turned around. "I meant to tell you, Matt. I've got orders to Melville."

"That's great, you'll do well, I'm sure," Matt responded.

"I know that you are tired right now, but let's get together tomorrow evening," Padgett said, walking off.

"Sure thing," Matt answered.

Paul smiled as Padgett left, "I'm glad that you let him handle the boat, Skipper. We still owed him one, for us playing taxi to those nurses that time."

Two days later, Padgett came looking for Matt. He found him writing a letter to home and one to Sheree. The last one that he'd write, he decided. He'd written one a week in the many weeks since his return from R&R. She had not responded to any of them. Matt had heard it said that a number of women in Auckland were married and their husbands deployed. Frank and Matt had discussed the possibility that this was the case with Sheree. That possibility was heavy on Matt's mind when he decided to write one more letter. If there was no answer, he'd do his best to put it down as one more wartime experience.

Looking up when Padgett came in, Matt smiled at his friend. "Present and accounted for, sir. Quick question, Matt," he said. "Did your TDY orders have a return date?"

"I don't think so, why?" Matt asked.

"How would you like the 174 to have a new paint job?" Padgett inquired.

Paul, who was sitting on his rack, answered at the same time Matt did, "I'd...we'd love it."

Padgett smiled, "The story will be that they patched and painted the 174 waiting on the dome."

"It sounds good to me, "Matt replied.

When Padgett left, Paul said, "Let's not tell the crew."

Matt smiled, "I bet you five to one, that they already know about it," Matt responded.

"Wait one," Paul said. Seeing QM2 Hall, Paul called him over. "Have you heard anything on how the repairs on the 174 are progressing?"

Hall stood and looked at the XO a minute. "You haven't heard? I thought that Padgett would have told you, 'Old Hickory' is getting a new paint job."

Paul nodded and turned to go back inside. He went over to his bunk and took out a five dollar bill and handed it to Matt. "I should have known by now to never doubt you, Skipper."

***

Matt, Paul, and Padgett went over to the small 'O' Club, that evening. They'd sat down and ordered when a group at a couple of tables over broke out in laughter. Matt turned and looked. One person though, with her back to Matt, looked very familiar.

"Excuse me a minute, fellows," Matt said, as he got up and walked over to the table.

Someone, seeing Matt approaching the table, said something to the group, so everyone turned to look at the handsome naval officer walking toward them. One of them pushed her chair back and stood up and walked to meet him.

"Matt Blue, you do turn up in the strangest places," she said.

"So do you, Karen," Matt replied. Karen introduced Matt to the people at her table.

Someone had put on some music, and Matt asked, "Care to dance?"

There wasn't a real dance floor, just a space up front between the bar and where the tables started.

"I'm here having my boat repaired," Matt volunteered, by way of an explanation. "What are you doing here?"

"Temporary duty," Karen said, and then the two fell silent as they danced.

When the song was over, Matt asked, "Want to go for a walk?"

"Sure," Karen replied.

They walked and talked for an hour. Matt looked at Karen. Standing under the palm trees, a gentle breeze was rustling the fronds and the moon was shining down on the still waters of the harbor. The moment was right, so Matt leaned in to kiss Karen. She put her arms around his neck and drew him to her.

After a long passionate kiss, Karen spoke in a low voice, "You don't know how many times I've wanted to do that."

Matt kissed her again and said, "We've always been in a crowd, but we are alone tonight."

"Lieutenant Matt Blue, your woman is ready to devour your body," Karen responded.

"We are not far from my room," Matt said.

They walked to his room, and Karen stood back in the palms as Matt went in and took the blankets off his rack and walked out. A couple of his crew saw him. They smiled but didn't speak.

Holding hands, Matt and Karen walked to a secluded spot. They spread the blankets and got under the top one. It was a bit warm but it helped keep the mosquitoes away. As they kissed, Karen unbuttoned Matt's shirt. He was soon returning the favor. The rest of the evening was filled in a hungry, passionate night of pure bliss. When their appetites were sated, they fell into a contented slumber.

Matt woke up first and kissed Karen's forehead, her eyes, the tip of her nose and then her lips and neck. Karen's arms encircled Matt's neck.

"Come here, lover boy," she said, and drew his body to her, feeling his chest crush her breasts, and feeling his heartbeat against her skin. "I can't tell you how lucky I feel, Matt. I've wanted you since the first night we were out to sea."

Matt, not sure how to respond, kissed her again. "We've got each other now."

"How long will you be here?" Karen asked.

"Two more days at the most," Matt replied.

She pulled him close. "Let's not waste a minute of that time, Matthew Blue."

CHAPTER TWENTY EIGHT

THREE DAYS LATER, MATT SAID goodbye to Karen. She had come down to the boat to see Old Hickory off. She had actually gone on board, and they had circled around to Blue Beach to let her off on the small pier.

The crew clapped and gave a cheer when Matt embraced and kissed Karen. They cheered again when she gave them a curtsy. Matt jumped back on board and said, "Take us out, XO."

Matt thought of that first night that he'd spent with Karen, as the 174 put Tulagi behind them. He'd walked her back to her quarters, in the wee morning hours. When he got back to his quarters, he tore up the letter to Sheree. She was suddenly a distant memory.

**

ARRIVING BACK AT THE BASE, Padgett's advice came in handy. Lieutenant Commander Singleton's boss was in Headquarters when Matt reported in.

"You stayed in Tulagi long enough to get a new paint job," the commanding officer said, accusingly.

"No, sir. We stayed to get the radar dome replaced. While we waited, we were lucky enough that they could take the boat in and repair the leaks and bullet holes, and then repaint her. I thought that was time put to good use since we had to wait anyway."

"I agree with you, Matt," Singleton chimed in.

"We finished our business and left," Matt said. Thankfully, the subject was never brought up again.

The next night, the 174 was given two assignments. One was to land ammunition and supplies for the army on one island, and then drop off a group of Alamo scouts, now called "snake eaters" by some, to another island. As the supplies were loaded on the stern of the boat, Matt looked at the stenciled labels. If PT boats were hauling in the small amount of supplies that the boat could carry, the army must be hurting.

"Why don't they airdrop this stuff?" Paul asked, while he and Matt were having lunch with Frank and Ted.

"The Japanese would see it," Ted said. "They'd setup an ambush if they could."

Thinking of Sergeant Belk and his guys, it made Matt shiver to think of the Japanese waiting for them in ambush.

"We'll be coming in from the north, barge hunting," Frank said.

"Yeah, don't shoot us," Ted added.

They all laughed but in truth, none of them thought it was funny. A number of lives had been lost to 'friendly fire.'

They watched the 172 boat head out of the harbor. For a moment, Matt wished that they were going with them. He and Frank had been together so long a trust had developed. It was a trust that didn't exist with everyone. The 172 boat was followed out by the 167, and the 171.

The supplies were loaded wherever they had room on the 174 boat. The Alamo scouts arrived. This was a different group but they had the same no nonsense look. The boat crew got the scouts situated, some sitting on crates, and others on the deck. They headed out with Paul at the helm.

Matt went aft to recheck the ropes securing the crates. He didn't want to lose anything if they had to do some sudden maneuvering.

"We already checked the supplies, Skipper." This was from Morales.

"Aye, we both did," Byhre chimed in.

"Good, then I don't have anything to worry about," Matt said.

"That's a fact," the two men replied in unison.

Matt had no reason to doubt them.

***

THE CREW OF THE 174 had developed camaraderie with the Army scouts, especially Sergeant Belk and his BAR man, whom they'd heard addressed as Braveheart. It was probably a nickname but nobody questioned it. He may have been an Indian, with his dark skin.

The guys in this new group were a bit standoffish, but that would probably change once they got to know each other. They made their rendezvous without being spotted by any Japanese planes, ships or barges.

Matt looked at his navy issue wristwatch. They were twenty minutes early for the scheduled arrival time. Of course, everyone knew the schedule was more a goal and far from an absolute. Matt motioned for Paul to lean in so he wouldn't have to shout.

"Cut your throttle back and let's idle about for a while," Matt said.

Paul gave Matt a thumbs up. Matt passed the word for the crew to keep a sharp lookout, even though it was unnecessary. No one replied or commented. They knew this routine as well as he did. Some would say that it was a game, but it wasn't anything like a game when the Japanese were doing their best to kill you. It was a time when 'silence was golden' and they all knew it.

The scouts' sergeant whispered to Matt, "I can't see jack." It was the first time any of the Alamo scouts had spoken since they left Lumbaria.

Time seemed to drag in the jet black ocean and tensions were high. Nobody would ever believe how eerie it was sitting in the middle of the ocean, in a small boat, waiting for something to appear and maybe snuff your life out in seconds. The ocean, at least, was fairly calm so the boat didn't bounce around too much. A small wave would occasionally lap against the hull.

"Plane, Skipper," L.Z. Gray said in a hushed voice.

It was probably ten seconds before Matt heard the drone of low flying aircraft. Every man on board, with the possible exception of the Alamo scouts, knew with the boat sitting still and leaving no wake, she'd be hard to spot. It didn't relieve any of the tension, however, when the sound of the plane was heard. It grew louder until it was directly overhead. They sat motionless until it passed and they could no longer hear the plane.

A few minutes later, Gill spoke, "There's the signal, Skipper, one red flash."

They would not return any signal, which could be seen and possibly alert any enemy in the area. They backed up to the little spit of beach, ready to flee, if necessary.

The Alamo scouts, without being asked, walked to the back and unloaded the crates to Sergeant Belk's men, who had been waiting on their arrival. This allowed Matt's crew to remain at their guns.

When Belk walked up, Matt took a handful of Tampa Jewel cigars out of his coat pocket, and handed them to him. A big smile crossed Belk's face and he gave an exaggerated salute. Putting the cigars in his shirt pocket, he took the last crate and waved goodbye as he disappeared into the night. A couple of the Belk's guys threw up their hands waving goodbye to Matt and the crew.

Back at the cockpit, Paul said, "Less than ten minutes, Skipper."

"Good," Matt said. Having the Alamo scouts unload had saved some time. He then spoke to Chief Ross, "You have our chart ready for Vella Lavella?"

"QM2 Hall does, Skipper," Ross said. Matt nodded his head.

Chief Ross had been delegating more of the routine tasks to David Hall. He needed the experience should the time come when he was the only quartermaster on board the 174 boat.

"Coffee?" BM2 Steffey asked.

"Sure," both Paul and Matt said.

Steffey and Gill went around giving everyone warm, black, and strong cups of the Navy's special coffee. Matt wondered if, after the war, would the thousands of men who had gotten used to the military coffee ever be satisfied with Maxwell House, A&P, or Folgers. His family had long been an A&P family. His mother bought beans that were ground right there in the store. One of the men at Melville said that he used coffee beans like snuff to keep him awake when on watch at night. Matt hadn't tried that yet.

❖❖❖

THE SOUNDS OF AUTOMATIC WEAPONS fire, and the boom of larger guns or bombs being dropped from planes was heard before they got in sight of Vella Lavella. *Our boats had not only found barges, but enemy planes as well*, Matt thought. The initial thought was to rush in and help, but they had to drop off the scouts first.

The sergeant, with the group, came up to the cockpit. "It looks like the battle is on the west side of the island. That should draw everyone's attention away from us on the east side."

Radioman Brown popped his head up, "There's all kind of radio chatter, Skipper. I believe that our boys are catching hell."

Matt wanted to send a signal saying, 'hold on, help is coming;' but he knew that radio silence on their part was imperative. They eased into their drop-off area and let the scouts off.

"Let's circle the island and come in from the north side," Matt said to Paul and Ross. He then added, "Spread the word, Chief."

"You've had the helm long enough, XO. Let me spell you for a while," Matt offered.

"Thank you, Skipper," Paul replied.

I should have relieved him earlier, Matt thought, *or let Chief Ross have a turn. It's something to think about later.* When they came around the island, Matt had Tony Brown send out a simple message.

"Old Hickory now on the scene," was the message.

They got a reply, "Welcome to the party."

Matt remembered Frank mentioning a report of eight Japanese barges. Well, they had the eight Japanese barges they'd expected, but the planes they hadn't planned on. A flare was dropped over the 171 boat, lighting it up like daylight.

"Open fire!" Matt yelled to the gunners.

The plane had its attention on the 171 boat, so Matt was sure that when his gunners punched .50 cal and 20 mm holes throughout the plane, it surprised the hell out of the pilot, if he wasn't already dead.

BM2 Steffey, Pappy, Gill, and MM2 Phagans were manning the 40 mm Bofors gun. This was their first actual battle against aircraft with the gun.

They had given the first Japanese plane hell, but they now had a second plane coming in to avenge the loss of his brother.

The 171 boat had come about and was adding its fire to that from the 174 boat. Fire flamed from the second Japanese plane's engine and it went down in the sea. With the two planes down, it didn't take long to handle the barges.

Brown came up, as they pulled away from the barges, and said, "The 171 boat is in a bad way. Two of the officers badly wounded and they are taking on water. They also have one dead gunner."

"XO, lay us alongside of the 171 boat and I'll go over," Matt said.

Paul leaned close and said, "That should be my job, Skipper." He was right so Matt just nodded.

Paul made a quick damage control assessment and then reported back. "Once she's planed out, the pumps should handle the water. The other officer is a new ensign so I should take her back." Matt agreed with him.

They brought the 171's wounded commanding officer and XO on board in case more damage was found and the boat had to be abandoned. The 171's commander had a nasty wound through his calf while the XO was wounded in the upper arm and shoulder. They dressed the wounds as they headed back to the base, letting Paul, in the 171 boat, lead the way.

As they neared the anchorage, Matt had Brown radio in for a couple of ambulances. The 171's boat chief would have to worry about the boat repairs.

CHAPTER TWENTY NINE

THE NEXT MORNING AT OFFICER'S call, they were told that the 171 would be out of action for awhile. Paul had already told Matt that by the time they'd made it in last night the water was up to the base of the motors. Matt had noticed that Paul had damn near beached the boat. A good thing or it probably would have sunk.

After officer's call, Lieutenant Commander Singleton, Frank, and Matt walked down to look at the 171. They had auxiliary pumps going and most of the water was out. The bullet holes were much more obvious now. The commanding officer and XO had been taken to Tulagi. Matt wished that he was going with them.

Matt joked with Roy Singleton, "Had I known that they were going there, I'd have found a way to get wounded." Roy smiled at that and laughed, he'd heard about Matt's nurse there.

After they looked over the 171 boat, Matt went back to their tent and Lieutenant Commander Singleton went to Headquarters. Before Matt got to their tent, he could hear Pappy playing his records. Thank goodness he'd gotten another record from some place, as they were all tired of Gene Autry. Matt recognized the song right away, 'I'm Walking the Floor Over You,' which was sung by Ernest Tubb. To Matt, he sounded like he was singing through his nose. However, the song had been a big hit and old Ernest had been very popular when the war started.

Frank called to Matt, as he walked over. "You saved the 171's bacon last night," he said, adding, "I'm glad that you came to help."

In truth, Matt had been told to drop off the scouts and return to base, which Frank knew. The brass just didn't specify which route to take.

"Did you think that I wouldn't?" Matt asked.

"Hell no, I was just hoping that it wouldn't be too late," Frank said.

It was Saturday and they had planned a boxing match that afternoon. Matt yawned and decided if he was going to the match, he'd have to get some sleep.

As he walked into the tent, Paul said, "You got a letter. A pilot who made the run to Tulagi dropped it off."

Matt tore open the envelope, since he knew who it was from. Karen's words filled his heart with joy. The letter was short, only a page and a quarter. He imagined that she had to write fast to get it in the pilot's hands before he took off. Matt read the letter twice, put it under his pillow and fell into a peaceful sleep.

Matt woke up with Frank shaking him. "Are you going to the match?" Matt put on his pants and boots, and carried a T-shirt.

The match was scheduled for ten rounds, but by the eighth round, both men were whipped. Neither man could toe the mark, and the referee called it a draw.

A guy put out the word during chow that they had planned to show a movie that evening. It was the same one they had shown twice, that Matt knew of. It was Gary Cooper's 1931, 'Fighting Caravans.' It was from a Zane Grey book. He decided to forgo the movie and catch up on his writing. Once he did that, he'd try to read one of the books that L.Z. had given him. It was the one by C.S. Forester about the Hornblower character in 'Beat to Quarters.' The book, 'The Gun' by Forester had been pretty good, so he'd try another one by the same author.

The next morning, breakfast was great. They had real eggs. Where they got the eggs from, nobody knew. Matt had two fried eggs. The meat was Spam. But even that didn't take away from the eggs. Matt ate his on bread: an egg sandwich with salt and pepper. He drank a glass of orange juice that, after putting some sugar in it, wasn't too bad. Frank and Ted came in as he was finishing his breakfast. He decided to stay back and have a cup of coffee with his friends.

Schedules had them separated a lot lately and Matt missed hanging out and patrolling with Frank and Ted. When you knew and trusted someone, it made patrolling a little bit easier. They all went for a walk, after finishing up at the mess tent, to let their breakfast settle. They walked by Headquarters, which Frank always called 'HQ'. They looked at the duty board but there weren't any patrols listed for that night.

"Dang, two nights without patrol," Ted said, looking at the list. "That worries me," Ted added. "It makes me think that the Japanese have something up their sleeve."

Paul walked up as Ted spoke. "I figure they always have something going on," he said. "I just try to survive it."

Paul handed Matt a note then. It said that they were getting another officer to replace Robbie, an Ensign David Christopher. He would report to them that afternoon. A visiting Chaplin had arrived that morning. A memo went out to all the boats and units.

"That's why there are no patrols tonight," Paul volunteered.

A service was held at 11:00 a.m. under the palms. It was a good service with the message being based on the Book of Romans, Chapter 10, verse 9. It basically said, 'if you declare Jesus is Lord and believed in the resurrection,' you would be saved. He only spent a few minutes on the war, saying the Japanese were Godless and for that reason alone, we would eventually become victorious. His statement caused some yeses and amens. Matt could picture his dad being an amen man. He'd done his best to make sure that their spiritual needs and growth had been taken care of.

As the service had been held under the palms, Matt knew the Chaplain was in good standing with the Lord. There had been a gentle, cool breeze blowing all through the sermon. When the service ended, they all realized how fragile life was and the goodness of Jesus Christ.

They walked back to their area, with Matt thinking back to the little church by the railroad tracks where he was baptized. *The Chaplin would have made a good Baptist preacher*, Matt thought.

***

LATER THAT AFTERNOON, EVERYBODY SAW a plane land in the harbor. A line of top brass got off and made their way to Headquarters.

"Damn," Ted said. "The man in front is General Douglas MacArthur. He's the man who escaped Corregidor in Bulkley's PT boat."

They'd all heard of that courageous affair at Melville. It certainly helped with public relations for the Mosquito Fleet, as they were called.

"We'll hear about this in the morning," Frank said. None of the men doubted that.

About an hour after the top brass arrived, they boarded the PBY again, taking the Chaplain with them.

Ensign David Christopher arrived that afternoon, as expected. They gave him Robbie's old bunk. After a few minutes, Paul and Matt knew that he'd fit in. They introduced David to the crew. They'd already prepared to meet the new ensign, as L.Z. quipped.

"We've prepared cocktails to celebrate your arrival," Ross said and handed David a cup. Paul and Matt were also handed cups... torpedo juice.

"To Mr. Christopher, welcome to the best PT boat around, the 174," Ross said, toasting the boat and David.

David raised his glass and seeing the men turn up their cups, he did the same. Only his was a full cup, while the others only had a shot. David's eyes watered and he coughed a couple of times, and then he chugalugged the torpedo juice. He licked his lips as he finished his cup. He held it up and asked, "Another cup."

This brought the men to their feet with cheers and applause. Ensign David Christopher had been successfully initiated and accepted by the crew.

Monday morning, they went to officer's call expecting to hear something after the brass had been there. Although, they never expected to hear what was passed on.

"Most of you know that we had top level guests this past weekend." Everyone laughed but the big man's name was never mentioned. "In our talks I told 'him' one of the issues in controlling the barge traffic was being able to see them. Therefore, in the future, when we set out on patrol, we will have one or more of the Catalinas, the Black Cats, with us."

These were planes that under the dark of night had sent tons of Japanese cargo and ships to the bottom of the sea. If they were indeed going out with with the PT boats, it would be a big help.

"Yeah, if they don't do anything but draw Japanese fire, it'll be a big help to us," Paul said. Something Matt wasn't sure about.

The barges didn't want to draw attention to themselves, anymore than the PT crews did. The commanding officer also alerted them that supply ships should be making harbor this afternoon. It had been expected yesterday, but ran into bad weather. It contained the supplies that they drastically needed for the base and PT boats.

As they were leaving the Headquarters building, the sounds of aircraft filled the air. The blast of the air raid siren quickly alerted them that it wasn't American planes. The officers all headed to their boats to get them out of the harbor. The planes would strafe them in another pass or two, they were sure.

Matt, Paul, and David got on board the boat just as their crew ran out on the beach. The engineers, Clark and Ruby, were huffing it. L.Z. banged his shin jumping on the boat. Steffey undid one line and then the other from the palm trees where they were tied. They heard gunfire from the planes as they focused on the supply ship. Clark and Ruby got one and then a second engine running. The third was proving to be contrary.

"You got the wing engines," Clark called up.

"It'll have to do," Matt said, and they took off to aid the supply ship.

Preacher was loading the 20 mm for Byhre. Steffey and Pappy were helping to get Phagans setup on the 40 mm. L.Z. and Morales reported that they were ready.

There were planes everywhere. The supply ship was at the entrance of the harbor. Her guns were firing but it was plain that they didn't have the experience or firepower that the PT boats did. One plane came in low to drop a bomb on the supply ship. He'd obviously disregarded the 174 boat. As he flew over, he flew into a barrage of fire that was so intense the plane exploded.

Tony Brown stuck his head up. "Headquarters says to defend the supply ship."

David Christopher glared at Brown, "What the hell do they think we are doing?"

Matt smiled, in spite of the gunfire all about.

Frank came on the radio, "We're the first ones out. You take the port side and we'll watch the starboard side of this grocery ship."

Paul laughed for a moment but hushed as L.Z. yelled, "Here comes another one."

This one was higher and was coming out of the sun. The gunners opened up enough to cause the Japanese pilot to pull out of his run and circle.

Clark called back, "You got all three engines, Skipper."

Thank you, Lord, Matt thought.

"One coming up our ass," Morales yelled.

The gunners focused on that plane. He dropped a bomb and then banked. Matt saw the plane drop the bomb and spun the wheel hard to starboard and pushed the throttles open. The bomb exploded where they had been, sending a big splash over the rear gunners.

The sudden move slung David Christopher to the deck. "Always hold on," Paul said.

"Lesson learned," he replied.

The planes left them then, but not before feeling the 174's lead.

"She's smoking," Morales yelled. "We hit her." He was speaking of the last plane.

The supply ship came by, with its crew waving and cheering. A harbor boat led it to its home for the next few days, at least. The captain saluted the PT boats, as they passed.

As they headed back to tie up the 174 boat, Matt said to Ross, "Get our scroungers out, most Ricky-tick." He was using the old gunny sergeant at Melville's favorite phase. "Let them know that we're the ones that saved their asses."

"Aye, Skipper," Ross replied. He went and spoke to L.Z. Gray and Pappy.

"XO, check to see when we can fuel," Matt said to Paul.

"Gotcha, Skipper," Paul replied.

CHAPTER THIRTY

T HE CREW WERE AWARE THAT they would probably, key word was probably, have some Black Cats spotting for them that night. This would eliminate their being surprised by Japanese gunfire, hopefully. The PT boats had learned to lay down a withering fire on barges until they'd destroyed or disabled them.

Lieutenant Commander Singleton came over to Matt before they left and said, "Matt, the Army has picked up evidence of some ambush spots to spring on PT boats. If we can coordinate the spots with the Army and the Black Cats, maybe we can be the one springing the trap."

Matt acknowledged the orders and went to tell Frank their orders had changed and that they wouldn't be heading out with him and the 157 boat.

Frank clapped Matt on the shoulder and said, "Well hopefully the Black Cat will do the work for you."

Matt smiled and replied, "We should have such luck."

The 174's crew rendezvoused with Sergeant Belk and his Alamo scouts. Each rendezvous had been at a different location. As he climbed on board, Belk walked over to Matt as David took them out. They shook hands and with a smile, Belk nodded towards the new ensign. "New meat, huh?"

If David heard what was said, he didn't show it. Belk pulled out a package from a pocket and handed it to Matt saying, "A little present from our journalist friend."

"Is he still roaming the jungles with you guys?" Matt asked.

Belk's reply was a blunt, "No! We are hearing that the action is moving to Vella Lavella." He then added, "We are expected to move out very soon so we may not see you guys after this trip."

"What about the Japanese in this area?" Matt asked.

"Barges have been taking them off," Belk responded. "They are probably taking 'em to Kolombangara. Some reports say there's thousands of Japanese there. That's my thoughts," he shrugged.

"I guess my question was, did the brass think that taking Vella Lavella would give them a good spring board for Kolombangara," Matt said. He remembered that they'd put out a group of scouts out on Vella Lavella and the plane attacks on their PT boats there. Other PT boats had been bombed and strafed since then. Several boats had taken a beating, not to mention those men who were wounded or killed. One boat was so beat up that it had to be towed back.

Matt couldn't help but wonder if once again the brass wasn't underestimating the resistance they'd run into. If they had, good people like the sergeant standing beside Matt, and his group, would pay the price.

Matt peeked in the envelope Hollis Walker had sent him. Pictures...he had guessed that. Calling to Gill, Matt told him to lay them on his rack.

Once they were away from shore, Matt had Radioman Brown radio the Black Cat base and confirm the coordinates. Someone was soon back on the radio confirming the coordinates for the rendezvous and a time…2130. It was 2100 now.

"Thirty minutes," Matt said to Belk.

"No problem, sir, it's not far," Belk replied.

Matt cut the engines to idle speed and bobbed along in the pitch black night. They had not bobbed about for long when L.Z. spoke, "Plane approaching, Skipper."

Matt touched his shoulder letting him know that he'd heard. They hadn't had too long to wait if that was their bird. The radio crackled down below.

Brown soon stuck his head up, "Be on the lookout for flares, Skipper."

The engines were all brought back up and were doing about twenty-five knots. They didn't have long to wait. A series of parachute flares were dropped, lighting up the area like daytime.

The Japanese had set up a field piece and several machine guns. The shoreline was lit up fairly well, but they didn't see any barges.

"See any barges, XO?" Matt shouted.

"No, sir!" he replied.

The flares were not the only thing lighting up the sky. Tracers from Japanese machine guns directed at the slow flying planes were putting on a show. Slow as the Black Cats were, they were still fast enough to get out of range before the Japanese could track them down with their machine guns.

"Let's join the ruckus," Matt said, trying to sound like one of the movie cowboys.

The Japanese had stopped firing, but the 174 knew where they were. Had the machine gunfire deafened the enemy? Did they not hear the boat as it crept in towards her target? Well, they were about to hear them.

"Let 'er rip, men," Matt said, still trying to mimic the movie cowboys.

The 174's gunners had marked the Japanese guns well. They poured a concentrated fire into those positions. The Japanese returned fire immediately. For a split second, Matt wondered if the sonar dome had been hit again as a shell passed over their heads. Seeing it there and intact, he thought *there goes a trip to Tulagi and seeing Karen again, if she's still there.*

Mail had been slow lately. You'd think that there was a war going on. Matt had taken the helm and tried to clear his thoughts. He made a turn to take them back out to sea and the beautiful darkness. The Japanese fire had been getting a bit too close.

Matt chided himself for letting his mind wander and lose focus on the enemy. Too many men depended on him to keep them alive. Thankfully, they'd not fired the field piece. Matt mentioned this to Belk, who was standing straddle-legged to keep from falling.

"May not have any ammunition," Belk growled. The good sergeant hadn't liked how close they'd come to the guns on shore. He spoke again, "Could be they're waiting on a barge to drop off a load of ammunition."

The enemy machine guns fell silent when the Japanese realized the PT boat was out of range.

As the PT boat maneuvered about, and changed positions, for the next pass, Matt asked the crew in general, "Everything alright. Anything need fixing?" He was sure that someone would speak out if need be.

L.Z. did speak, "Planes coming back, Skipper."

They all hoped it was American planes. L.Z. had gotten pretty good at distinguishing the sound of our planes from the Japanese.

But even he wasn't perfect. The 174 boat was still on the outside edge of their range but Matt told the guys to open up. Hopefully, they'd distract the enemy gunners away from the planes. It worked, but watching tracers coming your way would put a knot in anybody's gut.

Matt zigzagged and circled the 174, to throw the Japanese off. They didn't hear the Black Cats return with all the firing, so Matt was sure the Japanese didn't either. They did hear the explosions, however, as bombs dropped from the planes exploded. Orange flames lit up the black sky, replacing the flares that had gone out. Matt ordered the gunners to cease fire.

Morales took the camera from around his neck as he stepped away from his gun. He instantly started clicking away. "Pictures to confirm and proof of our action tonight," he said. Documented proof that was hard, for the brass, to discount.

The Black Cats radioed that they hadn't spotted any barges and were headed home. As the planes made for home, the wind was picking up a bit, and flashes of lightning streaked across the sky.

"It's between us and home," David volunteered.

Ross said, "Too much has gone right, so why not a storm just to keep everyone in our place."

"Mother nature," Paul said to David, who nodded.

Matt had already noted that it was between them and home. They changed course and headed to the drop off point for the scouts.

Braveheart, who with his BAR was laying on the bow as was his usual, shot his hand up suddenly in the air. "Cut your engines please, Skipper," he called in a voice just loud enough to be heard. It was the longest sentence that Matt had ever heard him speak. Generally, it was usually grunts that only Sergeant Belk understood.

Matt nodded to Paul, who cut their speed to idle. Braveheart pushed himself up off the deck and came to the cockpit.

In a low voice, he spoke, "Something is in the water. I saw it when the lightning lit up the sky."

Matt put everyone to looking over the sides. The water was black, and then came another flash of lightning. It wasn't a bolt that streaks across the sky, but a flash that starts from a long way off, and flickers, getting bright and then dying out suddenly. The water was black, yet they had no doubt that Braveheart had seen something. It might be important or nothing, just floating debris... or a submarine's conning tower. They circled back around at idle speed.

Everyone was silent. They knew the possibilities as well as Matt did. Through the tension, Matt wondered what David might be thinking. This tiny boat on a huge ocean searching for only God knew what.

L.Z., who was seated in his turret, was a bit higher up than the rest of the crew spoke up, "There it is, Skipper, just off the bow, port side."

They idled up to it and shined a red light over the side. It was a raft with three Japanese men lying on the bottom. Paddles were there with them.

Sergeant Belk spoke out in a firm voice, and then turned to Matt. "I told them to get up or be shot."

They didn't move, so the sergeant took his Thompson submachine gun, what he commonly called his 'tommy' off his shoulder. He fired off several rounds around the raft. Matt let his mind wonder, thinking *damn I'd like to have one of those.*

The firing of the Thompson stirred the Japanese. They awkwardly stood up but didn't raise their hands.

Braveheart with his BAR at the ready, spoke to Belk, "Watch them, Sarge. Make them raise their hands above their heads."

Belk asked if they spoke English. One of the Japanese men nodded, saying "I do."

"Have the men raise their hands or you'll all be shot. Braveheart, let go with a burst from the BAR for emphasis," Belk ordered.

The heavy sound of bullets alongside the raft, were only inches away and echoed in the night. This caused the Japanese to cower, or so they thought.

The English speaking Japanese man raised his hands, speaking in Japanese as he did so. He suddenly fell to the bottom of the raft and the guy behind him started firing with a pistol. The second man bumped the side of his leg and threw a grenade at the PT boat deck. It had barely landed when Belk set it flying with a swift kick. L.Z.'s .50 caliber and Braveheart's BAR turned the Japanese men into a bloody, tangled mess.

"Cease fire," Matt yelled. "Get the bodies on board before they sink."

Belk's men jumped in to help and the bodies were hauled on board just as the raft sank below the waves. A thorough search of the bodies was made. The Japanese man who did all the talking had a waterproof pack full of papers on him.

"He's an officer," Belk said, feeling how soft the dead man's hands were.

"The other two enlisted," Braveheart added.

Belk took off the Japanese's belt with the holster and pistol, handing them to Matt along with a short sword found in the raft as the bodies were taken out. "Keep these," he said, "and mail them home, but mail it one piece at a time, so that it won't get taken. Being an officer, you ought to be able to get your hands on a stamp that says 'Inspected'."

Matt looked towards the cockpit at Ross. He gave a slight nod that said I can do that. He probably meant that he did it all the time. Matt was thinking what a nice gift if would make for his dad.

Belk took the collar devices off the Japanese officer. "Show these to the brass, when you turn in those papers," the sergeant added. Matt nodded his head. "We were lucky that Braveheart spotted them," Belk continued. "I'm sure that they were dropped off by a submarine."

"Aye," Matt responded. The sergeant's comments made sense, Matt was thinking as they dropped the scouts off, how he'd like to have Braveheart as part of their crew. With Braveheart's eyes and L.Z.'s ears, nothing would get by them.

They dropped off the scouts, as had been previously arranged.

Belk whispered, as they got off the boat, "I wouldn't mention the souvenirs or show them off." Matt nodded and shook his hand.

⁕⁕⁕

BROWN RADIOED BASE AND LET them know that they were securing and heading home. It started raining immediately after starting back. Matt heard Paul say to David, "Told you so."

"At least, it will wash away some of the salt," David responded.

Morales was speaking with Ross, who was making his rounds. "I got pictures of the Japanese, if they turn out."

The rain picked up, and it seemed to be coming down in sheets, stinging their faces and skin as it pounded into them. The sea got up making a rough ride much rougher. Matt thought about sending most of the crew below. It would be just as rough, but maybe a little bit dryer.

QM2 Hall shouted out to get Matt's attention. "Radar contact dead ahead, Skipper, maybe a thousand yards."

Was it a real sighting, or was the radar just acting up due to the weather? Matt wondered, handing L.Z. his binoculars. Hopefully, he would be able to see more than rain.

L.Z. startled Matt, as he excitedly yelled, "Japanese submarine, Skipper, right off the bow."

Matt cut hard to port, missing the conning tower but felt the 174 boat scrub as they passed over the submerging submarine. Matt brought the boat around but only the periscope was above the surface and it quickly disappeared before their eyes. While they were circling around, they felt a vibration in the boat.

"Ready to drop depth charges," Matt ordered.

Pappy and Preacher ran over to the two depth charges. The sea was still bubbling where the submarine was going down.

"Let go with the two charges," Matt yelled. He didn't expect much but it was all they had. It would, at least, look better in a report, than having no action. Matt's immediate concern was the vibration. What was it from?

MOMM2 Clark came on deck. His appearance did not surprise Matt, but he dreaded to hear Clark's report. "We got propeller damage, I'm sure, Skipper," he said. "We need to slow down or we'll lose a shaft and maybe more. We may even need to cut an engine. I'll know in a few minutes," he added.

MOMM3 Ruby came on deck shortly. "More bad news," Paul said, seeing Ruby first.

"We need to cut the port wing engine," Ruby advised. "It's got a busted shaft seal and is leaking out. Clark said that it would be best if we could cut both wing engines."

Matt nodded and both of the engines were shut down. The vibrations immediately stopped, but would it last? They were able to make seven knots on one engine without feeling any vibrations. It was going to be a long night at that slow speed. Coffee was carried around to the crew by the newest man, Wheels Frongello.

When the squall finally passed and the rain had stopped, Gill and Steffey made grilled cheese sandwiches for everyone. They all ate in their soaked uniforms, but the warm coffee helped. Everyone was just glad that they were still moving. Matt thought, *running over the Japanese submarine could have left the crew a lot worse off.* They could have lost the boat like Kennedy did in the 109.

Morales moved forward, "I think I got a picture of the submarine, Skipper."

Matt knew that Morales was just trying to be helpful, but right then he didn't give a dang about a picture. Joe could sense Matt's mood and walked aft. Matt was suddenly glad that they had attended church last Sunday. Somebody up above had definitely been watching over them that night.

Paul and David were discussing the probability that the submarine had been the one to put the Japanese out in the raft. *Maybe they were just charging the batteries,* Matt thought, but he didn't comment on it. He didn't care. He suddenly had a longing for a hot bath, home, and Karen, and not necessarily in that order.

CHAPTER THIRTY ONE

A CROWD GATHERED AROUND AS THEY looked at the propellers. The crane on the supply ship had the stern on the 174 lifted up high enough that they could see the damage caused by running over the submerging submarine.

"Damn," Frank said. "Were you trying to use the props as a can opener and cut holes in the submarine?"

Lieutenant Commander Singleton and other officers from Headquarters were standing about and taking notes of the damage caused by running over the Japanese submarine.

"Thank God, she wasn't fully surfaced," Singleton volunteered. "Otherwise, her skipper would be bragging about how he had sunk one of the hated devil boats without firing a shot."

Ted, Frank's XO, spoke to the crowd in general, "I just wonder how much damage it did to the submarine's outer hull."

Matt said that he was doing twenty to twenty-five knots when he ran over the Japanese. "Those props are made of some good, hard steel. For them to look like they do, they had to have done some damage. They might not realize it now, but let the Japanese make a deep dive and see what happens. Maybe nothing...I don't know, but the pressure down that deep could cause the blasted thing to rupture. Again, I'm not into physics, so I don't know."

"We can only hope," Ted said.

"Well, we need that boat fixed, and quickly," Singleton said. He then added, "We can't do it here, so it'll have to be towed to Tulagi."

"Matt, come by Headquarters and pick up some orders after she's let back down," Singleton ordered.

"Aye, sir," Matt replied.

"Frank, is your boat ready to go?" Singleton inquired.

"Yes, sir," Frank said.

"Good, fill her up with gas and take a couple of extra drums along in case you need it," Singleton ordered.

"Will do, sir," Frank replied.

Before leaving, Matt gave the Japanese papers and collar devices that they'd taken off the Japanese to Lieutenant Commander Singleton. Taking them, Singleton looked at Matt and said, "This might be important. I'll send these up the line and let you know what I hear." He never did.

It was roughly two hundred miles to Tulagi. Making the trip during the daytime made them easy targets for enemy aircraft. This was their second time doing this, but being towed was more dangerous. However, most of the action was up north of them at the present time. That wasn't to say that some lone scout plane might not spot them, and consider them easy picking.

They left Lumbaria at 10:00 a.m. Frank and Matt had agreed that should a plane show up he'd cut the tow rope which would allow him to maneuver about. Thankfully, they didn't see anything.

"Dang, if it isn't kind of eerie, being the only two boats out here on this big ocean," Paul said.

"Yeah, it makes me think they are preparing for something big up north," Matt responded. Ross and Paul didn't speak, but they both thought the same as Matt did.

For a late lunch, Gill and Steffey brought around ham sandwiches and Kool-aid, or as it was commonly called 'bug juice'. Everyone ate in silence. A couple of guys asked to smoke which Matt allowed.

Gill did his magic, at dark, and they had donut sticks and coffee. They'd been underway a little over eight hours when Frank radioed that they were coming into the Tulagi Harbor. The tow was cast off and the 174 eased in under their own power.

Frank and Matt walked up to Headquarters, which was still in full swing. Frank looked at Matt and said, "For these guys to be working at…1920," he said after looking at his watch, "something must be in the works."

They were surprised even more when a woman walked up to the counter. The counter had been put up since Matt's last trip.

"May I help you?" she asked.

"I'm Lieutenant (j.g.) Matt Blue, skipper of the 174 boat," Matt said.

The woman smiled, and said, "So you're the one who tried to sink a submarine with your screws." She said this with a big smile.

"Guilty as charged," Matt confessed.

"I'm Carol Jenkins," the woman said, and then she looked at Frank.

"Lieutenant Frank Andruss," Frank said. "I'm his babysitter."

Carol laughed, "They are expecting you at the repair facility at 07:30 tomorrow morning. Your paperwork has already been sent over. Do you need billets for your crew?"

"That would be nice," Matt and Frank replied in unison.

A chief petty officer was at a desk behind Carol. "If you'll gather your men and come back here, sir, the chief will take you to your billets. You're late for chow, however."

"No problem, these guys will make do," Matt replied. He was sure a closed chow hall wouldn't deter his guys if they got hungry.

When Matt returned to the boat, he filled the guys in and told them to be at the boat, ready to go at 0700."

They then went to meet the Headquarters' chief. When both crews were settled in, Matt walked with Frank to the 'O' Club. He was hoping to find Karen there. Ever since he'd been told to take the 174 to Tulagi, she had been foremost in his mind. He didn't see Karen but he saw one of her friends that he'd met on his last visit.

"Matt…" she shouted. "It's good to see you." Her expression changed then, "Oh my, you're looking for Karen, aren't you?"

"Yes," Matt replied.

"I hate to tell you this, but we have been very slow here, so they sent her back to Noumea."

Damn, Matt thought. *Noumea, New Caledonia might as well be on the other side of the world*. He thanked Karen's friend and then he went back and sat by Frank. They each had a beer and then they walked back to their temporary quarters.

***

THE REPAIR FACILITY WAS READY for the 174 boat at 0730, the next morning. The supervisor asked how the props had been damaged so badly. Matt told him, with the supervisor shaking his head. While the props were being fixed, the bottom was checked and none of the scrubbed places were significant. However, some sort of putty was placed over the deeper scrubs, and painted over once the putty substance dried.

The following day, the supervisor told Matt that the shafts were okay, thanks to Clark shutting down the engines as quickly as he did. Clark, who was standing by the supervisor, smiled. Matt had been reading about PT boat's props the previous evening.

Finding Karen gone had been a big disappointment, so he'd pulled out his handbook and read about the props. He looked at Clark and said, "The specifications call for three aluminum-manganese-bronzes, right hand turning props, Tom."

Clark looked at Matt in disbelief when Matt asked if they'd installed the right props. "Skipper, we have three propellers of twenty-eight inches. They are definitely made of metal that looks to be aluminum. I don't know if they're made out of aluminum-manganese-bronzes material or whale dung." Frank slapped Tom on the back, and they all burst out laughing.

Once the boat was put back in the water, they took her out and tested the new props. Matt let her idle about at first and then pushed her up to twenty-five knots. She was as smooth as she could be. Matt motioned to Frank then, who was escorting them, in case trouble occurred, to let's let her rip. Matt opened up the 174's full throttle.

"She's doing forty-eight knots," Paul shouted.

Matt kept her there for about five minutes, and then he slowed her down to twenty-five knots. The crew was all smiles.

"She'll fly," Ross exclaimed. "Damned if she won't."

Clark came on deck, smiling, "She's smooth, Skipper. No vibrations or oil leaks, and the engines aren't heating up."

They took the 174 back into the harbor. Clark and Matt reported to the supervisor that all was right as rain. The supervisor filled out the paperwork and Matt signed it.

Matt, taking a copy up to Headquarters, asked Frank if he wanted to leave then or at dusk.

"We have to take on fuel," Frank said. "Let's leave at dusk. We can let the crews grab a meal and take a nap before we head back."

They reported to Headquarters and got things squared away. They had no problems refueling. Lunch that day was fried pork chops, so they all had a better than average meal. Matt never asked who, but somebody came up with two cases of Miller High Life beer. Everyone had two bottles, just enough to relax them for a good afternoon nap, hut not enough to get them drunk.

They were all up and rested by 1700 hours. Frank and Matt reported to Headquarters again, advising the duty officer that they were about to get underway. Both boats were ready, and at 1730 hours they were leaving the harbor. A Black Cat flew over waving its wings, just before dark. They'd been underway nearly eight hours and were nearing Rendova when they could see gun flashes in the distance.

Matt hailed Frank to come in close. "Don't you think we better radio the base and let them know we are coming in?" Matt asked.

"Yeah," Frank agreed. "Those guns are not small arms. We definitely don't want to become a casualty of friendly fire."

Brown radioed in to base and let them know that they were coming in.

CHAPTER THIRTY TWO

THE NEXT MORNING THE WORD was passed down that the Americans were making an all out landing on Vella Lavella. Frank and his crew, along with several other boats, had already left and had dropped off an advanced party.

The 174 boat had taken a group of Alamo scouts to the island, but he had dropped them off on the opposite side of the island from the advance party. The advance party had been under the impression that there were only a few Japanese on the island. They were wrong!

The Battle of Vella Gulf was a sea battle that had already taken place near Vella Lavella. Many of the survivors from the Japanese ships that were sunk ended up on Vella Lavella. There were several hundred, in fact.

The call from the advance party for reinforcements had gone out. The worst of all, this was that the Japanese were holding the area that the advance party had selected to be their landing.

The brass got an urgent call about a group of Alamo scouts that had basically become surrounded, and they were fighting their way back to a spot that they could defend with the sea at their backs. Time was of the utmost urgency.

Matt was the first person Lieutenant Commander Singleton saw as he rushed to our area. "Saddle up, Matt, we received an urgent call to rescue some Alamo scouts that the Japanese have pinned down."

David, who was standing beside Matt said, "I'll get the crew."

In less than ten minutes, they were underway, full throttle. Singleton had given the coordinates to Hall and Ross. The 174 boat rushed full speed to save their troops and got there just at dusk.

They could see the flashes from small arms fire. Gill radioed that they were coming in. The sergeant in charge said that they would all lie down if the gunners could pour in a barrage of fire from the boat's guns. Matt brought the boat in at half throttle for the first pass, and the 174's gunners poured so much lead into the jungle vegetation that it was swept clean. The Japanese directed their fire at the 174, but with little effect. When the 174 fired again, palm trees even crashed down like they'd been attacked by .50 caliber and 20 mm chain saws.

Firing from the Japanese had ceased, but the 174 boat made one more pass to make sure. They came in close then and picked up Sergeant John Belk and his squad. The last man on board was the BAR man, Braveheart. It was the first time that Matt had seen him without tons of ammunition. He had used it all up. There were only a few rounds left between the entire squad.

Belk shook Matt's hand and said, "You cut it close, Matt, but all's well that ends well."

They all knew that the ordeal had gotten to the sergeant. He'd never used Matt's name before, and seeing two of his squad dripping blood, and one body that had been brought with them, spoke volumes. They'd all heard it said that they never left a man behind, and now the 174 crew believed it. They got the wounded below and did what they could for them.

The 174 headed back to the base then with Paul at the helm. Brown sent word back for ambulances to be at the port.

When the scouts headed ashore, Braveheart nudged Matt and spoke, "I'll not forget."

The good news brought in by the Alamo scouts was that while there were lots of Japanese, they were only lightly armed. Rifles, pistols, a few grenades, and some only with knives or swords, and clubs. While it was felt that these survivors could not prevent the landing, they could create a problem.

The job of the PT boats was to escort the troop ship and to be on guard for aircraft and any Japanese destroyers.

Frank looked at Matt and said sarcastically, "With two torpedoes a piece, we can really do some harm to those destroyers."

The trade off for the other two torpedoes was the 40 mm Bofors, which was great for hunting barges but didn't do anything against a destroyer. The first wave of reinforcements proved to be a letdown for the PT boat crews.

Four fast destroyer transports arrived at dawn on the 15th of August. The initial landing took place without a single gun being fired. The troops were actually on shore in no time at all. They arrived at dawn and by 0645 a.m., the landing was over. If the PT boat's crew felt a letdown, the second wave move made up for it. For once, Matt was glad to see a large number of PT boats surrounding the troop transports. Only eight of the troop ships could off load troops on the beach at a time.

When the Japanese planes came in, the PT boats unmercifully filled the air with .50 caliber machine gunfire, 20 mm Oerlikon fire, and 40 mm Bofors and a few 37 mm guns that were carried in place of the 40 mm Bofors on some boats.

There was no way a plane could come in and target the troop transports without committing suicide. While the planes kept up a brutal attack, the troops of the second wave finished landing by a little after 0900 a.m.

The LST's came next. As slow as they were, Matt had no doubt that they'd get hit as they got into position to unload the troops. The Japanese, as expected, turned their attention to the LST's. The gunners on the 174 boat were exhausted from firing so much. The barrels on the .50 caliber guns had to be changed out. The loaders were all sweating. They were as worn out as the gunners.

The destroyers, out in the gulf, were still pouring it on and the 174's crew watched a zero explode in the air.

"Look," L.Z. said.

One of their planes had smoked another Japanese plane. Dale Byhre's gun had paused while waiting on ammunition from his loader. He shook his head seeing the last plane go down. "You'd think that one of the Japanese commanders could see that this plan isn't working out for them and recall the dang planes."

Preacher, who was a loader for Byhre's gun told him to hush. "I'd rather get rid of them now when it's in our favor for once, rather than when they're strafing us on the way home some morning."

Matt didn't hear Byhre's reply as Chief Ross and Wheels had a couple of coolers full of bug juice that they were taking around. A cup was tied to each spigot so everyone used the same cups. No one minded, however, as the bug juice went down a thirsty throat just fine.

By the time the last of the troops had landed, 4,600 men had been put on shore. Matt couldn't help but wonder what the troops felt like, as the troop ships and destroyers pulled away, disappearing over the horizon.

Brown stuck his head up and said, "Counting zeroes and dive bombers, the brass figures we downed forty-four planes today, Skipper."

"How many do you figure we got, Skipper?" L.Z. asked.

"All of them, so you better get busy with your paint," Matt said smiling.

This made the crew laugh. *When tired men laugh, you know they're okay*, thought Matt. As the PT boats secured and headed back to base, Matt couldn't help but wonder as Byhre had done, *Why would the Imperial Japanese Command waste so many planes and men?* It made Matt also wonder why that, even when a plan proved to be so obviously wrong, the local commanders were afraid to speak up to their superiors. Old Hickory's crew, while still at their stations, had relaxed and were joking with each other.

"I guess those Japanese will be singing sad songs about the fierce Devil Boats tonight," Dale Byhre said. "There was not a single ship sunk today."

"True, but I thought my barrels were going to melt," L.Z. answered.

The crew went on with each other, as Matt thought, *We've taken Guadalcanal and Munda Point on New Georgia, which gave us another airfield, and now Vella Lavella is ours. What's next?*

Glancing down at the fuel gauge, Matt also wondered when they'd move bases. They couldn't continue these long distance raids. Fuel consumption wouldn't allow it.

Paul must have read Matt's mind. "We'll make it, Skipper," he said, glancing at the fuel gauges. Matt smiled and said a silent prayer.

It was seventy miles from Vella Lavella to Rendova, and they'd been maneuvering since dawn. Yes, there was no doubt that they'd be moving soon...again, fuel demanded it.

***

THEY GOT THE NEXT DAY off, and all the PT boats were refueled. Chief Ross had the crew putting the 174 in ship shape order. Frank, David, and Matt went to the officer's call and came away shaking their heads.

The Black Cats had sighted a barge base on the north-eastern shore at a place called Horaniu. Two companies and a platoon of Japanese naval troops from Bougainville made it to Horaniu, in spite of the navy's attempts to stop them. The good thing was the American troops that had been landed were given orders to take the barge base. A few days later, it was reported that the Japanese had only put up token resistance. The Japanese, seeing the large number of American troops headed their way, hauled butt. Later that day, the American troops occupied the base.

"I'm glad it was them, instead of us," Ted said as they ate lunch.

The next day, seven PT boats under the command of Lieutenant Commander Leroy Taylor made the move to Vella Lavella Island in Lambu Lambu Cove along with one APC, to establish a forward PT base.

Vella Lavella turned out to be the most primitive of any PT base that they'd been too. Native huts set back in the trees, along with several tents, was it for housing? There was a small dock that the APC tied up to. This area was used for refueling. To tie up your boat, you found a sturdy looking tree hanging out over the water, and tied up to it. A destroyed Japanese barge had been driven up on the beach and left behind.

Morales had his camera out and was snapping pictures from different sides and angles. Byhre and Hall walked up to where Matt was standing. "We keep thinking that barge is going to start firing at us any minute, Skipper," Hall said.

Matt smiled and thought to himself, *They are not the only crew members with a touch of anxiety.* Seeing their new officer, Matt spoke, "That's what they look like without their teeth, Mr. Christopher."

The new ensign nodded and replied, "Yes sir."

Just before the 174 boat left Rendova, or Todd City, as it was commonly called, word had come down that the Rendova base was going to receive more facilities. Warehouses for supplies, repair shops, a better pier, and roads and fuel storage. Logistics dictated it. Tulagi was now too far away from the war, two hundred miles one way. It was a lot of precious fuel for a PT boat to use when needing repairs that couldn't be handled by the crew.

Orders came down then and several of the PT boats would go to Vella Lavella Island. Everyone stayed in tents for the month of October. Their assignments were nothing compared to the days of taking on the destroyers and cruisers during the days of the Tokyo Express. The enemy had not evacuated their troops from Kolombangara but had moved to the island of Choiseul. Some of the Japanese had been captured trying to make the crossing in native canoes. PT boats were called upon to land scouting parties on Santa Isabel and Choiseul.

They'd also been called upon a few times to pick up downed pilots and get them to Rendova. Basically, they hadn't seen any real action for a while. Every time the 174 went out, Matt had Ensign Christopher at the helm. It was a good time to check him out on the boat. They had just picked up a downed pilot when they lost another crew member.

The crew had just got the pilot out of the water when L.Z shouted, "Plane!"

Within seconds it seemed, a Zero came out of the clouds with his machine guns buzzing all about them. Matt took the helm quickly and thrust the throttles to full speed, zigzagging to make a harder target for the Zero. All the guns were firing, throwing up a barrage of hot lead. The Zero flew over, banked and then buzzed over and off to the port side of the 174. He flew up into the cloud's cover and when he came back it was directly at the bow.

The pilot knew his business. The 174's crew was looking directly into the sun. This attack was sudden and low...too low for the Japanese. Matt felt the wind on his face as the Zero passed over. They all felt the boat shudder as his bullets tore into the 174's bow.

Matt heard Christopher yelp as a bullet hit the deck by his foot. Matt then saw the gunners send everything they had up and into the belly of the Zero as it flew over. Fire, and bright orange flames immediately engulfed the plane and it exploded and went into the ocean.

QM2 David Hall burst through the chart house door. "It's Brown, Skipper. He's in a bad way."

Matt's heart sank. Dependable, loyal Brown was hit in the chest. He smiled at Matt and grabbed his hand. He died without speaking. The crew knew that Brown was gone by the time Matt came on deck. Brown had been with Matt from the very first. It was a hard blow to the 174 crew.

Ross, Wheels, Frongello and BM2 Steffey went around plugging and patching the holes where water was coming in. They made it to Todd City without further attacks or problems.

Matt had Gill radio and ask for an ambulance. The pilot had to be cleared by a doctor as per standard protocol, and Brown would be taken to a makeshift morgue. When they neared the base, Matt turned the deck over to Paul and went below to write his report.

Ross had the deck cleaned where Brown had been hit and Paul had the 174 refueled while Matt was at Headquarters.

The talk at Headquarters was that the New Georgia campaign was over. In retrospect, Matt wasn't sure that he'd ever been told that they'd been fighting the New Georgia campaign.

When he told the crew, QM2 Hall vocalized the thoughts of the entire crew, when he said, "If it don't mean we're going home, it don't mean jack, does it? I mean the war is still going on right?" Everyone agreed with him.

On the 14th of December, they were ordered to abandon Vella Lavella Island. Fortunately, the 174 was the first boat headed out through the narrow entrance. Unfortunately for others, a fire broke out. They were told a faulty fuel pump ignited the fuel dump and spread quickly to the ammunition dump. It was like a deadly fireworks show with ammunition exploding for hours.

The entrance into and out of cove was so narrow, the now roaring furnace so hot, that it blocked any escape. They lost the 239 boat to the flames. The blocked PT boats and the APC broke out their fire hoses and kept them going for hours before the fire was put out and it was safe for them to leave.

Matt and the 174 crew thanked God that they'd gotten out when they did.

CHAPTER THIRTY THREE

T HE TOP BRASS, IN THEIR infinite wisdom, had decided they didn't have to take an entire island to satisfy their need for a beach head to land troops and supplies, and to build an airstrip. Any Japanese on the island would be cut off from escape and supplies once the Americans dug in. Prior to the landing of Bougainville, it was decided that Treasury Island had to be taken so that supply convoys could be taken in close to the beach.

It fell to the PT boats to land a reconnaissance party on the island. The 174's orders were to land the party and avoid detection, if possible. They landed the scout party easily enough and only had one scare.

L.Z's incredibly sharp hearing picked up the drone of an aircraft. They cut their speed to idle and waited. Fortunately for them, the plane passed over without ever dropping down to check them out.

The 174 refueled the next morning. Ross had the men check everything during the day before they left again that night to pick up the advance party. They had been so inactive lately, that tempers between the men began to flare over minor stuff like Pappy's music or how someone dealt the cards. So when the job came for them to take out the scouting party, and then pick them up the next night, Matt was glad, and ready to be busy.

The sun was setting when they left the base. They made it to their rendezvous without seeing the enemy. When the advance party appeared out of the jungle, the 174 was surprised to see that they had several natives with them.

The lieutenant in the scouting party, came up to Matt. "Can you believe it's been three days without a smoke?" He was hinting for Matt to okay him to light up a smoke.

"We'll be home before you know it," Matt said.

The lieutenant took a deep breath and gave a sigh, and said, "The native chief says that there's only a handful of Japanese on the entire island, less than two hundred fifty of the rice eaters. The natives have agreed to act as guides when the landings take place."

Everyone knew that another landing was planned. Rumors were that PT boats would carry the first wave of troops in. The guys hearing the rumors settled down without tempers flaring, as there had been. *There's nothing like war to impress upon you that your life might depend on the actions of your shipmates.*

Mail caught up with them finally and they each had a stack of mail. Preacher got a box with crumbled cookies, which he allowed the entire crew to grab handfuls of the tasty crumbs. Pappy got some 78 rpm records and others got cigars, pipe tobacco, and such. Matt could smell the aroma of pipe tobacco as he went into his tent. *Dale Byhre has gotten a package*, Matt thought.

Matt went through Karen's letters, first putting them in order as to when they were mailed. He was sorting through the letters from home next, and then he found a letter from New Zealand, but he didn't recognize the name. It was from a Cora James. She lived in the apartment over Sheree's, and seeing his letters piling up, she felt that she should write him and explain why Sheree hadn't written. It seems that Sheree had developed pneumonia and had died in the hospital, a week after Matt had left. He suddenly felt his throat tighten, felt nauseated and he wanted to cry. He had noticed the sniffles the night he had held her, but he didn't think too much about it. He wondered if the alcohol in the drinks and wine hadn't helped with her cough, which hadn't been bad at the time.

Matt remembered his grandfather putting soft peppermint sticks in a pint of Four Roses bourbon and letting it melt. He said that it was the best cough medicine around. Had Matt known how bad Sheree felt, he would have taken her to a doctor, the hospital or someplace where she could have been treated. Matt suddenly wondered if he gave her as much comfort and pleasure as she had given him. Sitting on the edge of his cot, Matt's mind was racing over the news of Sheree's passing. He recalled comments by Reverend Lightfoot, their pastor, back at Eastside Baptist Church. Matt was upset over his dog dying after being bitten by a snake.

"Matthew, the Lord rarely lets something go away without replacing it with something better," the preacher had said.

Karen came to Matt's mind then. *Had she been God's gift to replace Sheree?* He finished Cora's letter. She had gone on and told him where Sheree had been laid to rest. Matt folded up the letter and wondered, as he sat there in the stillness, if he'd given Sheree a few days of peace. *Had he replaced something that she'd lost?* He'd never know the answer to that question, of course, but he sincerely hoped their time together had given her a brief respite. They had certainly eaten well, something that Matt didn't think she'd been doing, and that may have weakened her body.

The two of them had spent the time doing anything Sheree had chosen to do. Had he temporarily replaced a void, an emptiness in her life, something that had suddenly been taken away. Matt would never know, of course, but he sincerely hoped so. But now...how did he put it away? How did he get it out of his mind? He stood up and walked outside. Seeing L.Z. close by, Matt asked him for a match. L.Z. looked up at his skipper, as he fumbled in his shirt pocket until he got his matches and handed them to Matt.

Matt walked off a ways, and said a brief prayer and then struck a match. Cupping it in his hands, until it was fully lit, he set the flame to Cora's letter and burned it. Why? He couldn't tell you as he didn't know himself. Matt dropped the letter and watched it burn itself out.

When Matt turned back towards the tent, he looked up. The guys had gotten silent, and they were looking at him. Matt tossed the matches back to L.Z., who deftly snagged the box in midair with one hand and then he asked, "Are you alright, Skip?"

Matt didn't answer, he couldn't. He just lowered his head, so that they wouldn't see the emotions on his face.

Frank, seeing his friend was troubled, asked, "You okay, man?"

Matt nodded, but didn't speak. He couldn't. He walked back to his rack and wiped the tears away from his eyes onto his pillowcase. It took a few minutes to get his emotions under control, and his mind settled. He picked up the first letter from Karen then.

***

THE NEXT NIGHT SEVERAL OF their PT boats played transport service again. Frank had Lieutenant Commander Singleton on his boat as they went out. Rumors were, Singleton had done such a good job as squadron commander that he might be moving up the ladder.

Matt wished him nothing but luck as he'd been a good commanding officer, but he hated to see him go.

The advance party that night was made up a lot differently than the previous party. The whole group were New Zealand NCO's and natives from the island. Their job was to go in and cut enemy communications.

"Damn," Chief Ross said. "Talk about stirring up a nest of hornets."

It wouldn't take the Japanese long to know that they'd been sabotaged and also know the enemy was on the island. The landing went off without any contact with the enemy. The next day, their boats escorted the fourth transport groups landing on Stirling Island. Again, the landing went according to plans.

Matt was starting to believe the brass had finally got a workable plan together that wasn't costing them scores of American lives. The next day, Lieutenant Commander Kelly, their new commanding officer, arrived and they moved to their new temporary home on Stirling Island. It was also called the Treasury Base. The PT boats were given the job of blockading the southern aspect of Bougainville, the Shortland Islands and Choiseul Bay. The Japanese, unable to get destroyers or transports into the area because of the large number of Navy ships, reverted to their barges.

The barges would pick up Japanese troops that had escaped from New Georgia and had landed on Choiseul Island. The Japanese traveled overland on foot until they made it to Choiseul Bay. Barges would pick them up there and transport them at night across the Bougainville Straits to Fauro Island, of the Shortland Islands and on to Bougainville. Their route was the route the 174 had been assigned to blockade.

On occasion, a friendly Black Cat pilot would spot a barge and radio the location to them. They'd often drop a flare, lighting up a target. Unlike other barge hunting trips they'd been on, these barges would be full of soldiers with automatic weapons.

Three boats from RON 10 were assigned to patrol on that night. They were patrolling the Bougainville Straits, just off Favro Island.

Frank and Ted were closer to the northern end of Choiseul and the 171 boat was more to the south of them.

A Black Cat flew over, banked, and came back. He didn't have to call in the sighting as the automatic fire and the 40 mm cannon fire from the barges marked the spot for them.

"Damn, he's brave," Paul said. *Or dumb,* Matt thought.

The plane made another turn and came back again, but was much higher. The parachute flares did a good job lighting up the barges.

"There's three of them, Skipper," the chief said.

"I see them, Chief," Matt replied. What he didn't say was he hoped that Frank and the 171 boat got the word as well. "Gill," Matt yelled.

"Aye, Skipper," Gill replied.

"Radio our friends and let them know that we have enough to go around." Looking around the boat, Matt saw four people at the 40 mm gun, and three people at the 20 mm gun. The .50 caliber guns were both manned with a loader standing near. "Let's light 'em up, boys," Matt said and hit the throttle.

The 174 passed by the slow moving barges, with their guns blazing. Normally, when attacking a single barge, the gunners would duck down, but when it's three barges, it was a different story.

Each barge had a 40 mm gun that was equal to the 174's guns. Everyone heard the Japanese bullets puncturing their hull.

"Damn," Christopher yelled, as one bullet came close.

Matt called down to the engine room, thankful that nothing had gotten to them. "Change of tactics," Matt yelled. "We hit the front barge, turn out of range, and come up on the rear. We'll save the middle one until he's lost his friends."

They circled around out of range and came up on the rear barge They poured everything they had into it and then sped out of range, before the other two barges could bring their guns to fire. They made one more charge on the rear barge, and then got out of range. They then turned, hitting the front barge as they had the rear. By their second charge, they could see the barges trying to bunch up, but it didn't work. The middle barge collided with the front barge, throwing everyone to the deck. The 174 boat came in little closer and punched holes in the lead barge. They could see it taking on water. They kept firing and sped out of range.

Frank radioed that he could see the barges now. Frank could see men jumping out of the first barge, that was sinking, into the second one, as he went by.

They attacked the last barge, and as they sped away, Frank hit it with all his guns blazing. People were now jumping over its side, most of whom would drown before they would surrender. As the 174 passed the middle barge, it was being pulled down where it had tangled up with the front barge.

The 174's gunners started to fire and Matt yelled, "Cease fire!" The gunners didn't hear him, so he turned away. There'd been no return fire from the Japanese.

Matt looked over at Paul and David Christopher. "I haven't the stomach for shooting helpless people," he said.

They stayed away and watched the last barge get pulled down beneath the surface. Thinking they would pick up survivors, they got close to the Japanese in the water. But they would dive under or swim away.

"Some would say that we should turn the .50 caliber gun on them," Paul said.

"Let them," Matt responded, and then added, "I'm going down for a cup of coffee."

Frank must have felt the same way as they turned to follow the 174.

As Matt walked to the galley, he kept listening but never heard a shot fired. They called it a night. While Matt drank his coffee, he suddenly knew that they were going to win the war. *Hopefully, I'll live through it.*

CHAPTER THIRTY FOUR

T HE NEXT DAY WHEN MATT'S guys went to get ammunition, they were told that they could get about half of what they'd normally been given. When the chief came and told Matt that they'd been refused, he went to the ammunition dump. When he arrived at the dump, he heard a smart ass ensign tell Morales and Byhre that they needed to learn to conserve ammunition. Matt was glad that the ensign hadn't been talking to L.Z., otherwise, he'd lose a stripe again.

Matt looked at the ensign and said, "You're new aren't you?" The ensign nodded yes. Matt then said, "Walk with me." Looking back over his shoulder, he gave a slight nod.

Matt took Ensign Newberry down to the boat. "We took on three Japanese barges last night," he said. "They were shooting at us with 40 mm cannons and machine guns. Now, this is our boat. See all of those holes in it."

The ensign got big-eyed.

"Do you have any idea of how much enemy fire we were taking on?" Matt asked.

"No," the ensign admitted.

Matt said, hands on hips, "Well, Ensign, the next time we go out, I'd love for you to ride with us."

They stepped on board the boat, and Matt showed him the gas tanks. "There's nothing but wood between those tanks and the enemy's bullets. If just one bullet hits a tank you know what happens?"

"No sir."

"BOOM!" Matt shouted, and the ensign jumped. "We will all be dead very quickly. Hopefully, the explosion will kill you as that's better than being burned alive."

"I see," Newberry said.

They walked back to the ammunition dump and Matt's two guys were still there. When the ensign walked to the back, Byhre smiled and Morales winked. *We have our ammunition plus a reserve.*

***

SOME OF THE GUYS WERE throwing a baseball when Matt walked up to the area. It was much like their facilities at Tulagi when they'd first landed. The Seabees were building an airstrip, over 5600 feet long, someone had said, and they were getting tanks for a fuel farm. Matt had also noticed a pier was already being constructed. However, with all the skinny that was out there, the one piece that Matt held onto was they planned on a one hundred bed hospital, and that meant they'd need nurses. Matt had a recommendation that he was sure to put forward, and three if they'd let him.

The 174 was assigned to act as an escort that evening to a force of marine raiders to Puruata Island. The next morning, the Japanese on the island started to fire on the troops and ships associated with the main invasion of Bougainville. Everyone had been told that this was an allied invasion, so it was the PT's job to keep the Japanese busy on Puruata Island. The brass didn't want any of their allies shot by the Japanese that they should have already done away with.

"They waited long enough to decide," Ted said, as he passed a couple of beers to Paul, David, and Matt.

Matt looked at Frank, who replied to the unasked question about the beer. "Don't ask," he said. They sat under a palm tree, and finished their beers.

Ross walked up, "So no patrols tonight, Skipper?"

"No," Matt replied, and then he added, "but I'm sure you know about tomorrow morning."

"Yes sir," Ross said. He had his shirt off draped across his wrist. It partially hid a bottle of Miller beer.

Matt saluted with his beer and Ross returned the salute, and saying, "See you at 0600."

◆◆◆

MATT DIDN'T REALIZE IT, BUT looking at the map with Chief Ross, Frank, Paul, David, and Ted the previous evening, Puruata Island was only half a mile or less from the beach head on Bougainville. According to the Alamo scouts, who had reconnaissance the island, only a platoon of Japanese soldiers was garrisoned there, and that had been a week ago. There was no telling how many there were now. A barge or two a night with troops and guns could make the landing for the Marine Raider's Battalion hell.

On the first of November, troops simultaneously landed on Puruata Island and at Empress Augusta Bay on the west side of Bougainville. The landing on Bougainville met only a limited resistance. On Puruata Island, the landing was met with rifle and machine gun fire, as well as mortars and snipers. The PT boats patrolled along the coast and fired at troops moving in to reinforce the Japanese opposing the landing. The PT boats were only fired at once, and that was by rifle fire. Since the resistance was much more than expected someone decided to reinforce the marines ashore.

At 1330, the rest of the Marine Raider Battalion landed, bringing with it some self-propelled 75mm guns. When the entire battalion attacked, the Japanese pulled back. Half of the island had been taken by the time the fighting ended that day. The Japanese were not done yet, however.

The Japanese Navy sent a force of two heavy cruisers, two light cruisers, and three destroyers to attack the PT boats. The U.S. Navy had four light cruisers plus a destroyer squadron waiting on them. Most of the troop ships left the landing area as the combat ships readied for battle.

One of the Navy reconnaissance planes saw the Japanese ships and reported them. The American ships made radar contact at 0227 on the second of November. Matt's and Frank's crews sat on their PT boats and watched as naval gunfire, torpedoes, and attacks by enemy aircraft were all around them. They got off a few rounds at the planes, but for the most part they were out of their range, concentrating their fire on the ships.

The battle was broken off at daylight. Most of the ships were low on fuel and ammunition. When all was said and done, they had sunk one light cruiser and a destroyer. They'd damaged two more cruisers and two destroyers. Twenty-five Japanese planes had been shot down.

They'd lost nineteen that were killed and twenty-six were wounded. With the sinking of the Japanese ships, it was thought that they lost more than 650 killed. It had been a one-sided affair. Somebody later said that it was the last major naval action of the Solomon campaign.

The PT boat guys were just glad that they'd been mostly spectators and not actually called into battle. They'd all seen enough to know that their fragile little boats would never have stood up.

***

THE NEXT DAY, NOVEMBER 3RD, Commander Henry Farrow arrived with eight more PT boats, which Matt was happy to see. The Japanese up in the northern part of Bougainville continued to put barges full of men all along the coast and Japanese bombers attacked on the night of November 5th. They continued these nightly attacks until the end of the month.

Matt was glad that their nurse friends were not there during these nightly raids. At officer's call, one of the assistants told everyone that in thirty-three nights, the Japanese had dropped about six hundred bombs.

Matt could have kissed Frank when he said, "Apparently, *they* are not running short of ammunition."

Every PT boat officer laughed, while the ensign at the ammunition dump tried to make himself small. The PT boat commanders were, at first, assigned patrol duty, ten miles above and below the troop and supply landing point at Empress Augusta Bay. They fired at a number of Japanese planes and saw smoke erupt on occasion, but didn't actually see any planes go down. During the month of November, the 174 boat only had one barge encounter. The 172 boat was patrolling with the 174 boat. They were near the Buka Passage when the Japanese saw them. The Japanese turned tail and headed back to Buka Island, which still had a large amount of Japanese there.

Navy ships had been bombarding the island off and on for weeks. By the end of the month, the Japanese were trying to leave the island of Buka. Now the barge hunting became a nightly ordeal.

It was now the first week of December, and David said, as they walked down to the boat at dusk, "What a way to kick off the Christmas season."

"Welcome to the war," Paul quipped.

EPILOGUE

THE GROUP HAD SURE FIRE evidence, by the end of the month, that their boats had destroyed six barges and damaged another dozen. One of those sunk was the one Frank's boat and the 174 boat double teamed. When Matt gave the guys the numbers, he got the response he expected.

"Skipper, that's horseshit. We know that we sunk three by ourselves."

"I'm not arguing," Matt said,. "But remember, those words from the past, credible evidence."

"I wish we had that journalist with us. What was his name?" Preacher asked.

Pappy and L.Z. both answered, "Walker, Hollis Walker. Did we get credit for the plane we splashed?"

"Yes," Matt responded.

"We might as well have," L.Z. said. "She's already been painted on the side."

David Hall spoke up then, "We need to paint two columns. One that says sure kills and put what we know we got under it. Then the other column that says credible evidence."

"We can't," Morales said. "L.Z. doesn't know how to spell credible." This got a big laugh from the guys.

"Have you seen some of the new guys looking at our kills?" Mike Phagans said.

"Yeah, they're envious," Gill said.

"No need to be," Chief Ross replied. "If this war last much longer, they'll be able to paint some kills or they'll be dead." This shut everyone up.

When they got to base and everything had been secured, Matt went to his bunk to get a few hours of shuteye. There was a note on his pillow. He was to report to personnel the next morning to see the new squadron commander, Lieutenant Commander Taylor. To allay any fear that he might have over finding the note, someone was kind enough to add...not urgent. Get a good night's sleep.

Matt woke up and had to decide, *do I want another thirty minutes sleep. After all, it said not urgent. Or, should I get up and shower, then eat with Paul and David before heading up to the Headquarters tent.* He turned over and caught a whiff of his armpits. *Good Lord*, he thought. The decision was made for him. He got up and headed for the showers.

Matt's uniform looked terrible, but it was clean. They hadn't found the same number of native women to do the laundry as they'd enjoyed on Tulagi. Once dressed, Matt went to the mess tent. Paul had SOS and David was enjoying fried Spam. The Spam looked more appetizing than the chipped beef and gravy on toast. Matt wasn't sure who had come up with the nickname SOS, but it had to be economical or easy to store. Next to Spam, it was the most common breakfast meal. He'd heard on board ships that had been at sea for some time that it might be served up to three times a day. That would have meant that he would have missed a few meals.

This morning, David was talking about how Kennedy had totally lost confidence in both the Mark 8 and Mark 14 torpedoes, so he had the torpedo tubes removed from the 59 boat, adding a 40 mm Bofors and additional machine guns. He'd also somehow, got some armour plating installed in crucial areas.

"What I was telling David," Paul said, "is Kennedy has effectively changed the 59 boat from a MTB to a gunboat."

"I agree," Matt responded. Finishing his coffee, he told his friends that he'd see them later and headed up to Headquarters.

"Morning, Lieutenant," a petty officer said. "I'll get the commander for you."

Taylor came up right away and motioned for Matt to follow him to his space. "Morning, Matt," Taylor said as he sat down behind his desk and motioned for Matt to a folding chair beside his desk.

"Morning, sir," Matt responded.

"Coffee," Taylor asked.

"No, thank you, sir, I just finished two cups," Matt replied.

Taylor poured himself a fresh cup from a pot on a small burner that was on a small cabinet behind the desk. Setting his cup down, he said, "Lieutenant Commander Singleton had a lot of good things to say about you, Matt. Apparently, the people in Washington agreed with his assessment."

Taylor handed Matt a sheet of paper then. The heading across the top proclaimed it to be the "Navy Promotion List for Lieutenant." Near the top of the paper, underlined in blue ink was the name, Matthew Cox Blue.

"It's not even been two years," Matt said.

Taylor looked at him and said, "It hasn't been much more than a year or so, but we are at war, Matt, and promotion goes along with the needs of the Navy. However, looking at your records, your promotion from ensign to lieutenant (j.g.) took a while to catch up to you. You moved a lot in the beginning. Maybe it's the Navy's way of making it up to you." He said this with a smile. They both knew better than that.

Taylor reached inside his desk drawer and took out a small box. "Roy Singleton was so sure of your promotion, he left these for you."

Lieutenant bars, or—as they are affectionately called—railroad tracks, were in the box.

"They were Roy's collar devices, passed down to him," Taylor said. He then stood up and pinned the bars on Matt, and shook his hand. "See the petty officer so the paperwork can be done to get you paid as a lieutenant. After that, go enjoy the evening."

"Aye, aye sir," Matt said, trying to act according to naval protocol. "Thank you."

Taylor smiled and waved him off. Stepping out to the front, Matt was congratulated by everyone. The petty officer had already filled the paperwork out. Matt just had to review it and sign on the bottom line.

Matt was leaving Headquarters, when he saw a PBY landing. Matt veered a bit to see if it was top brass or who was getting off of the plane. The first person was a navy captain, a four striper. As Matt got closer, he could see more people deplaning. He could see it was not the top brass, but something they needed. It was medical personnel. They were all walking his way, headed up to Headquarters to check in.

Halfway back in this group were several nurses. Matt's face broke out in a big smile. What a wonderful day it was turning out to be.

There was three of the nurses he knew well and one he knew especially well. *Damn*, Matt thought. *I'm glad I showered this morning.*

One of the three nurses stopped the other two and holding out her arm, she pointed in Matt's direction. One of the nurses put her hand to her mouth, handed her bags off and started walking towards him. Matt rushed to meet her, not bothering to stop or salute the navy captain. As Matt neared Karen, she thrust herself in his arms and they kissed a long, loving kiss right there before God and everyone.

Suddenly, the air was filled with cheers and whistles. Word... thanks to the rumor mill, had gotten out to the 174 crew. They came down to congratulate Matt on his promotion. They received a show for their efforts. Everyone was clapping now, including the navy captain.

When Matt sat Karen back down, she spoke softly, "I love you, Matt Blue!"

He squeezed her hand saying, "And I love you." It came to Matt then, it was going to be a great Christmas. He just wished that he could take Karen home to meet his parents.

Paul, David, and the men walked up to all of them, "Congratulations, Skipper."

Karen looked at Matt and he pointed to the railroad tracks. She gave him another peck and said, "Congratulations and Merry Christmas."

TERMS

Boatswain's Mate – An enlisted man who looks to the maintenance of a ship or boat, inside out.

Cumshaw – To get/obtain by irregular means, usually exchanging favors, calling in debts, cutting corners or obtaining something on the sly.

GM (Gunner's Mate) – An enlisted man responsible for the mounting, maintenance and care of weaponry on a boat or ship.

MOMM (Motor Machinest Mate) – Enlisted man that was responsible for the machinery and engines on boats and ships.

Petty Officer – An enlisted person between the ranks of E4 to E9. They are the Navy's non-commissioned officers.

QM (Quartermaster) – Enlisted man that stands watch as assistant to officers, serves as a helmsman, responsible for the ship's navigation.

Rack – A cot or a place to sleep on ship or on shore.

RM (Radioman) – Enlisted man responsible for the maintenance, keeping radio receivers and transmitters tuned to correct command frequencies, known throughout the Navy as "Sparks."

Scuttlebutt – Slang term for rumor or gossip.

SOS – Chipped beef in a gravy usually poured over toast, known by most branches of the service as "Shit on a Shingle."

Torpedoman – An enlisted man whose specialty was responsible for the maintenance, stowage, and firing of torpedoes.

Torp Juice – Slang for alcoholic beverage made from 180 proof grain alcohol, taken from a Navy torpedo motor and mixed with a fruit juice, usually grapefruit juice, orange juice, and pineapple juice.

Black Cat– PBY Planes flew stealth missions over the waters of the South Pacific. They became one of the most important squadron names in American History. The black matte paint made the planes invisible nighttime predators. They were considered to be the savior, hunter, aggressor and supplier of the Pacific Theater during World War II.

SPAM – The Meat

During WWII, Spam's reach made its way to England and the countries of the Asian Pacific, where rationing and the presence of American troops saw the meat become a menu staple. "Having the sort of food that can survive in the tropical heat and be kept on a shelf for weeks and months was a huge boon." In England, SPAM was called specially processed American meat.

Tables: Military time, enlisted and officer naval ranks.

NORMAL TIME	MILITARY TIME	NORMAL TIME	MILITARY TIME
12:00 AM	0000	12:00 PM	1200
1:00 AM	0100	1:00 PM	1300
2:00 AM	0200	2:00 PM	1400
3:00 AM	0300	3:00 PM	1500
4:00 AM	0400	4:00 PM	1600
5:00 AM	0500	5:00 PM	1700
6:00 AM	0600	6:00 PM	1800
7:00 AM	0700	7:00 PM	1900
8:00 AM	0800	8:00 PM	2000
9:00 AM	0900	9:00 PM	2100
10:00 AM	1000	10:00 PM	2200
11:00 AM	1100	11:00 PM	2300

Paygrade	Rate	Abbreviation	Upper Sleeve	Collar and Cap
E-1	Seaman Recruit	SR	None	None
E-2	Seaman Apprentice	SA		None
E-3	Seaman	SN		None
E-4	Petty Officer Third Class	PO3		
E-5	Petty Officer Second Class	PO2		
E-6	Petty Officer First Class	PO1		
E-7	Chief Petty Officer	CPO		
E-8	Senior Chief Petty Officer	SCPO		
E-9	Master Chief Petty Officer	MCPO		
E-9	Master Chief Petty Officer of the Navy	MCPON		

Paygrade	Rank	Abbreviation	Collar	Shoulder	Sleeve
O-1	Ensign	ENS			
O-2	Lieutenant Junior Grade	LTJG			
O-3	Lieutenant	LT			
O-4	Lieutenant Commander	LTCDR			
O-5	Commander	CDR			
O-6	Captain	CAPT			
O-7	Rear Admiral (Lower Half)	RDML			
O-8	Rear Admiral (Upper Half)	RADM			
O-9	Vice Admiral	VADM			
O-10	Admiral	ADM			

Torpedo juice is American slang for an alcoholic beverage made from pineapple juice and the 180-proof grain alcohol fuel used in U.S. Navy torpedo motors.